THE ARCTIC CHASE

Also by Cap Daniels

The Chase Fulton Novels Series
Book One: *The Opening Chase*
Book Two: *The Broken Chase*
Book Three: *The Stronger Chase*
Book Four: *The Unending Chase*
Book Five: *The Distant Chase*
Book Six: *The Entangled Chase*
Book Seven: *The Devil's Chase*
Book Eight: *The Angel's Chase*
Book Nine: *The Forgotten Chase*
Book Ten: *The Emerald Chase*
Book Eleven: *The Polar Chase*
Book Twelve: *The Burning Chase*
Book Thirteen: *The Poison Chase*
Book Fourteen: *The Bitter Chase*
Book Fifteen: *The Blind Chase*
Book Sixteen: *The Smuggler's Chase*
Book Seventeen: *The Hollow Chase*
Book Eighteen: *The Sunken Chase*
Book Nineteen: *The Darker Chase*
Book Twenty: *The Abandoned Chase*
Book Twenty-One: *The Gambler's Chase*
Book Twenty-Two: *The Arctic Chase*
Book Twenty-Three: *The Diamond Chase*
Book Twenty-Four: *The Phantom Chase*
Book Twenty-Five: *The Crimson Chase*
Book Twenty-Six: *The Silent Chase*
Book Twenty-Seven: *The Shepherd's Chase*
Book Twenty-Eight: *The Scorpion's Chase*

The Avenging Angel – Seven Deadly Sins Series
Book One: *The Russian's Pride*
Book Two: *The Russian's Greed*
Book Three: *The Russian's Gluttony*
Book Four: *The Russian's Lust*
Book Five: *The Russian's Sloth*
Book Six: *The Russian's Envy* (2024)
Book Seven: *The Russian's Wrath* (TBA)

Stand-Alone Novels
We Were Brave
Singer – Memoir of a Christian Sniper

Novellas
The Chase Is On
I Am Gypsy

THE ARCTIC CHASE

CHASE FULTON NOVEL #22

CAP DANIELS

ANCHOR WATCH
PUBLISHING
** USA **

The Arctic Chase
Chase Fulton Novel #22
Cap Daniels

This is a work of fiction. Names, characters, places, historical events, and incidents are the product of the author's imagination or have been used fictitiously. Although many locations such as marinas, airports, hotels, restaurants, etc. used in this work actually exist, they are used fictitiously and may have been relocated, exaggerated, or otherwise modified by creative license for the purpose of this work. Although many characters are based on personalities, physical attributes, skills, or intellect of actual individuals, all the characters in this work are products of the author's imagination.

Published by:

** USA **

13-Digit ISBN: 978-1-951021-46-7
Library of Congress Control Number: 2023940993

Cover Design: German Creative

Printed in the United States of America

The Arctic Chase

CAP DANIELS

Chapter 1
A Permanent Withdrawal

Autumn 2009, St. Marys, GA

Something wasn't quite right. Everything was in place, just as it had always been at the First Community Bank on Osborne Street. The empty chair where Oscar had sat and slept for most of thirty years was still positioned by the door, but since Oscar, the only armed guard in town, had retired, no one had thought to move his chair or hire a replacement.

Lindsey was perched behind her window in the same position she'd been every time I'd come into the bank for years, but that morning, she didn't smile when Stone W. Hunter, my closest friend and tactical partner, stepped through the door behind me. Lindsey's eyes didn't brighten, and she didn't fidget in her seat. Since Tina Ramirez decided she wasn't interested in a life with a man who spent more time saving the world than he spent waking up beside her, Lindsey's attention toward Hunter had only grown. That morning, though, it wasn't adoration in her eyes. Lindsey's eyes were filled with the same look that Hunter and I had seen in the eyes of our enemies all over the world. The woman was terrified, but she was doing everything in her power to hold it together.

The man standing in front of her appeared to be a shade under six feet tall and around two hundred pounds. The kind of man who could be a handful if he'd been trained to fight. His feet were shoulder-width apart and pointed directly toward Lindsey. The muscles of his neck were relaxed, and his skin was clear and devoid of sweat. He wasn't nervous or afraid, but he didn't know Hunter and I were in the room.

Lindsey's eyes darted between Hunter and the man in front of her in two flashes almost too quick to see, but my partner didn't miss it. He let out a soft breath from between his pursed lips, and I nodded at his nearly silent signal.

I counted eleven people in the bank, but I couldn't see around the corner of the cashier's cage. There could've been more behind the partition. Other than Lindsey, three other bank employees were going about their morning routines as if everything were perfectly normal. Christen from the post office stood a few feet behind the man in front of Lindsey, and she was the antithesis of calm. The end of her typical ponytail trembled as if she were experiencing an earthquake no one else could feel. Christen was the reason most men in St. Marys would use any excuse to visit the post office. She was not only beautiful, but she was also one of the warmest personalities in town. Men routinely found themselves under Christen's spell, but that morning, she appeared mesmerized by something far more sinister than the mostly innocent flirtations she'd long since grown accustomed to.

I didn't recognize the four remaining people in the bank. Two of them held deposit slips or checks in their hands, giving them plausible reasons to be standing in line, but the two men, each standing with one hand in a jacket pocket and another near their waistline, looked way too much like the man at Lindsey's window.

Most people wouldn't have noticed the incongruity of the scene, but most people weren't Hunter and me. Of the few who would've noticed, most of them would've exited the bank as quickly as possible. Hunter and I had never been the type of men to run away from gunfire, and our reputations weren't going to change that morning.

Moving silently, Hunter sidestepped toward the vault, putting some distance between the two of us. He raised his hand in a friendly wave. "Hey, Lindsey. How's it going?"

My partner and the cashier had a long-running feud about the word *hey*. Anytime Hunter used the word, she would, without fail, reply, "Hay is for horses. Hellos are for humans." But that morning, she made no effort to acknowledge or scold him.

Our suspicions were confirmed. We were solidly in the middle of an armed bank robbery. We hadn't seen the "armed" part yet, but my partner and I were about to change that.

I eyed the two men with their hands still in their pockets and then cast my gaze on Hunter. He nodded and slid his hand inside his jacket. As if we'd rehearsed for weeks, he and I drew our pistols simultaneously, and I yelled. "Everybody down! This is a hold-up! If everybody does what I say, nobody's gonna get hurt."

Hunter let out a roar. "He said get down!"

All three tellers, including Lindsey, dived beneath the counter just as they'd been trained to do, and my partner put two nine-millimeter rounds into the base of the counter where it met the tile floor.

Chaos ensued, and screams filled the room. Hunter watched the man at Lindsey's window and everyone's favorite post office employee while I locked my eyes on the two men with hands still in their pockets. Christen hit the floor without a word and grabbed the bottom of her jacket. She yanked the jacket upward, revealing a suicide vest strapped to her body, and the bank instantly became the deadliest environment any of us had ever encountered.

The two men with their hands in their pockets moved as if they were somehow connected by an invisible link. Their hands slid from their pockets to reveal a pair of black plastic devices and in-dex fingers curled around triggers.

The man at Lindsey's window turned and laughed as if per-forming on stage. "You two either have the worst timing in the his-tory of bank robberies, or you're a pair of fools."

I glanced at his empty hands and gave the order. "Kill 'em!"

Hunter and I fired simultaneously, and the two men holding the triggers yelled like wild animals as blood gushed from the re-mains of their hands where the triggers had been only an instant before.

Hunter ordered, "Get on the ground, or your hands are going to be the least of your worries."

The two men grabbed their wounded hands and crumpled to the floor. Christen leapt to her feet and then kicked the closer man twice in the face until blood poured from his nose. With the first man squirming and bleeding to death, Christen drew an ink pen from her pocket and slashed at the second man like a woman possessed.

I scanned the area, continuing to piece together the scene, but Hunter was frozen on the man at the counter. "Get on your knees or die where you stand."

Hunter's icy tone sent chills down my spine, and I wasn't in his gunsights.

The man's laughter came to a close, and he leaned against the counter. "You won't shoot me. I'm an innocent bystander. I'm not even armed."

Hunter took a step toward him. "Not only will I shoot you, but I'll start with your kneecaps if you don't get on the floor right now."

The man held up two hands as if submitting to Hunter's demand, but from where I stood, it didn't feel right. The scene was far from secure, and we had two bleeding victims and an out-of-control postal worker still wielding her ink pen.

I got an arm around Christen's shoulders and pulled her from the bleeding man, but not before she delivered another torturous kick. The man's lips exploded when her heel caught him as he moved in the worst possible direction. He howled, and I tugged at the woman half my size.

It took several seconds for me to believe I had her under control, but her breath was coming hard and fast. "They were . . . going . . . to kill me."

"You're safe now. It's almost over," I said, but my words seemed to have no effect on her.

She continued thrusting toward the two men as I fought to keep her out of Hunter's way while he ended the confrontation.

I finally knelt with Christen still in my grasp, and she followed me to the floor. "I need you to hold still so we can end this and I can get you out of the vest. Do you understand?"

Still breathing as if she'd run a marathon, she said, "Yeah, but—"

"No buts. Just relax."

Hunter stepped toward the apparent leader of the group and motioned him to the floor with the muzzle of his Glock. "I'm telling you, man. I will drill through you if you don't get on the ground."

With his hands still extended, the man dropped to the floor, and in one swift, well-practiced motion, pulled a pistol from an ankle holster. The world around me flashed in slow-motion fits and starts as two muzzle flashes exploded from the man's pistol.

The speed with which he moved appeared inhuman, and his muzzle rose toward Christen and me. I threw her to the ground and rolled in front of her as I felt my pistol fire twice in my hand.

Hunter fired at least three rounds in the time I fired two, and the echoes of police sirens wafted through the smoke-filled air.

"Christen, are you hit?"

She shook her head. "I don't think so. Are you?"

I didn't know what she was going to do if I had been hit. Maybe there's some sort of super-secret postal procedure she knew to treat bullet wounds, but I said, "I'm okay. Just stay where you are."

I turned to survey the scene, and the sickening realization that Hunter and I were too slow poured over me. Both one-handed men were lying with their heads in puddles of their own blood, and the man at the counter rested against the sloped base with five holes in his chest.

I stepped back. "Everyone can relax. It's over now."

Hunter and I holstered our weapons, and I opened the front door as slowly as possible with my Secret Service cred-pack held high.

Two officers with weapons drawn stepped to within a few feet, and one of them asked, "Chase? Is that you?"

"Yeah, it's me, Chip. Hunter and I are inside. There's three dead bad guys and six innocents unhurt, but we've got a surviving hostage still in a suicide vest. It's Christen from the post office."

"Can you get everyone out while we get the bomb guy rolling?"

I held the door open, and Hunter herded the trembling customers and employees of the bank into the parking lot. With everyone out, I took a knee beside Christen, and she tugged at the vest like it was full of ants.

"Stay calm. Sometimes these things are rigged to go off if you try to remove them. We don't want that."

She was still trembling, so I took her hands in mine. "I know you're scared, but I'm going to stay with you until this is over. Okay?"

She shook her head. "I'm not scared. I'm mad. I wanted to kill those guys, and you beat me to it."

Laughter wasn't the appropriate reaction, but it was the only one I could muster. "Yeah, well, I think you gave them a good taste of your heel before they left this world. But we didn't shoot them. The guy at the counter did."

She peered across my shoulder. "Why?"

"That's the second-best question of the day. The first is *who*?"

Chapter 2
Crisscross Applesauce

Hunter laid a hand on my shoulder. "Get out of here, Chase. I'll stay with Christen until the bomb guy gets here."

Christen looked up at my partner. "Thanks for the thought, Stone, but both of you should get out of here. Casey is the only bomb tech the St. Marys PD has, and he's out of town this week. I know because we've been holding his mail for him until he gets back."

I stuck my head through the door just as an officer approached. "Chase, we've got a little problem."

"I know," I said. "Casey's out of town. What's your plan?"

"We're calling the state police, but it'll take some time to get them all the way down here."

I turned back to Hunter. "Get Mongo."

He held up a hand. "I'm already on it."

Five minutes later, our six-foot-eight-inch, three-hundred-pound gentle giant pressed through the door with a tool pouch beneath his arm. "What's happening, guys?"

Hunter shrugged. "Ah, you know . . . A few dead bodies and a pretty girl in a suicide vest. Just another day."

Mongo eyed the scene. "The two guys with their hands blown off were shot in the head from the direction of the cashier's counter. What's that about?"

"Their fearless leader put them down before Hunter and I could stop him."

"Interesting," Mongo said. "All right, let me take a look." He planted himself on the floor and whispered, "Crisscross apple-sauce."

Christen laughed. "Did you really just say crisscross apple-sauce?"

Mongo leaned in, studied the vest, and gave her a wink. "No, that's silly. Why would I say that?" He traced several wires with his fingertips and sighed. "You guys should probably go outside while Christen and I work some stuff out."

Hunter shook his head. "Nope. We're not going anywhere. We told Christen we'd stay with her."

She smiled up at him. "It's really better if you two go outside. Marvin and I can handle this, but I wouldn't mind if you called Singer and had him say a prayer or two."

Hesitantly, Hunter and I stepped toward the door, and Mongo said, "The GBI bomb techs will be here in about forty-five minutes. I can get you out of this thing in ten, but it's up to you."

Christen swallowed hard. "Let's go inside the vault, just in case you screw this up. There's no reason to kill anybody else this morning."

The giant helped Christen to her feet, and they disappeared behind the enormous door of the vault.

Hunter and I stepped through the door and into the parking lot to find our old buddy, the police chief, chewing on a cigar stump. "So, you two are robbin' banks now? Is that the game?"

Hunter said, "Work's been a little slow, Chief. We had to do something to supplement our income."

He planted his hands on his hips. "Yeah, I bet. Let's have it. How many people did you kill?"

"Just one this time," I said. "But he took out two of his own before we could stop him."

The chief scratched his head. "He shot two of his own men? On purpose?"

"There's no question about that," I said. "When he drew, he terminated both men with two perfectly placed shots before Hunter or I could get off a round."

The chief lowered his chin. "Are you telling me this guy out-gunned you *and* Hunter?"

I grimaced. "I wouldn't say he outgunned us, but he got two extremely accurate shots off in less than a second."

"With what kind of weapon?"

I dug the toe of my boot into the sandy surface of the parking lot. "This is where I get a little egg on my face. It was a nineteen-eleven, and I missed it. His pants never broke at the ankle. There was nothing to give away his concealed carry."

He stared into the blue morning sky and sucked air between his teeth. "A suicide vest on a federal government employee, two dead-man triggers, a guy fast enough to outgun you and Hunter, and a bank robbery on a Wednesday morning. What does that add up to in your head, Mr. Secret Service agent man?"

"You know I'm not really a Secret Service agent, right?"

He pulled a pouch of tobacco from his pocket and packed a chew into his jaw. "Yeah, but you've got yourself a set of credentials that say you are, and for us small-town, Southern cops, that's good enough."

I glanced back at the bank, thankful there'd been no explosion from the vault. "What does Wednesday morning mean, Chief?"

He spat a long stream of tobacco juice between his shoes. "It means there was less than twenty-five thousand dollars in that bank. The Brinks truck comes on Monday and Thursday. Even a third-rate bank robber would know that. Whatever those guys were after, it wasn't money."

"How long will it take you to get a solid ID on the dead guys?" I asked.

He sighed. "If I was a bettin' man—and I am—I'd bet those boys don't have a stitch of ID on them, and they've probably ground off their fingerprints."

"What about DNA?"

He laughed so hard he choked a little. "Why don't you come back to the police station with me, and I'll show you my cutting-edge forensic lab. The closest thing we've got to a DNA lab is a secretary—excuse me, an executive assistant—who demands that we do *not* agitate her."

I sidestepped another tobacco stream. "I thought the FBI handled all bank robbery cases."

He wiped his mouth on his sleeve. "They do, but thanks to you and Hunter, this one was over almost before it started. The feds aren't going to be in any hurry to get down here and stare at three dead bodies."

Before I could dig any deeper, Mongo and Christen came out of the bank, neither of them wearing a suicide vest.

The chief said, "I guess that means you disarmed the vest."

Mongo accepted a long hug from Christen and stepped beside me. "It's not exactly disarmed, Chief, but it's locked in the vault and waiting for a real bomb tech."

"Thanks, Mongo. I really appreciate you stepping up on this one."

The big man waved him off. "It's nice to have a few skills tucked away for times like this."

The chief turned back to me. "So, about that idea of yours . . ."

I shook my head. "I didn't say I had any ideas, but there's a lot about this morning that doesn't add up. It's not my monkey, and it sure isn't my circus, but we'll help if we can."

"Oh, you can help. It's just a matter of whether or not whoever you really work for will approve of you getting involved."

"From where I'm standing, Chief, I'd say we're already involved."

"Speaking of involved," he said, "I need yours and Hunter's guns. I'm sure you've got a backup."

I pulled my Glock, dropped the magazine, and cycled the slide. After pocketing the mag, I handed the pistol to the chief, butt first.

The chief turned and whistled toward a young officer who appeared to have no idea what was happening. "Smitty, get over here and bring an evidence bag and receipt."

Smitty dropped my pistol into the clear plastic bag, handed me a copy of the evidence receipt, and sealed the bag. The chief grunted and motioned toward Hunter. The procedure repeated itself, and our pistols were likely gone forever.

"Is there anything else you need from us, Chief?"

He sniffed and made a noise I'm certain my body has never made. "Yeah, about that . . . If I get you a good sample and some fingerprints—if they've got 'em—could you have your people . . . you know . . ."

"Only if you promise to give our guns back when this is over."

He shrugged. "Sometimes evidence slips through the cracks, and those *are* nice pistols."

I rolled my eyes. "Get the samples to Skipper, our um, executive assistant, and she'll get them through the system for you. It won't be official, though. You understand that. It's a favor for a friend."

If Skipper, the finest intelligence analyst in the business, ever heard me calling her an executive assistant, she'd serve my liver for dinner, but there's only so much truth one should ever tell the police chief.

He raised an eyebrow. "Are you calling me a friend, Chase?"

I shook my head. "I was talking about Smitty. Can we go now? Some of us have real jobs, and we're late for ours."

He said, "Should I ask for your passports so you don't leave the country?"

I chuckled. "Sure, Chief. Which ones do you want?"

"Get out of here, troublemaker. But before you go, thanks for what you did in there."

"Don't mention it."

Before Hunter and I made it to the Suburban, Lindsey ran from the corner of the parking lot and leapt into Hunter's arms.

She peppered him with kisses and leaned back to have a look. "Thank you, thank you, thank you a thousand times! You saved our lives in there, and I loved the two of you pretending to be the bank robbers. I knew you guys weren't just regular dudes. You're some kind of cops or something, aren't you?"

He returned her hug and wiped his face. "We're just concerned citizens, but we're glad we could help. Are you okay?"

She took his hand and looked up at him. "I'm still pretty scared. Maybe you should do something, like let me cook dinner for you. You know . . . to say thanks."

"I'll have to ask Chase. But that sounds good to me."

She shot a glance at me and then back to my partner. "Um, I was really just thinking of you, if that's all right."

I feigned shock. "That hurts my feelings."

Hunter threw a bullet he'd been palming at me. "You don't have feelings, Peg Leg. When are we leaving?"

"Not before the weekend," I said. "So, you've got plenty of time to have a homecooked dinner without me."

"How 'bout tonight?" Lindsey asked.

Hunter checked his watch. "What time?"

She giggled. "I'm off the rest of the day since the bank is closed, so anytime is fine with me."

"How about six?"

Lindsey danced on her tiptoes. "Perfect. You do like spaghetti, right? That's all I really know how to make."

"Spaghetti sounds great. I'll see you at six."

Chapter 3
The Talking Frog

Back at Bonaventure, that beautiful piece of land on the North River that had been in my mother's family since the late eighteenth century, I pulled the heavy door closed on our third-floor conference room and operations center.

Skipper, our analyst, sat at her typical position in front of four screens with two keyboards and panels of commo gear I'd never be smart enough to understand. As usual, she started the ball rolling. "Let's get this out of the way first. Nice job on the bank-robbery thing this morning. You guys are, once again, local heroes while I'm stuck in this dungeon and being called terrible names like *executive assistant*." She glared at me as if I were number one on her hit list.

I threw up my hands. "What did you want me to call you? Super spy?"

She huffed. "That would certainly be better than being called somebody's assistant—executive or otherwise. But I'll deal with you later. Right now, we've got work to do. Does anyone have anything for me before I bring Clark online?"

Clark Johnson was the team's handler and a former Green Beret. I'd learned more from him than everyone else in my life combined. Since he wasn't technically a member of the action team, he lived the good life on South Beach with Maebelle, a world-famous chef who just happened to be his wife.

Risking falling through the thin ice on which I was obviously skating, I asked, "Any hits on the DNA or prints?"

Skipper lowered her chin. "I don't know. Maybe you should hire an executive assistant and ask her . . . or him."

"What's it going to take for me to get out of the doghouse, and how do you know I called you that?"

She smiled the mischievous smile she was so good at. "I know everything you say and do, Chase Fulton. And don't you forget it."

"Noted."

She continued. "There were no usable prints, and so far, there aren't any hits in the DNA database. I've got Interpol on it, too, but it'll be tomorrow before I hear back from them. Do you have any guesses who these guys might be?"

I slowly shook my head. "No, but they're definitely not your run-of-the-mill bank robbers."

Skipper struck a few keys. "I've got some outside agencies on it as well, but whoever these guys are, they've gone to a lot of trouble to stay under the radar."

Mongo tapped the table. "I may be able to shed some light. The suicide vest they built had all the hallmarks of Khanjar Al-lah."

Singer, our Southern Baptist sniper, cleared his throat. "Khanjar Allah? The Dagger of God?"

Mongo nodded. "The soldering was a dead giveaway. As far as we know, there are only six bomb makers for Khanjar Allah, and all of them learned directly from the master, Yahir Al-Sayyed. Nobody solders like Yahir."

Hunter leaned back in his chair. "How do you know stuff like that?"

Mongo shrugged. "It's what I do. I look good, and I know stuff."

Hunter palmed his forehead. "Well, maybe half of that is true."

Skipper pounded away at her keyboard as if she were in a race. Without slowing down or looking up, she said, "None of the guys in the bank looked Middle Eastern, did they?"

I eyed Hunter, and he shook his head. "No, they looked like they could've been from right here. There was nothing distinctive about any of them until the boss shot the other two in the face."

Skipper spun in her chair. "I need you to be sure about that."

"Sure about what?" I asked.

"Are you sure he shot them directly in the face and not center mass?"

Another glance back at Hunter, and my memory was confirmed. "Yeah, I'm sure. He got one of them in the bridge of the nose and the other in the temple."

She stared at the ceiling for a moment. "Have you seen the security camera footage from the bank?"

"No, why would I have seen the footage?"

"I'm working a theory here."

Everyone leaned in. When Skipper worked a theory, things happened fast.

She clicked her pen against her teeth. "What if—and I'm just spitballing here—but what if he wasn't just trying to kill them, but also trying to eliminate the only other means we have of identifying them?"

"Facial recognition?" Mongo asked.

Skipper held up a finger. "Not just facial recognition, but also retinal scans."

Hunter punched the table. "No way! Nobody's good enough with a pistol to intentionally dot two different guys, right in the eye holes, in less than a second when me and Chase are an instant away from drilling holes in him."

Skipper held up her palms. "I told you it's just a theory, but don't get too cocky about who's the fastest gun in town."

Hunter gave me a wink. "I'd say me and Chase are tied for first now that we ventilated that guy's chest cavity."

She stared into the distance and bit her bottom lip. "How much time do you want me to spend on this?"

I said, "Let's brief Clark and see what he thinks, but let's move on for now."

She spun back to her console and typed for several seconds. Clark's face filled the large screen above Skipper's head, and I recoiled.

"Hey there, big fella! Could you back away from the camera a little? It looks like those nose hairs could use a little grooming work."

He moved away and said, "Sorry, I was trying to figure out why my camera mount won't stay where I put it. I heard a news story about a bank robbery up there this morning. Do you know anything about that?"

"We've got a little inside scoop, but we'll tell you about that when we finish the mission brief."

Clark settled into his seat. "Ah, yes, the mission brief. I'm sure you're excited about a little cold-weather operation."

"Not in the least," I said. "But duty calls."

"Indeed, it does," Clark said. "Let's start with the injured reserve. How're you doing, Hunter?"

"I'm good, but the doc says I can't deploy for at least six more months unless I'm working the TOC or something like that."

Clark sighed. "We're running out of operators. With my brother permanently grounded, and now you on the bench, we're down to just four, and what we're jumping into is no joke. I'm afraid we may have painted ourselves into a corner and thrown away the key."

I squeezed my temples. "You do know that's not how either of those sayings go, right?"

Clark waved a hand. "You know what I mean."

"No, actually, I rarely know what you mean, but let's hear it."

He said, "Let's start with the starters. Have you ever been to Arctic Survival School, Chase?"

"No, but I've studied the material."

Clark said, "I studied the waterboarding material, but that doesn't mean I know how it feels to be upside down in a bucket of water."

Mongo jumped in. "I'll keep him alive and teach him how *not* to freeze to death."

Clark shuffled some papers. "Okay, boys and girls, here's the deal. We've got a Russian submarine that got itself stuck in the ice in the Northwest Passage."

Singer interrupted. "How does a submarine get stuck in the ice? It never gets cold enough to freeze at the depths they run."

"Keep your shirt on, rifle boy. I'm not finished. It was supposed to be a routine training mission—whatever that means—but it didn't work out so well. Due to the latitude, the satellite coverage is weak, but we think the sub surfaced in flowing ice and launched some kind of surface party."

"Surface party?" I said. "What would they be doing on the surface in the Northwest Passage?"

Clark continued. "We don't know, but we do know the helmsman must've fallen asleep on duty because the sub drifted over some shallow water and ran aground. Some sort of mechanical problem must've followed because the sub didn't move after running aground. We think she's now frozen in place."

Mongo waved his pen in the air. "She's a nuclear boat, right?"

Clark nodded. "Yeah, she's an Akula-class boat named the *Pantera K-Three-One-Seven*. We believe she has the upgraded O-K-nine-V-M reactor. That would give her a hundred days of standard-duty duration, but if she's locked in the ice and not using power for propulsion, she could probably keep a crew of sailors alive for eight or ten months."

"What about rations?" Singer asked.

Clark said, "I don't know how the Russkies provision, but there may be a chance they could supplement their rations with polar bears, seals, and sea lions."

I jumped in. "If they're frozen in place, they might get lucky and a polar bear or two might walk by, but there won't be any sea lions or seals on the ice."

"Maybe they're eating each other," Skipper said. "It's not like it's unheard of."

Mongo said, "My question is, why didn't they launch a rescue effort and scuttle the boat?"

Clark said, "And we have a winner! I should've known it'd be you, Goliath. They did launch a rescue mission, and that's why we're neck-deep in frozen salt water on this one. The rescue attempt failed miserably, but that's not the cool part. The silver wrapping is *who* launched the rescue mission."

I said, "I'm pretty sure you meant silver lining, but don't keep us in the dark. Who's on the rescue?"

Mongo said, "Let me guess. The Chinese?"

"Bingo!" Clark said. "But it gets better. There must be something in the water up there because the Chinese icebreaker, *Xue Long*, puked in the sheets about fifty miles from the *Pantera*, and she's not moved an inch in over a month."

Mongo said, "It's pronounced *Shway-Lung*, and it means *Snow Dragon*. If I remember correctly, it's officially classified as an Arctic research vessel."

Clark said, "Anyway . . . as I was saying. The Chinese boat, *Chewy Lug,* or whatever, is a civilian boat. She was built in Ukraine in ninety-three and ninety-four, but she wasn't originally an icebreaker. She was an arctic cargo boat, but due to the hull design, she was converted to an icebreaker in ninety-seven by some shipyard in Shanghai I can't pronounce."

He paused to have a sip of whatever was in his coffee cup, and I said, "All this history is great, but where do we come in, and what are we supposed to do with a stuck Russian sub and a Chinese icebreaker?"

Clark returned his cup to a spot off-camera. "That's the tricky part. *Technically,* the Russians haven't declared the sub to be in peril, and they've launched no 'official' rescue effort. They're saying the *Snow Dragon* has nothing to do with any missing or disabled sub that may or may not exist."

"Ah!" I said. "That's why we got called up to the major league for this one. The Navy can't help because there's no official ship in peril, and the *Snow Dragon* is a research vessel that belongs in the Arctic."

Clark snapped his fingers. "You're pretty smart, College Boy, but that's not all. Since we did such a bang-up job in Cuba—bada-bing bada-boom—we're the goose that laid the talking frog."

I couldn't let that one go. "Wait a minute. Talking frog? Really?"

Clark looked offended. "Exactly. Don't you know anything? Stop interrupting me. This is serious. The Board pegged us for this one because of our stellar track record. Is that better?"

I nodded but didn't speak, so he continued. "Good. It would be relatively easy to plow in there with the *Lori Danielle* and pluck out the survivors, but as usual, we're not supposed to be where we are. We won't be riding to the rescue aboard the *LD* for this one, but our ice-breaking chariot will look a lot like her. Our research vessel is getting a paint job as we speak. When she comes out of the paint booth, she'll be the *Polar Explorer Three*."

I waggled my pen. "What are we supposed to do when we get up there and find the sub? We can't exactly walk up, knock on the hatch, and declare that we're there to rescue them."

"Forget about the sub," Clark said. "We don't think there's anyone still aboard her."

I asked, "Then we're going after the icebreaker?"

"Not exactly. We're actually going to find out what the sub was doing there in the first place, because whatever it was, it was *not* a routine training mission."

I slid my notepad away. "What does the Board think we are? Even if we find the sub, the only two things I know about submarines are that they float and sink. That's it. How are we supposed to figure out what their mission was?"

Clark put on that crooked grin of his. "Because you, College Boy, can read Cyrillic."

I leaned back in my chair. "I might be able to read Russian, but what makes the Board think there will be anything meaningful to read on that boat? If there was anything resembling classified material on that tub before the skipper got her stuck, the officers would've destroyed everything that would burn—especially anything detailing their mission."

Clark said, "Unless they damaged the reactor and exposed the ship and crew to radioactive material or radiation."

I tossed my pen onto the table. "Oh, great. So, we've got a Chinese icebreaker that's stuck in the ice but supposed to be able to operate in the heaviest ice on Earth, a Russian fast-attack sub that's probably radioactive, and polar bears, and we're supposed to march in there and figure out what the Russians had in mind when they stuck their sub under the ice. Is that about right?"

Clark gave me a nod. "That pretty much covers it, except for one thing. The sub's not *probably* radioactive. It's just *maybe* radioactive."

"Then I've got one more question."

Clark stuck his pen behind his ear. "Let's hear it."

"Since we're down a man, you're coming with us, right?"

The grin made its return. "I wouldn't miss it for the world, College Boy."

Chapter 4
My Favorite Things

I rolled over and pushed Penny's hair from my face and tried to focus on the clock, but grogginess wouldn't let my eyes come to life. I had no choice other than feeling for my ringing phone. "Yeah, hello?"

A voice that was way too happy said, "I'm really sorry to wake you, Mr. Fulton, but your horses are out."

I stretched, still desperately trying to focus on the clock. "I don't have any horses."

The caller seemed stunned, but Penny rescued me by pulling the phone from my hand. She stuck it to her ear, and I dived back into the pillow. I was relieved to know I was heading back to the spirit world, but my relief was short-lived.

Penny shook me. "Chase, wake up. The horses are out of the pasture."

"Whose horses?" I groaned.

"Ours!"

I rubbed my eyes. "*We* don't have horses. *You* have horses."

It didn't work. She gave me a shove, and I landed on my one remaining foot beside our incredibly comfortable bed. Apparently, I was about to wrangle some horses in the middle of the night, so I pulled on my prosthetic and my boots.

I grabbed a T-shirt from my dresser and pulled it over my head. "Okay, let's go get *your* horses."

She snickered. "Are you sure you're ready to go?"

I shook my head. "No, I'm not ready to go, but I'm sure I don't have any choice in the matter."

She opened the bedroom door and led the way downstairs. My prosthetic foot would never have any feeling, so I was forced to watch my right boot strike each tread of the stairs to avoid falling in my midnight stupor. It must've been step seven or eight when the reason for Penny's snickering became glaringly obvious to me. I stopped, shook my head, and turned back for our bedroom.

She giggled again, "Where are you headed, naked butt?"

"I'm going to get some pants so I'll have a pocket for a pistol to solve this horse problem."

Her giggling ceased. "Chase Fulton, if you ever say anything like that again, you can pick another bedroom."

I ran a hand through my hair. "Okay, fine. I'm just going to get pants . . . no pistol."

It took two hours to find all the errant equine and lead them to their stalls. Until we found the break in the fence, we'd have to keep them locked up, but I wasn't concerned about that endeavor. All I wanted was to be back in bed and sound asleep, but I should've known I wouldn't get my wish.

Mongo met me at the bottom of the steps leading to the back gallery at Bonaventure. "Oh, good. You're up. We can get started."

I yawned and stretched. "Get started doing what?"

"Learning how to stay alive when your blood is trying to freeze."

"Oh, goody. My two favorite things in one night . . . horses and the cold."

Mongo ignored me and stared down at his watch. "They should be here any minute."

"Who?"

"The guys with the freezer."

I started up the stairs. "Fine. Wake me up when they get here. I'm going back to bed."

"I don't think so," Mongo said. "I told Clark I'd teach you to stay alive in the arctic environment, and I can't do that if you're asleep."

I plopped down on the steps. "Okay, then. Can I at least have something to eat before whatever this is starts?"

"I'm afraid not. That's part of this morning's lesson. You'll understand soon enough."

The sound of a heavy truck on the driveway pulled my tormentor from the gallery stairs, and soon, a refrigerated tractor-trailer was backed into place beside our shop. The driver dragged a pair of heavy-duty power cables from the trailer and into the shop, and Mongo waved me over.

I followed him into the trailer and was immediately hit with a wall of frigid air. "Well, *that's* not what I needed this morning."

Mongo motioned to a wooden crate. "Have a seat, and let's chat."

I planted myself on the crate and started shivering within seconds.

Mongo played with the fog he blew from his lips. "So, what's the one thing you want right now?"

"I want to be back outside where it's sixty degrees."

"Exactly, and that's easy to accomplish here. We can simply step through that door, and everything about our world will change, but that's not true on the ice. Once we're in the environment, there's no magic door we can step through to end our suffering. That means we have to find a way to function when we're extremely cold."

He pulled a plastic bottle of water from his pocket, unscrewed the top, and threw the water all over me. I swatted at the incoming wall of water, but I was drenched.

He said, "Now what do you want?"

"The immediate thing that comes to mind is that I want to punch you in the throat for throwing water on me."

"This is serious, Chase."

I shook the water from my hands. "Oh, I know, and the lesson I'm probably supposed to learn is the importance of staying dry in a freezing environment."

"Very good, Grasshopper. Now, it's time for lesson number three."

He kicked the crate I was sitting on with his massive boot, and it shattered like glass, sending me crashing to the floor of the trailer. I pushed myself from the floor, but Mongo planted an enormous hand on my shoulder.

"Stay down there and pick through the crate for something to start a fire."

I pilfered through the splintered wood and found a thick plastic pouch with the words "Arctic Survival Bag 1 of 4" stenciled on the exterior. I tugged at the corners of the pouch, and my fingers ached as if they were on the verge of breaking off of my hands. "I can't get it open."

He leaned against the wall of the trailer. "Use your knife."

I shoved a frozen hand into my right front pocket, but I only found lint. "My knife is still upstairs. I've been playing cowboy with Penny all night."

He shuddered. "I don't know if that's supposed to be a euphemism for something I don't want to know about, but there's never any excuse to be without a knife, especially in a subfreezing environment like the one where we'll be operating. Here, you can use mine."

He pulled a small Ziploc bag from his pocket and tossed it onto the pile of debris from the destroyed wooden crate. I snatched the plastic bag and probed at the top with fingers I could no longer feel. Performing the simplest of tasks with frozen fingers was impossible, and I'd been in the environment for less than half an hour.

I finally pulled a splinter of wood from the pile and used it to probe the plastic zipper bag. It worked, and I was rewarded with a small knife frozen solid inside a block of ice about two inches thick. I looked up at the king of my frozen hell. "Really?"

He smiled and checked his watch. "It doesn't take long for frostbite to kick in, so you might want to get that fire going."

I threw the ice-encased knife to the floor and stomped it several times until the ice broke away. With frost forming on my beard, I grabbed the small switchblade and pressed the release button. Nothing happened, and I held it up toward Mongo. "It's broken."

He shrugged. "Ticktock. Ticktock."

I dug a thumbnail into the notch on the side of the blade and pulled with everything I had, but it wouldn't give.

"It's not mechanically damaged," Mongo said. "Think."

It's the ice. The mechanism is frozen, not broken. You've got to thaw it out, dummy.

I shoved the knife into my pants and waited for my body heat to melt the ice restraining the blade. Mongo laughed, and it only took a few seconds for me to know why. The frozen metal of the knife burned my skin as if it were made of red-hot iron. I snatched the knife from my pants and shoved it behind my knee, bending my leg to encompass the tool in the material of my jeans. By the time the knife thawed enough to open, I was shaking so badly I couldn't hold the heavy plastic survival pouch tightly enough to cut it open. I finally laid the pouch on the floor, planted a knee on top of it, and sliced at it with trembling hands. I won the battle and poured the contents of the pouch onto the floor of the trailer.

A flint and steel were the first items I grabbed with my mostly useless hands, but I didn't have the dexterity to strike the fire starter.

Mongo said, "Every task gets exponentially harder the colder we get. If we were in the gazebo just outside that door, you could've torn open the bag and had a fire started in seconds, but it's taken you thirty-eight minutes to realize you're crippled beyond the ability to survive in your environment. In another thirty minutes, your hands will be frostbitten so badly, they'll burn like fire until your nerves finally lose the ability to transmit their electrical pulses to tell your brain you're freezing to death. In an hour, you'll have zero dexterity, and your shivering will be so bad you won't be able to walk. Is this sinking in?"

My teeth chattered as I tried to say, "Yes."

He took a knee in front of me and whispered, "Now, imagine you've been in this environment for twelve hours and you've managed to stay alive by some miracle. Now, your body demands sleep. Do you think you'll ever wake up from that sleep in this icebox?"

I tried to shake my head. "No."

He reached out with a gigantic hand and grabbed my T-shirt. The material crunched as he broke the layer of ice that had formed from the water-bottle incident. He pulled up my shirt, exposing my red, blotchy skin. "Take a look at that. Your chest is almost to the point of frostbite, and you didn't even notice."

"I've got to get out of here," I said through chattering teeth.

He pushed open the door and helped me down the ladder. "Go get a shower to warm up, but start with cold water. You'll scald yourself if you start hot."

The sixty-degree air outside the trailer felt like a midsummer's day, and I sucked it into my lungs as if it were the breath of life.

After a twenty-minute shower, I was determined never to step inside Mongo's trailer again, but he had other ideas.

"There you are," he said. "I was starting to think you weren't coming back."

"I didn't want to, but I knew you'd hunt me down if I ran."

He motioned toward a green duffel on the gallery deck. "Check that out."

I emptied the bag's contents onto the floor and found a parka, gloves, an oversized knife, a flint and steel twice the size of the one in the trailer, a pair of waterproof pants, and a set of goggles.

He said, "Gear up, and let's try that exercise again."

I did as he said and pulled every piece of gear into place, and then back into the frozen world we went.

Within seconds of being inside the trailer, he threw two more bottles of water at me, but it ran off the parka as if I were a duck.

"Now, start a fire," he said.

I had four pieces of kindling from the broken crate burning in seconds. We doused the fire, and he ran me through two hours of tasks in the twenty-below-zero environment. As I worked through his puzzles, I learned that every piece of exposed skin burns in minutes, so I wrapped my face and neck with a balaclava.

Mongo pulled an MRE from his satchel. "Believe it or not, trying to eat in a frozen world is one of the toughest tasks you'll do. You have to keep your skin covered as much as possible and still get food in your mouth. Digestion will be slower because your body is working so hard to stay warm, but eating is crucial. We'll try to take in at least five thousand calories every twelve hours while we're on the ice."

He was right. Eating was tough, but I managed to get every morsel of the MRE down my throat. We melted ice with the hot pack from the MRE and drank at least a quart of water.

He said, "If we're not in a vehicle, we can't carry water. It'll just freeze, and we'll have ice in a world of ice. Believe it or not, dehydration is a real threat in the cold. We have to melt and drink at least a gallon of water per day, and more if we're burning calories."

My cold-weather training continued until Mongo was convinced I had learned enough basic information to survive while learning to adapt to a frozen world.

"Let's get out of here and get warmed up. We're going to spend enough time in subzero conditions. Do you have any questions?"

"None that can't wait," I said.

As we descended the ladder from the trailer, Skipper yelled from the gallery. "Hey, guys! Get in here. You're never going to believe what Scotland Yard found."

Chapter 5
Family Feud

It took longer than it should have for Mongo and me to crawl out of our arctic gear, but by the time we made it through the back door of the house, it looked like we'd turned the Abominable Snowman inside out with bright-white jackets, gloves, and parkas scattered on the yard.

The team was already in their seats when we pulled the op center door closed behind us.

I slid into my chair. "Okay, Skipper. Let's have it."

She held up a finger. "Not so fast. First, we have to go over some ground rules. My contact at Scotland Yard is absolutely back-door and under-the-table. He or she is still actively working cases, so if it gets out that she or he is sharing intel with us, that would be the end of a good career for her and an end to our inside contact. If we burn her, we have to be prepared to support her or him. This is the part where all of you nod and agree."

I said, "I heard you say *she* twice more than *he*, so I think it's safe to assume your contact is a woman."

Skipper grimaced. "I guess I deserved that since I work for a psychologist. Regardless, let's keep *her* a secret, all right?"

"We can do that, but we need to know that you trust her and the information she's feeding us is on the level."

Skipper paused. "I don't know her well enough to call her a trusted ally yet, but she's been truthful with me in the past, as far as I know. It doesn't rise to the level of *full* trust yet, but I'm not willing to out her."

"In that case," I said, "we need to make sure we don't feed her anything she could pass along to the wrong channels. So, let's hear what she gave up."

Skipper rattled the keyboard for a few seconds, and images appeared on the overhead screens. "Look at the guy on the left. His name is—"

Mongo cut her off. "That's Yahir Al-Sayyed, the Saudi master bomb maker for Khanjar Allah."

"Very good," Skipper said. "But how about this guy?"

Another headshot of a man with the hint of a Middle Eastern look filled the screen, and Mongo said, "Nope, don't know him."

Skipper said, "There's no reason you should. That's what makes my Scotland Yard contact so valuable. They keep dossiers on all sorts of characters. This one in particular is a guy named Pan Dahari. At least that's what one of his passports says his name is. He's believed to be from Turkey but doesn't seem to have a home address at the moment. His half-sister, Aiyla, is one of the wives of our favorite bomb maker, Yahir Al-Sayyed."

Singer furrowed his brow. "*One* of his wives? Islam forbids polygamy."

Mongo said, "Not always. There are provisions within the Koran allowing for polygamy in the case of the oppressed or orphans among women. Maybe our bomb maker likes loopholes."

Singer scratched a note on his pad and gave Mongo a nod.

Skipper continued. "Please tell me we're not trying to make Yahir out to be a good little boy."

Singer said, "No, I just want to understand him. I'm sorry I interrupted."

"Don't be sorry," she said. "We're learning together. So, back to the family ties. Pan Dahari is a bit of a shady figure, but he seems to be tied to the international banking network—as in, the electronic side. It's an extremely well-encrypted communication network, and Dahari may have even designed some software to provide security for the network. It's all a little fuzzy right now, but I'm piecing it together."

I said, "All of this is fascinating, but how does any of it tie our bank robbers to Al-Sayyed?"

"I'm getting there," she said. "Tell me what you *didn't* see any of the three robbers carrying during the attempted bank robbery."

Hunter said, "Bags."

Skipper snapped her fingers. "Exactly! They weren't there to collect money without bags. They were there to acquire something small and easy to carry, or they were there to commit an act of terrorism."

I said, "If it was pure terrorism, why wouldn't they have sent Christen in with the vest and blown the place to bits from the parking lot?"

Skipper said, "My thoughts exactly. I don't think it was an act of terrorism. I think they wanted something from inside the bank, but it wasn't their desire to blow themselves up. If it were, the vests would've been on the terrorists and not Christen."

"I hate to backtrack," I said. "We still haven't tied Al-Sayyed to the bank robbers."

Skipper waved a hand. "Sorry, I got excited. But here's the tie. Al-Sayyed is married to Pan Dahari's half-sister. We covered that, but this is where it gets weird. Aiyla has another half-brother named Nasir Osman. I know this is getting a little confusing for your testosterone-driven brains, but here's the zinger. Our lead bank robber's DNA sample very nearly matches Nasir Osman's DNA profile."

I blinked against the familial web Skipper was weaving. "So, the bank robber was Nasir Osman?"

She shook her head. "No, you weren't listening. I said *near* matches. That means Nasir Osman and our bank robber are definitely related and most likely share a common parent."

The air left the room, and everyone at the table sank in their seats.

Clark, who'd flown in while I was enduring Mongo's winter wonderland, had sat through the entire briefing without saying a word, but that came to an abrupt end when he said, "Get me a secure line to the Board."

"Wait a minute," Skipper said. "You're not burning my contact."

Clark lowered his chin. "I'm not worried about your contact. I'm worried about how many sleeper cells are waiting to hit banks all over the world."

"I'm a little ahead of you," she said. "I've already pulled the numbers. On average, there are twelve point three bank robberies per day in the U.S. The most we've ever had in a single day was forty-four, and that was on a Friday. That's the most popular day of the week for bank robberies, by the way, but yesterday, there were twenty-eight, and that's a new record for a Wednesday."

Clark pulled his headset from the shelf beneath his spot at the table. "Get the Board on the line."

Skipper said, "No. Wait a minute. What are you going to do? You can't hand this information to the Board. It's not ours to give away. I'm not going to let you do that to my source."

Clark slammed his hand on the table, sending an echo through the op center like thunder. "Here are your choices. Get the Board on the phone, or don't. I don't care. I have the responsibility to feed this intelligence—and that's what it is, intelligence, not information—up the chain. Whatever this is, it has to go to Langley.

It's that simple. If you won't get the Board on the line, I'll walk out of here and call them myself. It's my decision and my responsibility, and that's what's going to happen."

Skipper stood from her console and stared Clark down. "If you burn my contact, I'm done with you, I'm done with the Board, and I'm done with all of this. Good luck finding another analyst who can do what I do and who's willing to let you burn their informant network to the ground. Because it'll take me about thirty seconds to let every analyst on the planet know that's exactly what you did."

Suddenly, every eye in the room was focused on me, and every pulse rate must've doubled. I didn't know what to say, but that wasn't going to stop me from trying to get my train back on the rails. "That's enough. Everybody's right, and we're on the same team. Just take a breath. Clark, I'm starting with you. I cannot let you cost us our analyst. Every other member of this team, except her, can be replaced in a matter of months. There is no replacement for her, and if you'll take a beat to think about that, you'll see I'm right."

Skipper set her jaw. "That's right, Clark, and—"

I held up a finger in Skipper's direction. "Stop it. What you're doing is just as dangerous as what Clark's doing, so come down off your high horse and listen. I will not let you hold this team hostage beneath the threat of you walking out. That's not how we work. It's never been how we've worked, and we're not starting it now. If you don't want to be here, walk away. I never want anybody on this team who's anything short of a one-hundred-percent volunteer, and that goes for *everybody*."

Clark said, "I don't think you understand—"

I cut him off. "No, *you* don't understand. This is my team, and we work beneath you because we've bled and killed and fought beside you for so long that we've become one body with the same blood, sweat, and tears, and that's not going to change today. This team works because we trust each other implicitly, and we always do what's best for the team first . . . always."

Silence ruled the moment, but steam was still rising from Skipper's skull.

It was time for me to solve our problem, so I took a long breath. "Clark is right. This intel has to go up the chain."

Skipper stomped her foot. "No, it doesn't. Not at the expense of my source."

"Stop interrupting," I ordered. "The intel is too strong to sit on. Our first responsibility is to the safety of this nation, so the intel is going up the chain. It's that simple."

Skipper snatched her sweater from the back of her chair, but I held up a hand. "Stop! Clark is right, but you're right, too. We're not going to burn your source. She's too valuable, and you've spent too many years building that relationship. Here's how it's going to work."

I paused long enough to take a sip. "We're calling the Board—as a team—and we're going to brief our suspicion, but that's all it is right now . . . a suspicion. We're going to turn over the DNA samples and tell them what we suspect. We are not decision-makers at this level. This is so far over our heads, we can't even begin to imagine the implications. Now, I don't care which one of you briefs the Board. In fact, I think you should both do it, but whoever does it will not burn Skipper's source, under any circumstances. If Scotland Yard could make this connection, the CIA can certainly come to the same conclusion. It's that simple, and that's how it's going down. Got it?"

Skipper tossed her sweater onto the console. "I'll get the Board on the line, but—"

"No buts!" I said. "Do your job. That goes for both of you."

* * *

It took Clark and Skipper fifteen minutes to brief the Board, and every member listened intently before firing questions, but the first question out of the Board's mouth was, "Who made the discovery of the DNA matches?"

Clark opened his mouth, but Skipper muted his mic and said, "We have a secure and trusted source who made the discovery, but revealing that person's identity would serve no useful purpose. You have labs at your disposal that can connect the same dots in a matter of hours."

After a long silence, someone from the Board said, "Fair enough. We'll dispatch a courier for the DNA samples."

Disco, our chief pilot and retired A-10 Warthog driver, said, "We can have the sample on the ground at Andrews Air Force Base in a little over an hour."

A Board member said, "That's right. I seem to remember funding the purchase of a certain Gulfstream G-Four *Grey Ghost* for your team. Spool up the engines, and we'll have a technician meet you on the tarmac at Andrews in ninety minutes."

Disco stood and headed for the door, but the Gulfstream wasn't a single-pilot machine, so I stood with him.

Clark rose as well, but he didn't head for the door. Instead, he strode to within inches of Skipper's workstation. "I'm sorry. I was wrong, and you're too important to this team—and to me—for me to behave that way. It won't happen again."

Skipper pressed her lips into a thin line before saying, "I'm sorry, too. I shouldn't have threatened to leave. It wasn't right. I won't let that happen again, either."

The two stepped into each other's arms and hugged for a long moment.

When they separated, she said, "I really need Chase here for the Arctic mission planning. Would you mind flying with Disco?"

Clark sighed. "I guess if you're going to twist my arm, I'll suffer through a flight in that piece-of-crap airplane for the good of the team, but don't start expecting me to be so sacrificial."

Chapter 6
Painter's Block

"Well, that was interesting," I said.

Skipper spun in her seat. "Yeah, about that . . ."

I held up both hands. "It's over, and everybody kissed and made up. We can move on unless there's something you'd like to talk about."

In a rare demonstration of uncertainty, she ducked her head. "It's Tony."

Tony was Clark's brother and Skipper's husband, who'd been badly injured in the field with the team and would likely never deploy with us again.

"He's not doing great," she said.

The friend in me had a thousand questions, but the psychologist in me chose to shut my mouth and listen.

"He stopped painting, even though he's got orders for half a dozen more pictures." She paused, but I held my tongue, and she said, "The money would be nice, and I love seeing him paint, but he's just not feeling it. I can't get him to talk about it, but he misses the action, Chase. I'm starting to think he may be sliding into depression."

That was my cue. "Do you think he'd talk with me about it?"

She chewed on her pencil. "I don't know. Probably not as a doctor, but maybe as a friend."

"What do you want?" I asked.

She brightened. "I want my husband back. I miss him. He was so full of life, and every day was a new adventure, but now . . . I don't know. I'm worried about him."

We'd just stepped into a realm in which I had the duty to ask a difficult question. I leaned forward in my seat. "Look at me, Skipper. I have to ask. You're not seeing any signs of suicidal tendencies, are you?"

She slid her glasses up her nose to hide her attempt to wipe the tear from her eye. "You know I look everything up, right?" I nodded, and she said, "Okay, so I researched the warning signs, and the only thing that's a real red flag so far is one thing he said a few times."

"What did he say?"

She fiddled with her glasses again. "He keeps saying he doesn't want to be deadweight. He says he can't feel like a man if he's not contributing."

I listened to every syllable and said, "Selling paintings at half a million bucks apiece qualifies as contributing, doesn't it?"

She shrugged. "Yeah, but like I said, he stopped painting. He says he just doesn't feel like it."

I pondered the situation for a moment. "Let's put him back to work."

She stiffened. "He can't go back into the field with you guys. The doctors say—"

"I'm not suggesting deploying with us. I'm saying there's plenty of work for him to do that doesn't involve getting shot at."

"He's too smart to fall for that. He'll know instantly that you're throwing him busywork."

"It's not busywork. I'm serious about this bank robbery situation. If the Board keeps us on the Arctic mission, I'm not willing to forget about what those guys tried to do to Christen and our bank. I want to know what's really going on, and I think Tony may be just the guy to get it done."

The slightest hint of a smile came to her face. "He might like that idea."

"Get him up here," I said. "We'll brief it and put his butt to work."

* * *

Tony showed up fifteen minutes later, and we had him briefed up in no time. He took several pages of notes, and the transformation in his demeanor was astonishing.

I wrapped up the briefing with a bit of mental judo. "Now, listen. If you don't have time to devote to this project, we'll pass it to somebody else who can work it. It's too important to be a side gig."

He shook his head. "No, Chase, don't worry about that. I've got you. I don't know if Skipper told you, but I've really needed a project. I was getting a little down. The paintings weren't happening for me, and I'm not too good at sitting around. I kinda need something to keep me going. You know what I mean?"

"I know exactly what you mean. We're not sitters. We're men of action. You may not be ready to hit the road with us yet, but this bank robbery thing is weighing heavily on me. It means a lot that you're willing to take it on. I'll hook you up with the police chief and leave it in your hands."

"I'm ready when you are," he said.

We left Skipper alone to do whatever she does when we're not watching, and we headed for the St. Marys big-city police station.

* * *

"Chief, I think you know Tony Johnson, right?"

The top cop stuck out his hand. "I know who you are, but we've never shaken hands. It's nice to meet you, Tony."

"You too, Chief."

I said, "Tony is Clark's younger brother and a valuable member of our team. He was a rescue swimmer for the Coast Guard and exactly the man you want in the foxhole with you when the bad guys start lobbing rounds your way."

The chief inspected Tony from head to toe and back again. "I see. So, what brings the two of you to my office?" I shot a look over my shoulder, and the chief said, "You can close the door if it makes you feel better."

I pushed the door against the jamb and took a seat. "I'll cut to the chase because I know you're a busy man. I want you to deputize Tony and put him on the bank robbery case."

The chief dug at an invisible invader with a soggy toothpick. "That case is closed, Chase. All the perps are dead, and the bank never lost a penny except for the damage you did inside."

"I'll pay for that, Chief, but the case is far from over. You need to know what's going on behind the scenes."

I gave the chief an abbreviated and highly redacted briefing on what we'd discovered about the nationwide increase in Wednesday morning bank robberies.

"That's all very interesting, Chase, but what makes you think our little attempted robbery in our little town has anything to do with those others?"

Tony said, "I'll take this one, if you don't mind."

"Be my guest," I said.

Tony cleared his throat. "Think back to the scene of the attempted robbery. None of the three men killed during the attempt were carrying a bag of any kind. Just what do you think they were there to steal if they didn't have any way to carry it out of there?"

The chief leaned back in his massive chair and stared at the ceiling. Once the obvious question had washed through his head a few times, he inspected what was left of his toothpick. "And just what do you propose to investigate if I put you on the payroll, Mr. Johnson?"

Tony didn't miss a beat. "I think you may be misunderstanding, Chief. I'm *going* to investigate the attempted robbery, and I'm *going* to find out what was really happening with our robbery and a bunch of the others that morning. Chase and I just thought you might like to be in the loop when I do get to the bottom of it."

The toothpick went back into the chief's mouth. "Hmm. Do you have one of those Secret Service badges, too?"

Tony crossed his legs. "Not yet, but if you want me to have one, we can make that happen."

The highest-ranking law enforcement official in St Marys stood, pulled a hoop of keys from his belt, and unlocked a secure file cabinet. He returned to his desk and slid a silver shield across the desk toward Tony. "Don't arrest nobody. Don't shoot nobody. And for God's sake, don't get yourself shot with that badge in your pocket. Is all that clear?"

"It is," Tony said.

The chief directed his attention to me. "And he's still on your payroll, not mine. Capisce?"

I stood. "He doesn't need any money, Chief. He's got plenty of his own."

Tony studied the badge and shoved it into his pocket. "Thanks, Chief. Do you want my reports on paper or face-to-face?"

He spat the toothpick into the garbage. "So help me, kid. If you write any of this down, I'll shoot you myself."

"I thought that may be your answer. I'll stay out of your way, but I'll keep you in the loop."

The chief shook his head. "I'm pretty sure I'm going to regret this, and I'll probably have to testify about it one day, but go see Martha at the end of the hall. She'll take your picture and make you an ID, Detective Johnson."

On the ride home, St. Marys's newest detective said, "I really appreciate this, Chase. I was starting to feel pretty unnecessary around here."

"Let me tell you something, my friend. Everybody in this family of ours is equally important, except your wife. She's the best of us, so we're all smart enough to avoid comparing ourselves to her. We need you just as much as we need Clark or me. Don't ever convince yourself that you're any less important just because Hunter tried to kill you in the river."

It was Tony's turn to adjust his glasses. I'm not sure there was a tear coming, but he made the move look smooth. "Ah . . . Mr. Hunter."

"Why do you call him that?"

Tony put on a mischievous grin. "Because it drives him nuts. Who needs a better reason than that?"

* * *

When we made it back to Bonaventure, Clark and Disco were back from their errand to Andrews Air Force Base, and we reconvened in my favorite place on the Earth—the gazebo housing the eighteenth-century cannon overlooking the black water of the North River in my backyard.

Cuban Cohibas were lit, and Jack Daniel's Single Barrel was poured, but the best thing about my favorite spot on Earth that evening was the smile on Detective Tony Johnson's face when he said, "Listen to this, y'all. I've got to tell you this story that an old Korean War artilleryman told me about growing up in Richmond, Virginia."

Skipper grabbed his arm. "No, Tony. Don't tell that story. It's horrible."

He jerked away. "I'll have you know that's called assaulting an officer, young lady. You need to keep your hands off me."

She folded her hands like the perfect little church lady. "Okay, big boy. If you really want me to keep my hands off you, that's exactly what I'll do."

"Wait a minute," Tony said. "I'd like to retract that statement. I don't know what came over me. Clearly, I'm coming down with a fever, darlin'."

Skipper huffed. "That's what I thought. Are you really going to tell that story?"

He took a long draw from some of the best tobacco on Earth and let the white smoke encircle his head. "I sure am, pretty lady, and you're gonna sit right there and listen to it like it's the first time you've ever heard it." He took a swallow of the Tennessee sipping whiskey and sighed with great satisfaction. "So, I was sittin' around a fire one night listening to a bunch of old guys—like Mr. Hunter—telling stories from back in the day, and the talking stick finally made its way around to old Don, the epitome of a Richmond, Virginia, Southern gentleman. And this is the story he told. You're gonna have to forgive my poor imitation of his beautiful accent."

He cleared his throat, took another sip, and began. "This gentleman said, 'When I was a boy back in those days in good ol' Richmond, my fathah . . .' That's how he pronounced the word father." He said, 'My fathah owned an insurance company that sold policies that were payable by the week, and I'd go around collectin' a few cents from a few dozen customers every Friday in the only good suit of clothes I owned back in those days. As it was, I came to a house one day to collect, oh, seventy-five cents or whatever it was, and somehow the lady of the house had found out that my uncle was the baker in Richmond, and she just loved his bread. She went on and on about how much she loved my uncle and the bread he made until the idea came around to her that I ought to come inside and have a plate of her world-famous chitlins.'"

That got a good laugh, but he was far from finished. "I want you to know that I know how to spell chitterlings, but when Mr. Don from Richmond said the word, it came out *chitlins*. So, the story went on that Mr. Don went in and pulled up a chair, and out came Miss Lady with a heapin' plateful of soppin', sloppy, wet chitlins runnin' off every edge of that old plate. He said, 'I had eaten my fair share of chitlins back in those days, but I had neveh seen a mess of chitlins that sloppy and smellin' like they belonged back inside the old hog. But being from an upstandin', well-respected family, I had to keep up appearances, you know?'"

Tony had done a fine job of keeping his composure up to that point, but for some reason, his story sent him into a fit of laughter that was almost more entertaining than Mr. Don's chitlin story.

When he pulled himself together, he continued. "So, that old man said, 'After I put one bite of those dripping, wet, nasty things in my mouth, I knew there was no way I'd ever be able to get another bite down my throat, so I hatched a plan to do away with that plate of slop in front of me. I had two pockets full of paper envelopes for the insurance money I was supposed to be collectin'. I'd ease one of those envelopes out of my pocket and plop one forkful of those hog intestines into each one until that plate was clean. By the time I had exhausted my supply of collection envelopes, I'd put soggy sacks of chitlins into every pocket I could find, and that lady grabbed up my plate and said, 'Let me get you some more.' I thought I had made it through the ordeal, but she was almost too fast for me. Somehow, maybe by the grace of the good Lord, I got her stopped before she could pile another heap on my clean plate.'"

By that point, everyone in the gazebo was laughing too hard to catch their breath, but Tony wasn't finished. "Mr. Don said, 'By the time I made it to my old car, chitlin juice was runnin' out of every seam and pocket on my only good suit coat, and I had to throw that thing away. I drove that old car until the wheels fell off because I knew I'd never be able to sell it with the smell of chitlin juice oozing from every pore.'"

Chapter 7
Will I Get to Shoot Anybody?

Penny sat on the edge of our bed with her lip quivering almost imperceptibly. "This is the second worst part for me, and it gets harder every time."

I sat beside her. "Second worst? What's the first?"

She laid her hand in mine. "Knowing you may not come back every time you leave."

I squeezed her hand. "I know, but it's the nature of what we do."

"You're not going to do it forever, are you?"

I slowly shook my head. "No, nobody does it forever. Sooner or later, we get hurt, like Tony, or too old to stay in the fight."

She whispered, "There's a third option, and every time you leave, that's the one that keeps me awake at night."

"That's the one we don't talk about."

She lay back on the bed. "But it's the one I think about the most."

I spun and lay beside her. "Do you want me to quit?"

She closed her eyes. "You won't believe me, but it's the truth. I love you too much to ask you to quit. I watched what's happening to Tony, and it breaks my heart. There's something about the life you boys lead that you can't live without. Whatever it is, it's just as important as breathing to you, and I'd never take that away from you."

I brushed her hair from her face. "If you had known when we met, would you have—"

She pressed her finger to my lips. "Shh. I wouldn't change a thing, Chase Fulton. I love our life, and I love you."

We kissed and shared an hour of uninterrupted time, just for the two of us.

As we lay in each other's arms, she whispered, "Go. And don't say goodbye. I'll be here when you come home."

* * *

The *Grey Ghost* wasn't the typical business jet. The enormous door on the side of the airframe gave us the flexibility to change the interior configuration from the extreme luxury of bird's-eye maple finishes and the softest of leather seats to the pure utility of an empty space with cargo rollers on the floor for up to three pallets of equipment. When I raised the landing gear lever as we climbed out over the blue Atlantic east of St. Marys, our magic carpet resembled a dump truck far more than a Rolls-Royce. We had one pallet of seats for the team, one pallet of tactical gear, and an empty bay for the arctic gear we'd pick up along the way.

From the right seat, I managed the radios while Disco flew the airplane. Once in cruise flight, seven and a half miles high, he and I became little more than computer-systems monitors as we burned through the sky at just over five hundred miles per hour. We put the Great Lakes astern and watched Central Canada pass beneath us until the Anchorage Center controller said, "Grey-Ghost-One, descend and maintain one one thousand and contact Fairbanks Approach on one-two-seven point one. Good day."

I said, "Fairbanks Approach on twenty-seven-one, Grey-Ghost-One."

Disco programmed the descent, and I keyed the mic. "Fairbanks Approach, Grey-Ghost-One out of flight level two three oh for one one thousand with the numbers at Wainwright. We request the RNAV-two-five approach."

A friendly female voice filled my ears. "Good afternoon, Grey-Ghost-One, Fairbanks Approach. Wainwright altimeter three zero zero one, cleared direct CALOX, cross at or above three thousand. Cleared RNAV-two-five approach."

I read back the clearance, and she said, "I've never seen the Grey-Ghost call sign, sir. Is that an Army call sign?"

Disco chuckled, and I said, "No, ma'am. We're more of a humanitarian organization, you might say. We're pacifists. We don't believe in violence."

I could almost hear her laughing when she said, "Roger. Well, it's a cool call sign."

The United States Army Northern Warfare Training Center is administrated out of Fort Wainwright, but it's conducted at the Black Rapids Training Area, about a hundred miles southeast of Fairbanks, in the perfect vacation paradise . . . for penguins.

"Welcome to Wainwright, guys. I'm Sergeant Tyler. You're here to pick up the gear, right?"

I shook his hand. "Nice to meet you, Sergeant Tyler. I'm Chase, and these guys aren't memorable enough to introduce, but we need full kits for everybody."

His eyes fell on Mongo, and he chewed on his lip. "Well, we can suit up most of you guys, but the big guy's gonna be a problem."

Mongo said, "I'm sensitive about my size, Sergeant."

The soldier eyed me as if he couldn't decide whether to apologize or run. Finally, none of us could hold in the laughter any longer, and our giant said, "Relax, man. I brought my own custom gear, but I'm still sensitive about my size, so no fat jokes."

"Fat jokes?" Tyler said. "I was thinking more along the lines of having-your-own-gravity jokes."

Sgt. Tyler suited us up, and we loaded the *Ghost* with an additional ton of arctic gear and provisions.

We thanked him, and I asked, "Are you one of the instructors at the training center?"

He motioned toward a guy who looked more like a bush than a human. "No, I'm not, but he is."

The woolly beast of a man spun on a heel and threw up a hand. "How's it going?"

We waved back, but the man started walking toward us wearing a look I couldn't decipher. "Baby Face Johnson? Is that you?"

Clark squinted toward the burly man. "Kodiak?"

"Yeah, man. It's me. How and where have you been? I ain't seen you in . . . I guess fifteen years."

Clark stepped toward the man, and they hugged it out. "Guys, this is Kodi, but everybody calls him Kodiak . . . or at least everybody used to."

"They still do," he said as he shook hands and made introductions. "What are you guys doing all the way up here?"

We all waited in anticipation of how Clark would answer that question. He finally said, "We're on a rescue mission of sorts."

"Rescue mission?" Kodiak said. "Who are you rescuing? It don't much matter I guess since it's probably more of a recovery mission than a rescue. Nobody survives out there this time of year without some good gear and even better training."

Clark eyed Sgt. Taylor, and then leaned toward Kodiak. "Is there someplace we could talk?"

He waved a hooked arm. "Sure. Come on back here. I've got a pot of stew on."

We followed the woolly mammoth down a corridor to a break room of sorts with couches, a TV, and a kitchenette. He pulled the lid from the pot and gave it a stir. "Y'all want a bowl?"

Before we knew it, we were sitting around a table eating Kodiak's Alaskan stew out of paper bowls with plastic spoons. Well, most of us were using spoons, but Mongo had forgotten his table manners again.

Kodiak gave Clark a look. "So, what's really going on, man? You're not still SF are you?"

Clark wiped his chin. "No, my Special Forces days are behind me. We're all 'silly-villains' now, but Mongo was a Beret. Disco was Air Force. The quiet guy who looks like a sniper looks that way because he's one of the best. He was a Ranger. The ugly dude who likes to think he's in charge is OGA."

Kodiak lowered his chin. "Other Government Agency, huh? This is quite the motley crew you've got here, Baby Face. What's really going on?"

"Have you still got a clearance?" Clark asked.

"Yeah, of course. In fact, I just renewed it. Everybody at the school has to have a TS. They can't have us teaching this stuff to the bad guys."

Clark said, "Before we go any further, me and Kodiak go way back. We did Jump School together when we were privates. We hung together all the way through SF Q Course, but we never operated together once we got our Green Berets. I wonder why that is?"

Kodiak roared with laughter. "Because, brother, me and you would've burned the world down if they turned us loose together."

"Did you retire?" Clark asked.

"Yeah, I did twenty years and eighteen days and retired as a master sergeant. How long have you been working with this bunch?"

Clark finished his last spoon of stew. "Long time, brother. Do you like it up here?"

"It's home, I guess, but I'm gone in twelve more days. They're doing cutbacks, just like everywhere else. We've got a bunch of young guys with families and kids to feed, so I took the incentive pay to bug out and left the young guys drawing paychecks."

Clark raised an eyebrow at me, and I gave him a subtle nod. He asked, "Have you got anything lined up?"

Kodiak shook his head. "No, I figure I'll do some backcountry guide work and bum around until something comes up. You know, man, that's how it's been most of my life. Things just fall into my lap when I need them."

Clark waggled his empty bowl. "The service around here sure is slow."

Kodiak kicked Clark's chair hard enough to scoot him clear of the table. "You know where the pot is. I ain't your waitress."

Clark refilled his bowl and slid it onto the table. "Say, Kodiak, would you mind giving us just a minute? We need to talk about how much we can tell you without going back to jail."

"Sure, man. No problem."

When the door closed behind him, Clark said, "He's a solid dude, and he bleeds red, white, and blue. It wouldn't be a bad thing to give him a shot at the team since Tony's out of the game and Hunter's still on injured reserve."

I leaned back in my chair. "It's been fifteen years since you've seen the guy. Do you really want to vouch for him with that much time between you?"

Mongo said, "I've heard of him, but I've never operated with him. He's got a good reputation, as far as I know."

Clark said, "I say we ask him some questions, brief him up on what we're doing, and see what he says. We could use an extra man who knows how to stay alive up here."

"It can't hurt to ask him some questions," I said, "but if we don't like his answers, or if they don't check out, we press on without him."

Clark stuck his fingers into the corners of his mouth and whistled loud enough to wake the dead.

Kodiak came back through the door like a dog called to dinner. "If this is turning into a job interview, I ain't cuttin' my hair or shaving my legs."

"What makes you think this is a job interview?" Clark asked.

"Just a hunch. How's the pay and insurance plan?"

Clark booted Kodiak's chair toward him. "The pay stinks, and Mongo is the closest thing we've got to a medic, so he's your insurance plan. Sit down, you old goat."

We quizzed him pretty hard for ten minutes and called Skipper to run a background check.

She called back half an hour later. "He's cleaner than any of us. It looks like he stays off the grid most of the time. He's got a stellar service record and perfect performance appraisals as a Department of Army civilian. His clearance is up to date, and he's got money in the bank. Have him pee in a cup and put him to work, as far as I'm concerned. Is he cute?"

"I don't know," I said. "I can't really see him."

Skipper said, "What?"

"Never mind. It'll make sense when you meet him."

An hour after putting the first spoonful of Kodiak's stew in my mouth, I offered him a temporary assignment. "We're headed north to look for a submarine that may be abandoned and an icebreaker that's stuck in the Northwest Passage. The pay is twenty-five hundred a day, and I'll pay you for thirty days, even if we're not gone that long. After that, we'll decide if you're a square peg in a round hole. Interested?"

He closed one eye and leaned toward me. "Will I get to shoot anybody?"

"Only if they look like they're about to shoot at us."

He stuck his hand out, and our team became exponentially more likely to survive and thrive in the frozen north.

Chapter 8
Same Planet, Different World

Clerical tasks have always been a mystery to me, but I was smart enough to recognize the importance of *some* such tasks. Sending a federal government employee on a mission to locate and investigate a stranded Russian submarine that even the Russians were ignoring wasn't something the cake-eaters in DC were likely to approve. In fact, they were far more likely to hang all of us from frozen gallows if we tried. Nothing about our mission was official or remotely authorized by any arm of the Washington, DC, beast.

I asked, "When is your official end date, Kodiak?"

"Twelve more days."

"That'll never do. Twelve more days will mean twelve more inches of ice, and we're not interested in having our ship pinned in with the Russians and Chinese. If you're okay with it, I'm going to make some calls and get you fired."

He lowered his chin. "If you're paying me twenty-five hundred a day, feel free to backdate my last day as long as you want."

Skipper answered on the first ring. "Chase, I'm glad you called. Tony already has something on the bank robbery. It wasn't a robbery at all."

I cut her off. "That's great. Has he tied it to the other attempted robberies that day?"

"Not yet, but he's—"

"Tell him to keep working, but we've got a more pressing issue at the moment. I need you to get Kodiak fired."

She said, "I thought that might be coming, so I've already laid the groundwork. When do you want it effective?"

"Yesterday would be optimal, but we'll take what you can get."

She rattled some keys. "I'll call you back in five minutes."

As usual, she was ahead of schedule, and my phone chirped after only three minutes. "Okay, he's all yours."

"You're the best, Skipper. We've got some flying to do, but I'll check back in with you in twelve hours. In the meantime, keep Tony working the bank issue, and I need you to open a Cayman Islands bank account for Kodiak with seventy-five thousand."

"You got it. But don't you want to hear what Tony found?"

I checked my watch. "Can you do it in three minutes or less?"

Instead of answering, she started briefing. "We think we know who the lead bank robber was. By all indications, his name is Yusuf Osman, the brother of Nasir Osman, who is the half-brother of Aiyla Al-Sayyed, the wife of Yahir Al-Sayyed, the bomb maker. Don't try to keep up. Just remember the name Joseph Olson."

I shook my head in confusion. "Who on Earth is Joseph Olson?"

She said, "Just listen, and I'll tell you. Joseph Olson has at least one Florida driver's license, and we think he's the head bank robber you killed."

A glimmer of light was cutting through the fog in my brain. "Okay, but how is this Joseph Olson guy tied to Yusuf Osman?"

"Tony thinks they're the same guy."

I planted myself in the nearest chair. "What else do you know?"

She grunted. "*Know* is a strong word. Right now, we just *suspect*, but we're working to tie it all together. Olson has forty-four mini-storage lockers rented all across the country that are being paid for from the same bank account. Tony wants to get a look in as many of those storage lockers as he can."

"Put him on the road," I said. "But how did you come up with the idea that Joseph and Yusuf are the same guy?"

"I ran known-alias searches for everyone we knew in the terrorist group—Khanjar Allah, Dagger of God—and Yusuf and Joseph kept popping up together. That's why I say we *think* instead of we *know*. Right now, it's all a little shaky, but we're tightening it up by the hour."

"You keep saying *we*," I said. "How much time are you spending on this thing?"

She huffed. "I'm not going to neglect you and the Arctic mission. There are some things I can do that Tony hasn't learned yet, so I'm supporting him at the same time I'm taking care of you. You know you're my priority."

"If anybody can multitask, it's you, so I'm not concerned. Keep me posted if anything changes on the Russian or Chinese front. I'm planning a flyover of the coordinates where we think the sub is stuck. If the reactor is still churning, it'll be the warmest thing in the environment, so we should be able to see it."

She said, "I'll work on some thermal imaging for you if I can find a satellite that can see that far north, but no promises."

"Do what you can. We'll talk again in twelve hours or less."

Without another word, the line went dead, and I pocketed my phone.

By the time I made it to the plane, Kodiak was stowing his gear on the pallet, and Disco was plotting a course on a paper chart.

I called into the cabin. "Do you need anything?"

Kodiak looked up. "I'm good on gear except for arms. I can get mine, but it'll take an hour or so for me to get home and back."

"We've got you covered unless you're partial to your own. We've got a full complement of M4s and Glock nine-millimeters. There are four SR-25s, and Singer has his heavy long guns. If you need anything more than that, we've got time for you to run home."

He said, "That covers it. I don't have anything to add to that collection except a grenade launcher."

"We've got a pair of forty-millimeters and four dozen flares."

He pulled a strap tight and secured the loose end. "In that case, it sounds like we're ready to go."

Through some transaction I don't care to understand, the Army topped off our fuel tanks and even sent out a pair of mechanics to give the *Grey Ghost* a once-over to make sure she was prepared to operate in the arctic environment.

After the mechanics gave the thumbs-up, I climbed into the cockpit beside Disco and went through the start-up checklist. "How far is it to our first set of coordinates?"

He pulled up the flight plan on the multifunction display and pointed to the waypoints. "That's the icebreaker. There's no meaningful reason we need to spot it as long as the engines are running. She may be aground, but she won't be cold enough to freeze up and disappear in the ice. We shouldn't have any trouble spotting her, even from high altitude."

"What about the Russian sub?" I asked.

He slid his finger across the screen. "If the coordinates we got from the National Reconnaissance Office are close, she should be right there."

"How far is that from civilization?"

"That's the interesting thing. They're less than a hundred fifty miles from a copper mining outpost called Kugluktuk. The navigator on the sub should've known the local geography before he let the captain stick their nose into the passage."

I said, "The navigator got them grounded on a sandbar, so I'm not sure we should give him much credit for knowing the Inuit villages."

"You make a good point," he said. "Let's go take a look and see if we can spot a big black superstructure sticking out of the ice."

I leaned into the aisle and yelled, "Seal the hatch, and we'll go sub-hunting."

Clark hefted the cabin door closed and checked the seals on the cargo hatch. "Sealed up and ready to go."

Climbing out of Fairbanks, we paralleled the western boundary of the Yukon Territory until we crossed the Arctic National Wildlife Refuge and its razor-sharp mountains.

I watched the beauty pass beneath us. "That's some of the most rugged terrain on the planet down there."

Disco leaned toward his side window and peered toward the earth. "It's hard to believe how much difference a couple thousand miles make."

I was almost mesmerized by the beauty. "It's the same planet, but definitely a different world."

Disco looked over his sunglasses. "That's pretty poetic for a gunslinger. Are you sure you're not hiding the mind of a philosopher behind those Ray-Bans?"

"There's no philosopher in me, my friend. Singer may have a sprinkle or two, but not me."

He scanned the instrument panel as he looked away. "There she is . . . The Beaufort Sea and western end of the fabled Northwest Passage."

"It looks awfully icy from here," I said.

"I guess that means we'll learn just how tough the hull of the *Lori Danielle* is, huh?"

"She's never let us down before," I said.

He chuckled. "We've also never put her in water that's twenty below zero and full of ice that can cut through steel like butter."

We turned east over the water, and everything changed. Instead of the pristine mountains with their honed edges jutting into the sky, the world became an icy, white expanse as far as the eye could see. The earth looked like a barren, frozen wasteland where it was all but impossible to determine where the earth stopped and the frozen ocean began. I couldn't imagine any creature thriving in such an unforgiving environment, but I was only hours away from doing exactly that.

Disco's voice pulled me from my world of wonder. "We're coming up on the coordinates for the sub."

I spun in my seat and called into the cabin. "Stick your faces in the windows and look for anything resembling submarine parts sticking out of the ice. We're getting close."

My team pinned themselves to the windows and peered earthward as we penetrated deeper into the frozen world. Some elevation relief appeared on the horizon, but nothing like the mountains behind us.

I asked, "How thick do you think the ice is?"

Disco said, "Hopefully thin enough for our ship to crush but thick enough to walk on."

We continued our reconnaissance at three hundred miles per hour with our eyes trained on the blinding white surface beneath us. The multifunction display on the panel showed the delineation of the land from the sea, giving us a reference of where not to look. There was little possibility of the sub being anywhere except the water, but I'd learned to always expect everything except logic in our line of work.

We made several passes in a one-hundred-mile grid over a narrow neck of the Northwest Passage bounded by Inuit-owned land of the Nunavut Land Claims Agreement, but nothing resembling anything man-made appeared beneath us.

Disco asked, "How long do you want to search?"

I checked the time. "Let's spend thirty more minutes then head to Prudhoe Bay."

That turned out to be a wasted half hour we'd never get back. Nothing but snow and ice showed itself.

"Are you okay up here by yourself for a few minutes?"

Disco said, "Sure. I'll be fine. Are you ready to turn for Prud-hoe Bay?"

I nodded, slipped from the cockpit, and took a knee in the aisle. "Did anybody pick up the sub?" Heads shook, and I said, "That's not great news. It means we're looking in the wrong place or the reactor isn't running and the boat's covered with snow and ice. Either way is bad."

Clark said, "Skipper's on the satellite hunt, right?"

"She is, but the satellite coverage this far north is sketchy, to say the least. We're headed to Prudhoe Bay now, and we'll overnight there and get an update on the *Lori Danielle*. Keep your eyes on the surface for the next few minutes, just in case we get lucky and catch a glimpse of something black."

Kodiak asked, "What's the *Lori Danielle*?"

I turned back for the cockpit. "You'll see soon enough."

Chapter 9

The Threat

Like most of Alaska's North Slope region, Prudhoe Bay is a tiny community built around the oil industry. The bay itself is little more than an inlet with an island in the middle. The map of the bay reminded me of Charlotte Amalie on Saint Thomas, but nothing about the climate resembled the Caribbean paradise.

Disco greased the Gulfstream onto the Deadhorse runway and brought us to a gentle stop in front of the hangar that would be the *Grey Ghost*'s home for the next few days . . . or weeks. Several airplanes that looked like they'd outlived their airworthiness were scattered around the airport. Some had blankets wrapped around the engine cowlings, but some were frozen to the ground, neglected by both their owners and Mother Nature.

I couldn't tell Penny how much I liked the name Deadhorse for an airport and community, but I had my own private chuckle.

We deplaned and shivered against the frigid air.

A man in coveralls rolled up on an aircraft tug and shut down the engine. "You guys must be the environmentalists. You ain't come up here to shut down the oil wells, have you? 'Cause if that's why you're here, you and that nice airplane probably ain't making it out of Deadhorse, and I dang sure ain't putting you in one of my hangars."

At that point in my life, I'd been threatened by everyone from Russian oligarchs to the Cosa Nostra, but until that moment, I'd never had a man look me in the eye and send chills down my spine.

I was trained to stand toe to toe with practically any man and duke it out, knowing I'd likely come out on top, but disarming the guy on the tug required a skill set that had nothing to do with the pistol behind my right hip or the strength in my fist. "I married a North Texas girl with black crude in her veins. We're not the kind of environmentalists you're thinking about. We're here to make sure you can keep pumping that black gold without anybody messing up what you've got up here."

The man jumped down from the tug and stuck out his hand. "A North Texas girl, huh? I got me one of them, too. They're a handful, ain't they?"

"They sure are, but I wouldn't trade her for a thousand city girls."

He slapped me on the shoulder. "Me neither, partner. I'm Pecos."

"Pecos?" I said. "Really?"

He shrugged. "Naw, not really, but that's what they call me. I made a little money on a claim just northeast of Pecos that nobody else believed would produce a single barrel. Since then, everybody just calls me Pecos, and they listen when I point to the ground and tell 'em they's oil down there."

"So, what are you doing driving a tug at the airport?"

"I do this 'cause I like it. I been flying all my life, and since I made my money in the ground, I can do pretty much whatever I want, and I want to run an airport nobody else wants. So, I guess it's welcome to Deadhorse. How long you stayin'?"

"'Til we find what we're looking for," I said.

He nodded toward the least filthy hangar on the field. "Well then, since you and me have the same taste in women and being left alone, that hangar's all yours as long as you need it. There's a bunkhouse upstairs in the back, and we'll keep the big doors shut so that Gulfstream of yours won't freeze to the floor."

"I appreciate that, but we probably won't spend much time here. We're meeting our ship in a day or two."

He squinted, but with only one eye. "Your ship? What kind of ship are you talking about? A spaceship? You'll be able to drive an Abrams tank across that bay in another week. There ain't no ship captain in the world who'd stick his nose in that water 'til spring thaw."

"Like I said, we aren't the kind of environmentalists you're thinking about. We'll stay out of your way, but we probably won't be in the hangar for more than a couple of days. We'll be out on the ice most of the time, but the plane will appreciate your hospitality."

His eyes began to work together again when he raised both eyebrows. "On the ice? What kind of psycho environmentalist are you? You can't survive out there on the ice. That's crazy. I think you probably ought to head back to Texas, big boy."

"I'll make a deal with you. If we're not alive and back to pick up our airplane in thirty days, you can have it."

"Have what? The plane?"

"Yep."

He took a long, slow look at my team of misfits. "Care to put that in writing?"

I pointed a finger at him then back to myself. "We both married North Texas girls, Pecos. That practically makes us kin. If you and I make a deal, it's stronger than any writing on any paper will ever be."

He climbed back aboard his tug. "I like you, Tex. Now, don't get yourself killed or frozen to death out there. If I wanted a Gulfstream, I'd order one and pay for it in cash."

We set up camp in what Pecos called the *bunkhouse*, but *penthouse* would've been a better moniker. As beautiful as Bonaventure was, I didn't own any piece of furniture that came close to the décor of the hangar's bunkhouse.

Clark let out a long, low whistle. "This ain't bad. I may need to stay here, rename this place 'the op center,' and run this mission in my pajamas."

I held up two fingers. "Two things. First, you're not running this op, and second, you're not running this op, so don't get too comfortable."

Kodiak messed with his massive beard. "Just so there's no confusion, can you run down the chain of command for me?"

Clark said, "Sure. It's like this . . ."

I cut him off. "Before ol' broke-back former-action guy muddies the water too much, here's how it goes. I run the team. Mongo is second-in-command. And Clark is our handler and liaison between us and the Board. The Board is a collection of individuals who funnel our funding and dispatch us on the missions they select for us. It's that simple."

He steepled his fingers and stared at the ceiling. "So, who do you answer to? The Pentagon? Langley?"

"That's where the waters muddy themselves," I said. "Although we coordinate operations with government agencies from time to time, we're not officially part of any government organization. There are at least twenty similar teams to this one who work beneath the Board. I know this because we're team number twenty-one."

I shot Clark a look, and he took the floor. "What College Boy is trying to say is we're pretty independent. Believe it or not, there have been a couple of times when the president himself has directly recruited our involvement in a mission. That's rare, but it happens. Our boy Chase had a chummy relationship with the previous administration, but our ideals fall a little across the aisle from the present bunch in the White House."

Kodiak said, "Really? The president?"

I waved a hand. "Those were exceptionally rare missions, and even on those, we acted independently of the federal government."

Kodiak seemed to ponder the arrangement for a moment. "I like the independence, but what happens if we get busted in some third-world pothole?"

Singer stepped out of his shell by bouncing a rubber ball off Kodiak's forehead. "That's why Chase is paying you twenty-five hundred a day instead of six hundred. If we get rolled up, we're not coming home in a nice clean box with a flag draped over us. In fact, we're probably not coming home at all."

"So, you do it for the money," he said.

Singer gave him a toothy grin. "Nope. *You're* doing it for the money. The rest of us don't have a daily rate. We do it because we've got people at home we love. About three hundred million of them. The pay doesn't matter anymore. We do this because it's the right thing to do, and we're the right people to do it. If you stick around long enough, you'll understand."

Kodiak leaned back on the sofa and seemed to process Singer's speech. "If you guys aren't getting paid, how can you afford to pay me seventy-five grand a month?"

Singer poured a mound of coffee grounds into the filter. "I didn't say we're not getting paid. I said we don't have a daily rate. We've been blessed beyond our craziest imaginations, so we don't think about the paycheck anymore. We think about what we can do to make the world around us safer, better, and freer."

Kodiak looked toward Clark and pointed at Singer. "Is this guy for real?"

Clark kicked back in his recliner and put on his trademark crooked grin. "He's just getting started. You'll think you're at an old-time tent revival before the day is over. Singer is our Southern Baptist sniper. Just wait 'til you hear him sing 'I'll Fly Away.' You'll tear up."

Kodiak closed his eyes and slowly shook his head. "I've signed on to the island of misfit toys."

I said, "You're not the first to call us that, but when the shooting starts, you'll be surprised by the depth of hell these guys can pour onto the bad guys."

He pulled his hat down over his eyes. "From time to time, everybody needs a gunfight."

* * *

Skipper picked up on the second ring. "Hey, guys. How's it going?"

"Not bad," I said. "We're getting settled into our temporary home you scored for us in Prudhoe Bay. Pecos is quite the character. You could've given me a little heads-up on that one."

She giggled. "Yeah, I could have, but letting you stumble into him sounded like a lot more fun."

"Okay, but your definition of *fun* is a little different from mine. I've got two things. First, where's our boat, and second, do you have any new information on the bank robberies?"

"Let's start with question two. Tony is on his way to Kansas City to check out a pair of robberies."

"A pair? Were they successful?"

"That depends on what their mission was. I don't think they're connected, but Tony has another theory. They got away with sixty-five thousand at First Community Bank, but the crew that hit a little bank in the suburbs met the same fate as the ones you and Hunter put down."

"Is it rare to have more than one robbery in a city like KC?"

"It is. That's exactly why I don't think they're related. The crew who scored the sixty-five K was a team of two, and they were both Americans by birth and have criminal records."

"What about the dead guys?" I asked.

"We're not sure yet. That's part of the reason Tony is headed out there. Just like the dead guys here, the Kansas City crew doesn't seem to exist, and judging by the video surveillance, they weren't carrying any bags, either."

"What's your theory?"

"What makes you think I have a theory?"

I chuckled. "You always have a theory, so let's hear it."

She huffed. "Oh, all right. It's a working theory, though, so don't expect to be impressed. I think it's an enormous ruse to test the American banking system."

"Test the system for what?"

"That's the part I don't know yet, but unless you're the FBI, there's really no way to study bank robberies. It's not like there's a bunch of hold-up videos on YouTube you can watch. You pretty much have to either commit or witness a bank robbery to know how they go down. That makes me believe that whoever is behind the mass of attempts that day was conducting research and development."

I thought about her theory for a moment. "But why the suicide vest?"

"I can't find the logic in that one yet, but we do know there were three other hits that day with vests involved. One was foiled, but the other one killed the wearer and six customers."

"Where were they?"

She clicked a few keys. "The one that didn't go off was in a place called Shipshewana, Indiana, an Amish community about forty miles east of South Bend."

"Amish? I didn't know they used banks."

"I don't know if they do or not, but there are people there who aren't Amish. We're getting off track. The point is, that bank and town are even smaller than St. Marys. It's just too weird."

Before the robberies took control of my brain, I said, "Let's talk about the ship."

She stroked a few more keys. "She'll hit the ice northwest of Prudhoe Bay in twelve hours. We'll get an ETA from Captain Sprayberry when he encounters the ice. If it's mostly floaters, he'll be there in less than twenty-four hours, but if it's solid, there's no way to predict how long it'll take the *LD* to make her way through the ice."

"Sounds good. In the meantime, keep me posted on the bank thing, but I'll be focused on the mission here."

"Before you go," she said, "there's one more thing you need to know about the bank robberies."

"Sure. What is it?"

She lowered her voice. "One of them happened at a bank on a military base in Alabama."

Chapter 10
Focus!

It wasn't as comfortable as the gazebo back at Bonaventure, but someone—I assume it was Pecos—had built a deck on top of the hangar with natural gas heaters and Adirondack chairs arranged in a semicircle around a table reminiscent of King Arthur's. My team of noble knights had a long history of finding places to sit, talk, and think, and the rooftop deck was perfect for exactly that.

"Is this your first time?" Kodiak asked as he studied his first cigar with the team.

I watched the white smoke drift from the tip of his Cuban. "First time for what?"

"Being above the Arctic Circle."

I closed my eyes and drew a map in my head. "Clark and I were in Finland on a mission once."

Kodiak continued admiring his cigar. "How'd that one go?"

"We're still alive, and we got the job done."

Clark kicked my boot. "But you did have a little boo-boo and almost froze to death in the Moscow River."

Kodiak leaned forward. "I thought you said you were in Finland."

"We were, but not for long. We'll tell you the whole story someday after you've met Anya. It won't make sense until then."

"Who's Anya?"

Mongo closed his eyes and slowly shook his head, but Clark perked up. "Ah, she's nobody important. Just Chase's first real girlfriend."

It was Kodiak's turn to perk up. "Now, I have to hear the story. Do tell."

Before I could cut him off, Clark said, "Suffice it to say that she's a 'moderately attractive' former Russian SVR officer who cut Chase's tongue in half with a fighting knife on one of his first missions."

"That's not exactly correct," I said.

Clark raised an eyebrow. "Which part?"

"She wasn't my first girlfriend."

Clark took a draw from his cigar. "Oh, I thought you were going to protest the 'moderately attractive' part."

"Well, that part's wrong, too."

He said, "Oh, really? Let's get Penny on the phone and see how she feels about the description."

Kodiak jumped in. "Slow down. You're adding women too fast for me to keep up. Who's Penny?"

I boxed out Clark and got the rebound. "Penny is my wife, who is exponentially more beautiful than Anya."

The wooliest and newest member of our team pointed toward the North Pole. "Since we're talking about beautiful things, take a look up there."

With the sun hiding somewhere well south and far beyond every horizon, tentacles of green gently lumbered their way across the northern sky until I was captivated beyond words by the scene unfolding in front of me. As the arms softened from sharp-edged streaks of green, willows of reds and purples and colors I can't name joined them in a timeless dance like nothing I'd ever experienced. The eerie power the waves seemed to possess left me entranced, and I could almost feel the ends of my immortal soul reaching out to join the beseeching lights as they clawed at Heaven's floor. The longer I watched the magic and majesty of nature's elegant, heavenly dance, the smaller and less significant I felt. Fabulous and unstoppable forces would always exist above and beyond our reach, making everything I would ever do somehow less important, while at the same time, boundless in a world filled with misery, sadness, and anguish. But those lights—those living, arching, reaching lights—cried out for solace and purity and goodness, as if only I could hear them, while everything around me fell silent and humble and dark.

"I guess we're not meant to understand some things, huh?" Kodiak said.

Mongo said, "We understand the aurora borealis. Believe it or not, they start on the surface of the sun as plasma that we call coronal mass ejections and are thrown into space at unbelievable speeds. When this CME finally makes it to Earth in two or three days, it collides with our magnetic field and is funneled toward the poles as charged particles. When those particles collide with oxygen and nitrogen in our atmosphere as they reach the magnetic poles, they present as lights in the polar sky."

Kodiak threw a thumb toward our giant. "So, he's the one, huh? There's always one in every crowd."

I laughed. "Yep, he's ours, and we love him, but I bet Singer has another opinion about what causes the lights."

Our Southern Baptist sniper exhaled a long stream of white smoke. "Nope. I'm sure it happens just the way Mongo says it does, and for me, that's just more proof that God is one heck of an astrophysicist."

Kodiak drew a circle in the air with his fingertip. "Is this how it is?"

"What do you mean?" I asked.

"This," he said. "It's like one big goofy family."

"I've never used those exact words to describe us, but we'll take it. Yeah, this is how it is when nobody's shooting at us, but when bullets start flying, we're all business. You'll see."

He leaned back in his chair and stared into the sky. "Man, I never thought I'd find this again after I left Special Forces. You guys are all right."

Clark said, "Don't fall in love with us yet. The last guy we picked up at the last minute for a mission went home with a broken hip. Your opinion may change when we're dragging you off the battlefield next week."

"I've been dragged off battlefields all over the world, Baby Face. I figure it'd be an honor to have any one of you guys doing the dragging next time it happens, but if I get to pick, I choose Mongo to do the dragging."

I spent the next several minutes enraptured by the awesome beauty of the northern lights before finally checking my watch. "I guess we should hit the sack. We've got some more grid-flying to do tomorrow, and with any luck, our ship will come in."

* * *

Dawn came, and the *Grey Ghost* propelled us into the arctic sky for another day of sub-chasing. We flew the same grid we'd flown the day before, but the sun was at a different angle, so I hoped the new perspective would give us a glimpse of our target.

After two hours with our eyes pinned to the frozen world beneath us, Disco said, "Maybe we should go check on the icebreaker and make sure it is where we think it is."

"Sounds good to me," I said. "Every piece of ice is starting to look like every other piece down there."

I briefed our backseat crew, and Disco turned us toward the co-ordinates where Skipper believed the icebreaker to be. A Gulf-stream business jet may not be the perfect platform for airborne search missions, but ours could certainly cover a lot of ground in a little time. We ate up the one hundred miles in less than twenty minutes and slowed to our search speed.

I motioned toward the windshield. "That was easy."

Disco looked up. "Well, would you look at that? If that's not a Chinese icebreaker, I'll eat my boot."

"I've smelled your boots," I said. "I can't recommend them as an entree."

We flew over the ship at three thousand feet and squinted against the gleaming ice in hopes of seeing any sign of life.

"See anybody alive down there?" I asked.

Clark shook his head. "It looks abandoned. It's a diesel boat, right?"

"Yes. The intel Skipper picked up is that she's propelled by a seventeen-thousand-horsepower, low-speed diesel with a single screw."

Clark said, "She's not making smoke, so anything on board is likely frozen to the deck, including the crew if they didn't get off."

"Do you see the helicopter on deck?" I asked.

He stared back out the window. "No, it's not on the helipad, but that doesn't mean it's gone. It could be in a hangar bay. We'll have to get aboard to know for sure."

We made several passes over the ship, desperately straining to see movement.

Disco said, "I'm thinking about buzzing the deck to wake 'em up if there's anybody down there. What do you think?"

"Give it a shot," I said. "If anybody's alive, they'll be happy to see us, even if we don't speak Chinese."

In true Top Gun fashion, Disco buzzed the tower. It was actually the superstructure of the icebreaker, but close enough. We made enough noise and passed within a hundred feet of the crippled vessel.

As if he were back in his beloved A-10 Warthog, Disco pulled the nose up and executed a 180-degree maneuver, reversing our course for another pass on the ship. He said, "Keep your eyes open and fingers crossed that they don't have a deck gun."

"Why would they shoot at us?" I asked. "We're their only hope of rescue."

Our chief pilot put on a look of utter disappointment. "They're Chinese. They'd rather shoot us down than admit they had to be rescued by Americans."

"Touché"

Bullets didn't fly, and crewmen didn't appear. Either the ship was abandoned, or everyone on board had frozen to death.

Clark called from the main cabin. "Hey, Chase. Get back here a minute."

I slipped from the cockpit and took a seat across from him. "What is it? Did you see movement?"

"No, but I've got an idea I want to run past you."

"Let's hear it."

"Let's say we spotted both the icebreaker and the sub. Which one would be safer to approach and board?"

"Obviously, the icebreaker. It probably has a civilian crew and few, if any, weapons on board."

"Exactly," he said. "So, if we got to choose, we'd pick the icebreaker. We found it, so I think we should board it."

"To look for survivors?" I asked.

He shook his head. "Finding survivors would be a good outcome, but it's not our primary mission. Our mission is to find the sub and figure out what it was doing up here. Try to stay with me. The sub ran aground, right?"

I nodded. "That's what we believe."

He continued. "The icebreaker was dispatched to rescue the sub crew, right?" I kept nodding, and he said, "If they were coming to rescue the crew, they had to know the coordinates of the sub. If we can make our way on board that ship, we'll find the true coordinates of the sub."

"Yes, but everything will be written in Chinese. I speak a little Mandarin, but I can't read Mandarin or Cantonese."

"How about Skipper?" he asked.

"She doesn't read or speak any Chinese."

"No, you dingbat. I know she doesn't speak the language, but can she wave her magic analyst's wand across it and translate it into English?"

I palmed my forehead. "I'm an idiot."

Clark sighed. "Sometimes."

I saved a waypoint in the GPS and recorded the coordinates of the crippled icebreaker. It appeared she plowed her bow onto a piece of earth or a wedge of ice she was unable to break through, leaving the bow damaged and the vessel most assuredly stuck.

"Let's head back for the sub site for a couple more passes before we give up. If we don't pick it up, we'll board the Chinese ship and go shopping for a location."

Disco turned us around and headed back toward our search grid. An hour into the continued search, Disco reached over and gave me a shake. "Are you okay?"

I shook myself from my stupor. "Yeah, sorry. I'm okay. I was just thinking about the bank robbery."

"The bank robbery? Are you serious? You're second-in-command of a jet airplane flying two thousand feet above one of the most unforgiving environments on the planet."

I grabbed my water bottle. "You're right. I'm sorry."

He said, "This isn't like you, Chase. You don't get to lose focus. Before this mission is over, you'll be in absolute command of a ground force of men—including me—who'll unquestionably follow you into that frozen hell down there."

I sat there like a fourth grader in the principal's office awaiting my paddling and dreading the call to my mommy.

Disco said, "Forgive me if I'm overstepping here . . ."

"No," I said. "You're not overstepping anything. You're exactly right."

He seemed to consider a thought before saying, "I have the airplane. Tell me what's going on with the bank robbery."

I leaned back in my seat. "It's not a singular event. I'm sure of it. There were too many other robberies and attempted robberies that day, but that's not the problem."

The look on his face said I had his attention, so I said, "There's a solid tie between a Middle Eastern bomb maker and one of our dead bodies in St. Marys."

"I know that part. What else?"

"Tony and Hunter are piecing it together, but one of the robberies happened on a military base in Alabama."

He froze in place. "Who would have the stones to pull that off?"

"We'll know soon. Other than Redstone Arsenal and Fort Rucker, can you think of any other bases in Alabama?"

He cast his eyes to the overhead panel for a moment. "Maxwell Air Force Base in Montgomery, Anniston Army Depot, and a small Coast Guard base in Mobile are the only others I can think of."

I tried to picture a map of Alabama in my head, but until we knew which base and which bank, it wouldn't matter if I could draw the whole state from memory.

Disco asked, "You don't think the bank robberies have any-thing to do with this mission, do you?"

"No, I can't imagine how they'd be connected. Middle Eastern terrorists don't spend much time in bed with China and Russia unless you buy into the old adage, the enemy of my enemy is my friend."

He stared out the window for a moment, then turned back to me. "Look, Chase. I understand you've got a lot on your mind, so if you want to delay this mission or scrub it completely, I think I speak for the whole team when I say, if we're going out on the ice, everybody, especially you, has to bring his A-game. If you can't do that—"

Before he could finish, Singer's baritone rang out from the cabin. "Tallyho! Ten o'clock, maybe three miles!"

Chapter 11

Dog Ears?

Bank robberies were immediately the last thing on my mind as I strained against the glare of the sun on the icy world beneath us in search of what our eagle-eyed sniper had spotted ahead and left. Disco reduced power and made a gentle turn to put the site on our nose. Judging distance on the ice was almost impossible, but if anyone could do it, it would be Singer.

"I'm going to dirty up," Disco said as he lowered the flaps and landing gear and reduced our speed to as slow as possible. The closer we drew to the mound in the ice and snow, the more it re-sembled the bow of a submarine.

We brought the airplane about, and I called into the cabin. "We're going to take it down the left side. See what you think."

Disco aligned us about a quarter mile to the northwest of the bulge in the otherwise flat surface and cruised by at a hundred fifty knots.

I watched our passengers from the cockpit. "What do you think?"

Clark said, "If that ain't it, it's missing a good chance to be. How far are we from Skipper's coordinates?"

I did the math. "About ninety miles."

He asked, "Did we know the sub's course prior to running aground?"

"By all indications, it was working westward through the Northwest Passage, presumably planning to return to the east coast of Russia through the Bering Sea and into the Pacific."

I snapped several pictures of the snow-covered object and recorded the coordinates only seconds before Disco said, "We burned a lot of gas down low, so unless you need a little more time on target, we should head back to Deadhorse."

I said, "We've got everything we need. I just hope that thing is our missing sub."

I zoomed in on my multifunction display and studied the suspected sub's position. "According to the map, that mound is at least a couple hundred feet away from the water."

Disco glanced at the screen. "Don't put too much stock in the map overlay. This far north, the GPS has an inherent error due to the limited number of birds we can pick up, and the map projections aren't as accurate as they are closer to the equator. Two hundred feet out of the water, according to the map, is likely still in the water, considering the error."

"I guess we'll find out."

He set the autopilot to take us back to the airport and asked, "Have you heard from the *Lori Danielle*?"

"Not yet, but Skipper said they could be here as soon as tonight."

We landed and taxied to the ramp, where Pecos was sweeping snow off the wings of a massive airplane.

Disco said, "It's been a long time since I've seen one of those."

"What is it?" I asked.

"It's a C-Forty-Six," he said. "It's sort of the big brother to the DC-Three. There are a few of them up here running cargo to remote villages. There are a lot of places that aren't accessible any other way, so the cargo planes are their lifeblood."

I gave him a playful punch. "That sounds like a good gig for you when you get too old to run around with us trigger-pullers."

"Thanks to you trigger-pullers, I don't *need* to work anymore. I do this because none of you can navigate. You'd be lost all the time without me."

"It's hard to argue with that. We'll get you a combat Hover-ound with a mounted fifty-cal when you get decrepit."

"I'll take one of those now," he said. "That sounds like fun."

* * *

The Wi-Fi at Club Deadhorse—as we'd come to call our temporary home—wasn't exactly high-speed, so it took a few minutes to transmit our pictures, video, and flight data to Skipper back in the temperate zone of coastal Georgia.

"Okay, got it," she said. "It looks like the outline of a sub in the pictures, but it's a long way from the water."

I gave her the speech Disco had given me an hour earlier, but I wasn't convinced she bought it.

She said, "You may be right about the reliability of the GPS position in the *Grey Ghost*, but the global maps are a lot more accurate than they used to be. I was tracking your satellite phone most of the day, and there were times when the GPS position of the phone indicated that you were several hundred yards away from the airplane. I assume you weren't floating around in the air at three hundred knots without an airplane, were you?"

"As far as I know, I stayed inside the cockpit all day."

"That's what I thought," she said. "Now, let's plot these coordinates and see what we find."

Her keyboard must've been smoking based on the sounds of rattling keys beneath her fingertips. A few seconds later, she said, "Yeah, it could be. It's close enough to the water, and remember, they did run aground, so it had to be shallow."

I said, "We'll call this our best first shot. We'll be able to use the magnetometer from the *Lori Danielle* if we can get close enough to fly the chopper to the site."

She said, "Oh, I forgot to tell you, but you'll have a new toy when the ship arrives. I wanted to keep it a secret so you'd be surprised, but I guess that's not tactically appropriate."

"Keeping secrets from us isn't a great plan while we're in the field."

"Fine," she said. "Just spoil all my fun. It's a hovercraft—sort of a mini LCAC. You know, the Navy's landing craft air cushion."

"Yeah, I know what an LCAC is, and this is the perfect environment for it. Do you have any specs?"

"Not really. A couple of the machinists from the *LD* built it while they were bored in dry dock."

"I'll have to tell Captain Sprayberry to give those two machinists an extra ration of rum if their creation works."

"I guess you'll see tonight," she said. "They're making great time through shallow patchy ice and should be in Prudhoe Bay before dark. You should go down and provide a welcome party for them. Remember, though, she's not the *Lori Danielle* anymore. She's the *Polar Explorer Three*—at least temporarily."

"That sounds like a good idea, but I'm not a fan of the new name."

It sounded like she was clicking through electronic pages of notes. "Do you want an update on the bank robbery investigation?"

I had a moment of indecision. Everything inside me burned to know every detail, but the mission at hand had to take precedence. "No. Unless you need something from us on the investigation, just hold the briefing until we complete our task up here. I've got enough on my plate."

"Whatever, but Tony and Hunter interviewed Christen, and she had a lot to say."

I glanced across my team and reaffirmed my responsibilities to them. I was on the verge of taking them into an environment that would kill most men in a matter of days, if not hours, and they deserved nothing short of my full attention. "Tony and Hunter can handle it. I trust them. The rest of us are staying laser-focused on this one."

* * *

My phone chirped, and Captain Sprayberry's voice filled my ear. "Afternoon, Chase. This is the newly christened *Polar Explorer Three* with a new ETA. We'll be in Prudhoe Bay in an hour."

"Right on time," I said. "We've been scouting locations, and we've got a couple of sites that look interesting. We'll see you when you make the bay."

We crammed a collection of sandwiches down our throats and dressed for the conditions.

It took fifteen minutes to make our way from Deadhorse to the water's edge at Prudhoe Bay in a borrowed four-wheel-drive van that Pecos just *happened* to have warmed up and cleaned for us. Finding anything warm or clean was a real treat in the wilds of the frozen north.

When the helmsman brought the ship to a stop half a mile from the shoreline, Clark said, "I'm a little embarrassed to admit that I thought she'd lay alongside the dock. I guess I didn't think about the depth."

I laid a hand on his shoulder. "Don't be embarrassed. I expected the same."

Kodiak chuckled. "I have two questions. First, is that your ship? And second, do you have a plan for getting aboard her? Prudhoe Bay is about eight feet deep, so there's no way that boat's getting anywhere near the shoreline unless it sprouts wings and flies over here. And there's no chance of getting a dinghy through that ice."

"I have two answers. Yes, that's our ship, and believe it or not, she can fly . . . sort of."

He nodded in apparent approval. "Not bad."

I asked, "How far can we walk on the ice?"

"Until you can't."

Clark said, "Yep. Same old Kodiak."

"I'm not being facetious," he said. "There's no way to know how thick the ice is without chopping it up. You might walk all the way to your ship, or you might be wet before you take ten steps. I'm not going to risk it."

I pointed to the ship. "Fortunately, none of us have to risk it. Here comes our ride now."

The MH-6 Little Bird lifted off the deck and cut across the bay at top speed. The pilot spun the chopper around with its tail facing us and its nose pointed back out to sea, but it never altered course.

The skids of the Little Bird kissed the frozen earth a few feet away, and Kodiak said, "That guy's good. Did you steal him from the One-Sixtieth?"

The 160th Special Operations Aviation Regiment, known as the Knight Stalkers, was one the most elite flying units in the world, serving as the ride of choice for Army Special Forces and other operators who needed the best pilots on Earth to drop them into, and pluck them out of, hellholes all over the globe.

I shielded my face against the rotor wash. "No, that pilot didn't come out of the One-Sixtieth. We had to settle for what we could afford."

Gun Bunny, our Norwegian goddess of all things aeronautical, leaned through the door of the chopper with her blonde hair rippling in the wind. "You boys need a ride?"

Kodiak shook his head. "Let me guess. That's Anya."

Mongo threw an arm around the former Green Beret. "Not even close, my man. Not even close."

The ride to the ship was a brief endeavor, and almost all of us made our way to the combat information center seconds after touching down.

We settled into our chairs, and I took a quick head count. "Oh, boy. Disco's missing again."

Clark gave the table a knock. "I'd bet dollars to dog ears he's wherever Ronda No-H is."

I rolled my eyes. "Dog ears? You know it's donuts, right?"

"I love donuts," was the only answer I would get from the master of the King's English.

Kodiak examined the CIC. "You guys don't mess around. Is this really yours?"

"Sort of," I said. "Officially, I think it's on lease to an offshore research outfit out of Australia that may or may not really exist, but when they're not using it to study microscopic bacteria on fish eggs or some such craziness, they let us use it as our home away from home."

The burly woodsman pulled off his parka. "I sure hope you boys like how I shoot, 'cause I could get used to a life like this."

When I finally found Disco, it turned out that Clark was right, as usual. Our chief pilot was inseparable from the ship's purser, Ronda No-H. They'd been . . . "friends" for a while, but the nature of our work kept Disco ashore with us most of the time, and Ronda's responsibility was to the financial survival of the ship.

I stuck my head into her small office and motioned toward Disco. "Is he bothering you?"

She smirked up at me. "Absolutely . . . in all the right ways. Please tell me you're not taking him out to get shot at tonight."

"I wouldn't dream of it. But I can't make the same promise for tomorrow."

Chapter 12
Going Nuclear

The rest of the evening was spent marshaling equipment from the Deadhorse airport hangar to the *Polar Explorer III*. I was determined to rid her of that horrible moniker as quickly as possible. Nothing about the polar regions, except perhaps the northern lights, called to me in any way. Getting back to the little latitudes I loved so much was high on my list of priorities for the coming days.

With our gear aboard and stowed, Clark and I sat inside the hangar bay beside our Little Bird and stared out over the freezing sea. "Hey, College Boy. Do you ever wonder what single decision in our lives brought us to where we are?"

I raised my steaming mug of coffee in salute to my handler. "I think about it all the time, my friend, and I don't think it's a singular decision. I think it's a collection of decisions made over a lifetime, and any one of them could've sent us in a different direction."

He grunted. "I'm not getting sentimental in my old age or anything like that, but I'll tell you one thing, kid. I sure am glad our bad decisions brought us together."

Catching compliments from Clark Johnson is like catching falling stars, so I wasn't going to let the moment get away.

"I feel the same. I'd have been dead a long time ago if you hadn't wandered into my life."

He took a swallow of his coffee—or whatever was in his mug. "Ah, somebody else would've taught you to stay alive if I hadn't been around, but I didn't just *stumble* into your life. You must've forgotten how we met."

"I'll never forget that day. You flirted with Anya to make me jealous and get me off my game."

He cut in. "Two things. First, I wasn't flirting with her. She was flirting with me, and who can blame her? I mean, look at me. I'm a catch. Second, you didn't have any game back then. You were a baby giraffe trying to learn to walk."

"And you were sent to kill me."

He let that hang in the air for a while before saying, "I'm glad I didn't have to do it."

"Me, too. Have you ever had to pull that trigger?"

He turned to face me. "Do you mean on one of our own?" I nodded, and he said, "Only once, and you were there. In fact, you did it, too."

"What are you talking about?"

He set his mug on the deck. "Remember the Montana job? We took out a whole team of guys who'd once been on our side."

I stared at my boots for a long moment. "I've never thought about it that way. I don't like that we had to do that."

He stood, folded his chair, and stuck it on its hook by the door. "I don't like that we have to do any of this stuff, College Boy, but somebody's got to do it."

I stowed my chair beside his. "What are we really doing here?"

He pressed the control to close the hangar door. "I've been asking myself that same question for three days. If we find the sub and it's full of dead Russians, what are we supposed to do with them? Are we going to drag their frozen bodies back to the ship?"

I opened the walk-through door from the hangar into the interior of the ship. "Worse yet, what are we supposed to do if we find the sub and there's nobody aboard—alive or dead?"

He stepped through the door and checked the corridor for prying eyes and ears. "Our orders are to locate the Russian sub, determine the mission it was on, and report that back to the Board."

"There's no chance anybody's alive in that boat if that was the sub we found today."

He drummed his fingers on the bulkhead. "Why would they shut down the reactor?"

"If they abandoned ship, there would be no reason to leave the reactor running, so maybe they ran aground and determined there was no chance of getting the sub off the hard. Maybe they shut it down and started walking."

Clark traced a line on the deck with the toe of his boot. "How hard is it to shut down a nuclear reactor? How long does it take?"

"We're going to need Mongo," I said. "I wouldn't know a nuclear reactor from a washing machine, but I suspect he knows all about them."

"Let's wake him up."

Clark and I crammed ourselves into Mongo's cabin that would've easily been large enough for three normal-sized humans, but our giant would never qualify as normal.

He rubbed the sleep from his eyes. "You woke me up because you want to know how to shut down a nuclear reactor? Are you serious?"

"We're thinking about the sub," I said. "If that mound in the ice is the sub, that means somebody shut down the reactor. Otherwise, the sub would've stayed warm enough to keep the snow and ice off the hull."

He sat up and checked his watch. "I've got to find a team that keeps normal business hours."

"Just tell us about the reactor," Clark said. "Then you can go back to dreaming of enormous women, or whatever you dream about."

"It's really not that complicated," he began. "When the reactor is producing power, there's a chain reaction that happens inside the reactor core. The reaction is maintained by keeping the number of neutrons produced higher than the number absorbed. That's called the critical condition. You're with me so far, right?"

My eyes were already glazed over, but I said, "Sure. Assume we're still with you."

He rolled his eyes. "Anyway, to shut down the reactor, you have to diminish that critical state into subcriticality. This is done by lowering the control rods between the fuel elements inside the core so they can absorb all the neutrons produced by the core."

Clark looked as if he understood what Mongo was talking about and said, "Yeah, yeah . . . What we really want to know is how long that process takes."

Mongo shrugged. "Seconds. As soon as the control rods are lowered between the fuel elements, the chain reaction stops."

I leaned in. "So, the reactor can be shut down in seconds?"

"Yeah, but you still have to deal with the heat. The fission products inside the fuel elements are radioactive and generate a ton of heat. You have to do something with that heat, or you'll have a meltdown. You've heard of a meltdown, right?"

Clark and I nodded, but I wasn't sure why.

Mongo continued. "Managing that heat is often done with water infused with boron. I don't know how it's done on a submarine, but your premise is all wrong. Just because the crew abandoned the sub doesn't necessarily mean they shut down the reactor."

I asked, "Wouldn't the reactor keep the hull warm enough to keep the ice off the hull?"

"Modern reactors regulate themselves by producing power on demand, so it's possible the reactor is still running at extremely low output and not producing enough power to keep the hull warm in this environment. It's pretty cold out there, and you have to remember the sub has two hulls. The inner hull may still be above freezing, but the outer hull that's exposed to the elements will be a lot colder and less affected by the reactor."

Clark twisted to look at me. "Did you get any of that?"

"I think I got the important part. The reactor could still be operating, and there could still be living souls on board the sub."

Mongo held up a finger. "Wait. There's another possibility. The core could've become unstable and shut itself down to protect the reactor and contain the radioactivity. That's how most reactors behave, but who knows what kind of safety protocols the Russians have in place?"

I squeezed toward the door. "That's enough for one night—and maybe one lifetime—so you can go back to sleep now, and Clark and I will go outside and talk about stuff we understand."

Mongo said, "Before you go, have you considered the possibility of the submarine being used as a dirty nuclear bomb?"

I froze. "Why would the Russians sacrifice one of their nuclear subs as a suicide bomb?"

Mongo raised an eyebrow. "Why do Islamic extremists blow themselves up on purpose?"

Before I could answer, he said, "For the greater good. Think about it. Russia is the world's leading producer of natural gas, but we're catching up. What better way to stop natural gas production in the West than contaminating the world's largest natural gas field off Prudhoe Bay, Alaska?"

I locked eyes with Clark. "It's time to wake up the Board."

It took exactly six minutes to have the team assembled in the CIC and Skipper at her workstation back in the Bonaventure op center. Clark briefed the situation with Mongo, filling in the technical data along the way.

Skipper seemed to take the news in stride and was all business. "I don't know how long it'll take me to get the Board online. Do you need all of them?"

Clark gave me a checking glance, and I shook my head. He said, "No. Whoever you wake up first, get him on the screen. I don't want just a voice. I want to make sure Chase can look him in the eye and do some of that psychologist stuff to see just how surprised he is to hear the news."

Skipper said, "Stand by. I have two of them coming online now."

Seconds later, a pair of disheveled faces appeared on the CIC main monitor, and Clark went to work. "Sorry to wake you, gentlemen, but we have a situation."

One of the faces cleared his throat. "It's part of the job, Mr. Johnson. What have you learned?"

"We found the icebreaker, and she's obviously derelict and dead on the ice. We'll be happy to salvage her for a hefty fee while we're here, but that's not what this call is about."

The man said, "Don't rule that out just yet. We may find a way to use that to our advantage, but we'll come back to that issue when we've resolved the more pressing issue. Please continue."

Suddenly, a third and fourth face appeared in boxes on the screen, and Clark took the floor. "Gentlemen, we believe we found the Russian submarine. If we're correct, it's about ninety miles northwest of the coordinates where we believed her to be. We've not put hands on her yet, but there's a protrusion in an otherwise flat surface that stretches for over fifty miles in every direction. If the protrusion isn't the Russian sub, it's certainly something that looks a lot like one."

Clark paused, took a drink, and shot a thumb toward Mongo. "Our resident big brain has a theory that the derelict sub may be acting as a dirty nuke to contaminate the Prudhoe Bay natural gas field. As absurd as that sounds, it could explain why the Chinese were so willing to get involved. I have a theory that the Chinese may have been here to rescue the Russian sub crew and get them out of the area before the contamination began. Keep in mind, we haven't verified any of this yet. It's all supposition at this point, but I'm not willing to dispatch a team into a potential dirty nuke environment without some thorough investigation."

One of the men said, "Of course not. If you did, we would remove you from duty immediately. If she's within range, we can dispatch a sniffer from the USS *Ronald Reagan* in the Pacific to detect the presence of radioactivity."

Skipper said, "Sir, the *Reagan* is involved in an exercise near Kwajalein Atoll, and involving the U.S. military in this may be the worst foreign policy decision ever made. We might as well install some more bugs in the Watergate Hotel while we're at it."

Silence ruled the moment until Mongo spoke up. "It's not hard to build a sniffer if we don't have a Geiger counter on board. We can easily deliver it by drone with remote telemetry back to the ship."

Every eye turned to me, and I gave the order. "Find Big Bob, the chief engineer, and build us a sniffer."

Chapter 13
Let's Move

Mongo and Kodiak hit the door running, leaving Clark, Singer, Disco, and me in the CIC with Skipper and the Board on monitors.

"What's our move if we detect radiation?" I asked.

"Retreat," came three voices through the overhead speaker.

A Board member said, "You found the icebreaker, right?"

I said, "Affirmative, sir."

"Any signs of life on board?"

"No, sir."

"Can you board her?"

"Affirmative, sir."

He cleared his throat. "Sniff the probable submarine site ASAP, and if you don't get a hit, board the icebreaker posthaste."

I let the scenario play out in my head. "We'll be outnumbered at least thirty to one if we board the icebreaker and the Russian submarine crew is on board."

The man laughed. "You're practically tier-one operators with zero accountability, far superior firepower, and the element of extreme surprise. Nobody on board that ship expects American commandos to raid their vessel. If they put up a fight, crush them like cockroaches."

The look on Clark's face mirrored mine, and he said, "Taking down the Russian sailors is one thing, but taking out a civilian crew of a civilian ship in distress? That's a violation of at least a few hundred maritime laws."

The spokesman for the Board said, "Silence the members, please, and give us five minutes to wake up the president."

Skipper touched a finger to her ear and gave me a wink the instant before a black line stretched across each of the Board members on the screen. She said, "Listen closely, guys. From their end, it appears they're silenced and we can't hear anything they say, but clumsy ol' me got confused and accidentally silenced *you* instead. We'll hear everything they say, but they can't hear us. Don't react to anything you hear."

We listened carefully and pretended to talk with each other while the Board members discussed our dilemma. To my surprise, a voice said, "I'm sorry to wake you, Mr. President, but we have a situation."

He briefed the president and then listened intently. We couldn't hear the voice on the other end of the line, but the man said, "Thank you, Mr. President. We have one of our best teams on site and ready to move."

The speaker came back to life. "Okay, gentlemen. I just got off the phone with the president, and you're authorized to use deadly force in the interest of the United States of America, the citizens of Canada, and other nations who may suffer tragic ends should you allow this atrocity to play out."

Clark said, "Forgive me, sir, but I want to make certain I fully understand our mandate and authority here."

"You heard me loud and clear, Mr. Johnson. The president himself authorized your mission, and we're prepared to dispatch as many teams as you need to complete your mission."

Clark didn't back down. "We don't have time to wait for another team. We've got work to do, but you should dispatch a team of cleaners to pick up the broken pieces when we're finished. We'll report back within twelve hours with a sitrep."

Clark glanced my way, and I gave a sharp nod. He said, "Cut the line, Skipper. We have our orders."

The faces disappeared, and Skipper said, "Nicely done, Mr. Johnson."

Clark grinned. "Sometimes the younger gorillas have to slap the silverback around a little to earn some love from the lady monkeys."

I closed my eyes and tried not to laugh, but no one else resisted. When the moment passed, I stood with the intention of finding our big-brained giant, but the hatch to the CIC opened before I could take a step.

Without preamble, Mongo filled the opening. "Here's the plan. I figure the lightest two pilots we have are Disco and Gun Bunny. We've got three fifty-five-gallon drums of jet fuel. That puts each barrel at three hundred seventy-five pounds of fuel, plus the weight of the barrel for a total of four-oh-five each. The shipwrights are mounting and plumbing one barrel inside the Little Bird to almost double her range of two hundred thirty miles. The target is a hundred ninety miles away."

I held up my hand. "Slow down. Just give us the big picture. We're not engineers."

Kodiak said, "I've got it, big man. We can shuttle two barrels and set up a FARP with the hovercraft while Disco and what's-her-name run toward the target with one of the Geiger counters."

Mongo jumped in. "They'll have to land and wait to take measurements. The rotor wash makes it impossible to take an accurate reading while airborne."

"I got it," I said, "and I like it. But what's a FARP?"

My all former-military team got a good chuckle out of that one, and Clark finally said, "It's a forward arming and refueling point. Think of it as a makeshift gas station."

I ignored the embarrassment I wanted to feel. "Her name is Gun Bunny, by the way. And how many Geiger counters do we have?"

Mongo held up two fingers, and I said, "Perfect. Mongo and Kodiak, you're with me on the hovercraft. Disco, brief Gun Bunny and get her ready to go at first light. We'll press forward with the hovercraft, set up the FARP, and be ready for your turnaround."

Disco said, "If we don't get a hit on the Geiger counter along the way, we'll fly to the suspected sub site. Why not take the magnetometer and check for a chunk of metal under the ice while we're there?"

"How much does it weigh?" I asked.

No one said a word, so I grabbed the handset to the onboard comms and punched a key.

Seconds later, a voice said, "Go for engine room."

I asked, "How much does the magnetometer weigh, and how big is it?"

The engineer said, "The airborne version is four feet long, a foot and a half wide, and weighs one-twenty-five without batteries."

"Can it be run from the electrical system on the Little Bird?"

"Sure it can," he said. "That's why I gave you the weight without batteries. It's a simple connection, and we already have a hard point on the starboard-side skid to mount it."

"Rig it, ASAP."

"Yes, sir."

I locked the handset back into its cradle. "Let's move."

Forty-five minutes later, Mongo, Kodiak, and I were dressed head to toe in all-white arctic survival suits and riding the hovercraft over the rail of the *Polar Explorer III* beneath her deck crane.

We touched down on the ice with the hoisting gear still in place, and Mongo said, "Don't cast off until we're at one-hundred-percent power with steady temps. I do *not* want to fall through this ice."

The hovercraft's twin jet engines whistled to life and came up to full power as the internal turbine temps settled right on the numbers.

Mongo inflated the skirt, flew the machine just above the ice on a cushion of high-pressure air, and gave the order, "Cast off all lines."

Kodiak and I disconnected the cables from the crane, and we were soon gliding across the frozen surface at a remarkable speed. The cabin of the hovercraft wasn't exactly comfortable for the three of us, but it protected us from the wind as we soared across the ice at seventy knots.

As we sailed eastward, I said to Mongo, "I didn't know you could pilot a hovercraft."

His face was hidden behind his layers of insulation, but his eyes showed amusement. "Neither did I, but I'm having fun learning as we go."

At our speed, the frozen world in front of us passed as flashes of white beneath the three-quarter moon hanging low on the southern horizon. An hour into our trek, Mongo brought the machine to a hovering halt and slowly let it settle to the ice.

"What if the ice gives way?" I asked.

Mongo pointed to a row of three green lights at the left of the panel. "If the sensors detect water, three inflatable pontoons will automatically fill from compressed air cylinders, saving the ship and crew."

"Ha! Those guys thought of everything except heaters and comfortable seats."

"It's still a work in progress," he said. "We'll make modifications until we get it just right."

"We?" I asked.

He rubbed a gloved hand across the panel. "Me and this girl are going to be spending a lot of time together."

"Irina may get jealous."

The big man shrugged. "She can hang out with us if she wants. She's got that Muscovite blood, so she'd be right at home in this environment."

"I think she's pretty comfortable eight thousand miles west of Moscow."

Kodiak asked, "What is it with you guys and Russian women?"

I threw up both hands. "Not me. He's the one who married one. I just got caught in a Russian honeytrap once, a long time ago. I'm perfectly content with my North Texas girl."

"Let's take a reading," Mongo said.

We pulled the Geiger counter from its case and powered it up. After ten minutes on the ice, the device hadn't offered so much as a chirp, so I said, "It looks like we're clean here. Let's soldier on."

That's the instant the ice-covered world around us exploded into utter chaos. The crack of automatic-weapons fire cut through the predawn stillness, and my senses piqued. The fire had come from a 5.56-millimeter rifle, so it wasn't the Russians or the Chinese, but it was still the last sound I expected to hear at that moment.

Kodiak's voice cut through the air like a sword. "Get on the hovercraft!"

Another burst of rapid fire echoed through the darkness, and the sound of Kodiak's boots striking the ice ahead of me filled my head with a thousand questions.

What's he shooting at? What's happening? Are we being attacked?

Before I could answer any of my own questions, every light on the hovercraft bloomed, illuminating a half-acre swath in front of the machine, and what I saw terrified me far more than any Russian submarine crew or Chinese ice-breaking sailor. Two massive polar bears galloped straight at Kodiak as he ran toward me, firing into the air behind him.

I lowered the muzzle of my M4 and sighted on the lead bear, but an instant before I pressed the trigger, Kodiak yelled, "No! Don't kill them! Mount up!"

He slid to a stop between me and the rushing bears. Mongo's light show had done nothing to slow them down. Kodiak shoved me as he turned to face the fast-approaching maneaters. At that moment, my brain did something I never would've imagined it would do, as I was suddenly overtaken by the beauty of the enormous creatures and filled with disbelief. I never remember seeing a polar bear before that moment, but the fleeting moment passed, and I was flooded with the instinct to simply survive. I could stop both the bears with a half dozen well-placed rounds, but Kodiak was obviously set on leaving our potential killers alive.

The turbines of the hovercraft rose in pitch and volume until the roar of the machine consumed every other sound in our frozen world. The lights of the craft sliced between us and the bears, and Mongo spun the machine, giving Kodiak and me an instant to grab the stern rail and hit the ramp, but his lack of experience with the craft sent him and our only hope of survival sliding wildly past with the bears still thundering toward us.

Kodiak laid down a wall of lead into the snow and ice in front of them, but the creatures didn't slow. My newest teammate and I were seconds away from becoming polar bear porridge, and our options were dwindling quickly. He dropped the magazine from his rifle and shoved a fresh one into the well. He'd clearly come to the same conclusion as me, and we raised our rifles to trade the bears' lives for ours.

As I pressed the fabric of my gloved finger into the trigger, a wall of fire erupted in my peripheral vision and filled the air with belching orange flames and black roiling smoke. The stream of liquid fire froze our attackers in their tracks and seemed to mesmerize them.

As Kodiak and I ran for the hovercraft, Mongo kept pouring fire toward the bears until we were safely aboard. We collapsed to the deck, and Mongo flew us to the northeast at easily four times the speed the bewildered bears could make.

Chapter 14
Like Butter

"Why do you have a flamethrower?" I asked as I caught my breath.

Mongo said, "Everything around us is frozen, so I thought a little bit of *actual* firepower might come in handy."

"That's my Mongo . . . always thinking."

We continued our trek toward what we believed to be the Russian submarine as the southeastern sky showed the first signs of daybreak at the top of the world. Everybody loves a beautiful sunset, but I've always preferred the life-giving emergence of our nearest star on the opposite horizon. The weight of our mission began to lay heavily on my mind.

Kodiak pulled me from my haze. "This may not be the best time to ask this question, but who were those guys on the monitors in the CIC last night?"

I lifted my head and scanned the lightening desert of ice in front of us. "As a matter of fact, this is the perfect time for that question. Those guys are four of the members of an organization called the Board. Their identities are protected, but suffice it to say we know who they are and what brand of kitty litter they use."

"Interesting."

"They usually hand down assignments to Clark, who hands them down to us, but we always have the freedom to turn down missions individually or as a team. No one is forced to work on a project he doesn't feel good about."

He met my gaze. "Is that true for you, as well?"

His question hit me squarely in the chest. "I haven't really thought about that. We've never spelled it out, but I believe we have an unspoken agreement within the team that if I turn it down, I'm doing so as the spokesman for the team. I can't imagine the rest of the guys going to work without me."

He lowered his chin. "What? The whole team works exclusively for you? They don't contract out?"

Mongo saved me from explaining our situation. "Twenty-five hundred a day is the part-time pay rate. The rest of us are on salary."

The bearded polar bear lover leaned back against the bulkhead and seemed to let Mongo's words wash over him.

I changed the subject to avoid turning the conversation into a salary negotiation. "We need to talk about the polar bears."

"Yeah, I know," Kodiak said. "I should've put 'em down, but I just couldn't do it."

I took half a step toward him. "You're not going to let that happen when the next bears turn out to be Russian submariners bearing chopped-off AKs, are you?"

Somewhere beneath twenty pounds of arctic survival gear and thirty pounds of beard, I suspect he wore a look of understanding. "Don't worry. I love polar bears, but I can't say I feel the same about Russki sailors with AKs."

I continued my stare. "There's nothing more important than the successful completion of our mission, and we must be willing to sacrifice anything that stands between us and mission success, be it man, beast, or mindset. I'm glad we didn't have to kill the bears this time, but we'll never put our mission at risk by being unwilling to eliminate a threat."

"Understood," he said.

A lot of men would've tried explaining their justification for their actions, or lack thereof, but Kodiak didn't fall into that group. He was clearly a soldier through and through, even if he had a soft spot for bloodthirsty bears.

Our second stop sent Mongo onto the cabin top with a pair of binoculars in his hand on his first-ever polar bear watch. "Okay, guys. It looks clear. Do your thing. I'll sound the alarm if our furry friends make another appearance."

We dismounted and set up the Geiger counter, but the needles never moved.

Back aboard the hovercraft, I plotted our position and tried to dial the sat-phone while wearing oven mitts. When I finally succeeded, Skipper answered almost before it rang. "Go for ops."

"We're on the ice thirty-five miles from the suspected sub site, and zero radiation detected. I'm starting to feel good about this thing."

Skipper sighed. "Come on, Chase. You know better than to say things like that. Don't start feeling good until everybody is home, clean, dry, and warm."

"You're right, as usual. Is Disco airborne yet?"

"Look to the west, and you'll probably hear them coming."

As if on cue, the unmistakable buzz of the five-blade rotor atop our MH-6 Little Bird helicopter broke through the whistling wind of the frozen world. Disco was a remarkable fixed-wing pilot, but that morning's demonstration of rotary-wing, aeronautical wizardry came at the delicate touch of our resident chopper master, Gun Bunny.

The machine approached at high speed and descended toward us like a hawk diving on prey. The chopper spun two-hundred-seventy degrees, and the skids touched down on the railing of the hovercraft as gently as a mother's kiss.

We shielded ourselves against the rotor wash, and Kodiak asked, "Why did he land up there?"

I dug a toe into the ice. "That wasn't a *he* who made that landing. Disco's good, but that was Gun Bunny's work. The surface area of the skids is small, and the chopper weighs almost three thousand pounds, so *she* wasn't willing to risk falling through the ice if it's too thin here."

Both pilots climbed down from the chopper and pulled off their helmets, but it only took a few seconds of exposure to the frigid air for them to redon their headgear.

"How's it look?" Disco asked.

Kodiak held up the Geiger counter. "Clean as a whistle."

Disco tightened his scarf around the exposed skin of his neck. "In that case, we'll press on. We're showing just over thirty-four miles to the target."

Kodiak took a step forward and stuck out a gloved hand. "We've not been formally introduced. I'm Kodiak, and these Neanderthals keep calling you Gun Bunny, but I just can't bring myself to call you that."

She stuck her hand in his and laughed. "It's okay. My mom named me Barbie, but I prefer Gun Bunny. I was an Apache pilot in the Army, so the call sign made more sense back then."

"No kidding? An Apache pilot, huh? That's impressive. I think I was a cook, or maybe an admin clerk when I was in the Army. Who knows? I may have even saluted you back then."

She nodded vigorously. "I can see it. You've got that admin-clerk look about you, and I was never much for being saluted. It all seemed a bit silly to me. I figured you cooks and clerks on the ground didn't care what I wore on my shoulder while I was laying down hellfire missiles to cover your egress."

Kodiak cocked his head. "Was that you?"

Gun Bunny gave him a wink. "Probably."

I cleared my throat. "Maybe we can continue the dating game back on the ship, but I'd sort of like to get out of the cold sooner rather than later, if you two don't mind."

She said, "We'll need some clippers and a razor before I pick bachelor number one, but I'm ready to press forward to the sub site. Just give the word."

I stared out over the barren landscape and turned to Mongo. "I'm going with them. You two set up the FARP here, and we'll be back to refuel within an hour. Keep your sat-phones handy in case we need a little ground support."

I climbed into the Little Bird with the pilots, and we were eastbound in seconds after lighting the fire. The chopper's heater was a pleasant relief, and I could almost feel my blood starting to thaw.

"There she is," Disco said after fifteen minutes in flight.

We flew over the protrusion from the ice at less than fifty feet, and it looked even more like the nose of a submarine from that range.

"Let's get down there and take a reading," I said.

Disco spun in his seat. "We'll come to a hover and let you out, but with the ice still being thin, setting down on the skids isn't a good idea."

I grabbed the Geiger counter and gave him a nod. He brought the bird to within inches of the ice and hovered as steadily as if we'd already landed. I stepped off the skid, and they flew a few hundred feet away while I brought the electronics to life. I walked the perimeter of the enormous protrusion, waiting for the needle of the Geiger counter to come to life, but it never happened. At one point, I wondered if the device was actually working.

After convincing myself there was no radioactivity threatening us or the polar bears, I waved for the chopper, and they once again hovered just above the deck as I climbed aboard.

"Nothing. If that's the sub, she's not leaking anything that'll eat our flesh."

Disco said, "I guess that means it's time to wave a magnet over it and see which way it swings."

I knelt on the floor of the chopper between the two pilots' seats and fired up the magnetometer. We lifted off and slowly hovered toward the mound. As we made our first pass, the machine lit up like a Christmas tree.

I reset the magnetometer and rechecked the reading. "I think we found our missing sub. Let's figure out how she's lying under the ice."

We hovered in expanding circles around the prow and determined a line of magnetic signatures extending to the southeast for almost a hundred fifty feet.

"That's odd," I said.

Disco looked down at me. "What's odd?"

"Do you remember how long the *Pantera* was?"

"Not exactly, but I seem to remember it being almost four hundred feet. Does that sound right?"

"It was an inch shy of three hundred sixty-two feet, according to the data sheet Skipper gave us, but whatever this is, it's less than half that length."

Disco asked, "Could she have broken up when she ran aground?"

"It's possible. That would explain why there are no survivors. The crew would've frozen to death within minutes."

"Maybe it wasn't frozen over yet, and some of the crew might have made the surface."

"I don't know," I said. "Even if the surface weren't frozen yet, it would still be tough to survive out here after being wet. There's nothing in any direction for miles."

Gun Bunny said, "I suggest we fly a grid with the fuel we have and search for the other half of the sub. If it broke up, it wouldn't be far away."

"Let's do it."

We flew a grid pattern expanding away from the portion of the sub we found.

"Nothing," I said. "There's nothing metal within a mile of that thing."

Disco tapped on the panel in front of him. "We're out of fuel. We can't stay here any longer."

I shut down the magnetometer, and we flew the fifteen-minute route back to the hovercraft.

"Well, what did you find?" Mongo asked as soon as I stepped from the chopper.

"We found something long, narrow, and metallic, but not long enough," I said.

"Anything radioactive?"

"Not so much as a blip. But if that thing is the sub we're looking for, it's less than half of it. The *Pantera* was over three hundred sixty feet, but we've only got about a hundred fifty feet of metal under the ice."

Mongo considered the scenario. "It could've broken up on a ledge, and the separated section could've settled directly beneath the part you can measure."

I pictured his description in my head. "That's a good theory, but there's only one way to know for sure, and that's to cut a hole in the ice and dive it."

Mongo shivered. "That's not the only way. In fact, that's not even a good way. Regardless of how we do it, we need the *Lori Danielle* for close support."

"You mean the *Polar Explorer Three*," I said.

"Whatever. We have an excellent ROUV on board with lights and cameras. If we can get the ship within five miles of the sub site, we can launch the ROUV and get high-definition video of whatever's down there."

Kodiak raised a hand as if he were in grade school. "What's an ROUV?"

Mongo laughed. "It's a remotely operated underwater vehicle. Think of it as an underwater drone."

"Got it."

I dug a heel into the ice. "Now, I guess we just need to know how thick the ice is so we'll know if we can get the ship close enough to launch the rover."

Kodiak stared down at the frozen surface of the planet beneath our feet. "I'd bet it's no more than a foot thick right now, but we'd have to auger into it to know for sure."

"I've got a better idea," Mongo said as he climbed back aboard the hovercraft.

A minute later, the massive man was burning a hole in the ice with his beloved flamethrower. He made short work of the task and said, "Nanook of the North was right. It's about eight to ten inches. The ship can plow through that like butter."

As I studied the hole Mongo melted in the ice, I said, "That gives me an idea."

Mongo smiled his clairvoyant smile somewhere beneath his wrap. "And that's why you're in charge, Dr. Fulton."

Kodiak watched the exchange like a fast ping-pong match. "Doctor?"

I waved a hand. "It's a long story. Don't worry about it." I turned to Disco. "Let's get you fueled up and back on the ship. We've got work to do."

Chapter 15
Look What We Found

It took ten minutes to refuel the chopper, and soon, our pilots were slicing through the arctic air on their way back to the *Polar Explorer III*.

I ushered Mongo and Kodiak back aboard the hovercraft. "Take us to the submarine."

Mongo brought the machine to a sliding stop fifty feet from the protruding prow, and I said, "Let's see you open up a window to our world with your new favorite toy."

Mongo shouldered the fuel tank and hefted the flamethrower beneath his arm. Beginning his work six feet above the frozen surface, he waved the smoking orange flame across the wall of ice we hoped contained the hull of a Russian nuclear submarine. It was slow work, but our giant went about the task with the same precision he did everything else in his life. He wasn't always the most patient Goliath, but he was certainly always thorough.

The ice slowly melted and ran from the vertical wall in streams and then quickly refroze as it pooled around Mongo's feet. Ten minutes into the task, the unmistakable black metallic surface of a submarine emerged through the ice.

Mongo lowered his fiery wand. "Looks like a sub to me."

"Me, too," I said. "Do you have any data in that supercomputer you have for a brain about where the markings would be on a Russian sub?"

He shrugged. "I'm afraid that's outside my wealth of knowledge, but Skipper could find out in seconds."

"Tell me something good," were her first words after picking up the phone.

"We found a submarine," I said.

"That's definitely something good, but is it the right submarine?"

"Is this place littered with grounded subs?"

"Not that I know of, but it's nice to be sure."

"That's exactly why I'm calling. We need to know where to find the markings on a Russian nuclear sub. Mongo melted a hole through the ice shroud this one is wearing, but it's just a black metal tube until we find something to identify it."

"Give me a minute," she said. "I'm pulling up pictures now." A few seconds later, she said, "I'm sending a couple of pictures to your sat-phone. The *Pantera* has a strange array of white marks across her bow, and her draft markings won't be numbered. They're delineated in meters with a longer mark every five meters."

"You're the best, Skipper. Thanks."

I pulled up the pictures and showed them to Mongo. He grunted. "We don't have enough fuel to go sniffing around for draft marks on a hull this size, but I'll take a pass at that crazy white line on the bow."

The flamethrower roared back to its full strength, and our giant became a crazed dragon on a fire-breathing strafing run. The sound of the pressurized flame felt alien in the world we inhabited. Prior to its growl, the only sounds were the ceaseless wind cutting across the frozen plains and the occasional crushing collision of massive fields of ice pressing against each other in their relentless battle to claim what little unfrozen expanse remained. Hearing the fires of hell battle the freezing expanse gave me the sense of standing between two worlds and wishing to occupy neither.

Despite my inches-thick layers of protection from the killing elements surrounding me, a chill more akin to the dread of a coming terror than to the hatred of subzero wind cut through my soul, and I began to tremble. "Are you cold?" I asked Kodiak.

He didn't look away from Mongo's work. "No, I'm good. You okay?"

"Yeah, I'm all right. Just not climatized yet."

He slapped me on the back. "Give it six or eight more years. You'll be fine."

"I don't want to give it six or eight more minutes. Humans don't belong up here."

"I'll take that as a compliment," he said. "Humans are soft and easily distracted."

That's when distraction came in the form of 7.62mm incoming fire. Rounds bounced off the newly exposed black skin of the sub and pierced the air around us.

Like a mother throwing her arm across her child in a car crash, Kodiak shoved me to the ground, and we low-crawled for the cover of the massive submarine.

Mongo spun to investigate our mysterious dive for the deck, and a round pierced the fuel tank strapped to his back. A stream of highly flammable liquid death poured from behind the giant as the realization of our situation struck him like a freight train. He shucked the rig from his shoulders and tossed it away from the hovercraft, our only means of escape.

With practiced wordless battlefield communication, he glared at me, awaiting a direction-of-fire call. I pointed through the frozen undersea prowler in front of us, and he sprinted for the back of the bulge above the ice. Kodiak and I had occupied the closest piece of real estate that would provide us with protection from the assault, but we'd chosen a position that was impossible to defend. With the massive wall of ice and metal in front of us, we were little more than cowering children hiding beneath our beds.

Kodiak rolled onto his back and assessed the ice wall in front of us. "Get me up there!"

He let his rifle hang from its sling against his chest and took three strides away from the obstacle. I stood with my face pressed against the wall and my knees slightly bent. Kodiak took two running strides, planted one boot on the back of my calf and another on my shoulder, then shot up the side of the sub like an arctic Spider-Man. With his feet splayed out and dug into the ice of the mound, he raised his rifle across the crown of the Russian war machine and poured lead onto the battlefield.

I moved with all the speed I could muster and joined Mongo at the stern. "How many?"

He shook his head. "I can't tell yet, but we need some help."

I ripped the bulky glove from my hand and crushed the keys of my sat-phone. After an eternity with incoming rounds dancing through the air above my head, I hit the key that was guaranteed to garner an answer.

"Go for ops."

"Skipper, we're under small-arms fire at the sub site. Unknown number of aggressors firing from the northeast. Get that chopper back out here."

She said, "There's no armament on the Little Bird. They stripped everything off for fuel."

I swore under my breath and slammed my back against the sub. A billion thoughts poured through my head, but none of them improved our situation. Over the roar of the gunfight, Kodiak yelled, "Ammo!"

Mongo peeled off and sprinted around my boots, then he tossed four magazines skyward, and Kodiak caught them in pairs. He continued laying down fire and scanning the battlefield. "They're flanking to the northwest. Save the hovercraft!"

I yelled into the phone, "Find us some reinforcements!"

With that, I shoved the phone into my pocket and leapt to my feet. I ran in a straight line as fast as my bulky gear would allow while keeping the sub between me and most of the incoming fire. When I believed I'd created a sufficient angle, I juked to the right and directly toward the hovercraft. If they put enough rounds on the craft, we'd be not only in the coldest gunfight of my life, but also a long way from the ship, with no way home.

A round tore through the shoulder of my over suit, sending white insulation into the air as if I'd run through a cloud. The whistle of the passing round sounded like airborne death, but the pain didn't come, the blood didn't come, and I never broke stride. If I'd been the actual target of a sniper, he would've fired again, sending a round through the center of my chest, but the glancing blow had to be nothing more than a lucky potshot for me, and a near success for the hapless shooter.

I dived onto the hovercraft and slithered into the pilothouse. The machine came to life just as it had been designed to do, and I inflated the skirt as I shoved the controls to their stops. The device lumbered to the right as if struggling against an invisible force anchoring it in place. Nothing I did increased its speed as the heavy chunk of aluminum and I crawled across the ice like an errant snail. Finally, the turbine generated enough force to return the craft to its former glory as a nimble speed demon. Learning the controls as I maneuvered out of the line of fire wasn't the optimum scenario, but it was better than letting the magic carpet succumb to the ravages of flying lead.

Whoever our attackers were didn't particularly matter at that moment. My only concern was my team's survival and escape from the gunfight. Any earlier desire I had to defeat the gunmen melted like the ice beneath Mongo's flame when I realized we could likely escape if I could just get Mongo and Kodiak back on board.

In my haste to learn to fly the hovercraft, I hadn't given any thought to the control input that would stop it. I raced toward Mongo's position at the lower end of the bulge and did everything I could think of to slow down, but nothing seemed to work. I was left with only one option: slamming into the sub.

Can the machine survive the collision? Can I survive it? Will it capsize and become nothing more than an inverted dying beast?

There was little I could do to answer or manage any of those questions, so I soldiered on with escape in my eyes and two tons of hovercraft in my hands.

Mongo saw me coming and probably understood my inability to manage speed. He paced his run as closely as possible to my approach speed and leapt aboard as soon as I was close enough. Without hesitation, he shoved me from the controls and angled toward Kodiak.

Our survivalist caught a glimpse of our approach and lifted his feet from their grip on the ice. He slid, feetfirst, and bounded from the ice and onto the ramp at the rear of the craft a second before Mongo turned perpendicular to the sub and pressed the machine to her limits.

When we finally made our turn to the southwest, hopefully out of range of the shooters, Kodiak was first to speak. "I estimate twelve to fifteen—definitely AKs, indistinct white camo, unknown affiliation. My guess is not infantry-trained soldiers."

Mongo nodded. "I agree. They weren't very good shots, and nothing about them said they knew anything about small-unit tactics."

I said, "I guess that makes us the three luckiest guys above the Arctic Circle, huh?"

Kodiak stuck a finger inside the bullet hole in my jacket. "I'd say so. That didn't find any flesh, did it?"

"No, I'm good, but I'd better call Skipper off. She's likely to have the Canadian Air Force en route."

"Go for ops," she said with no sign of anxiety in her voice.

"We escaped unharmed, so call off any backup you had headed our way."

"Roger. Stand by."

She came back on the line seconds later. "Okay, the cavalry is standing down. What happened up there?"

"We're not sure yet, but it's safe to say that somebody knows we're here."

Chapter 16
Home Sweet Home

"Let's put this together," Skipper said. "Give me what you know for sure, and we'll go from there."

I said, "The things we know are few. That's definitely at least part of a submarine. The gunmen were using AKs. And they were a small, poorly trained unit of less than twenty."

"Were they in uniform?" she asked.

"They were in the same white camo we're in, with no insignia that we could see."

She was silent for a moment before asking, "Do you think they were trying to kill you or just scare you away?"

"Why would that matter?"

"It matters because it helps us understand what they think we are. You were a team of three men using a non-military hovercraft. If they think we're just harmless civilians, it makes sense for them to just try and scare us away, but if they thought we were military or paramilitary, they might intentionally avoid killing us to prevent this from becoming an international incident."

"That's pretty deep thinking," I said. "It's over my head, to be honest. Whoever they are, they know we found the sub, and they know we have automatic weapons and a flamethrower."

"A flamethrower?"

"It's a long story, but Mongo's involved."

"Oh, okay. It makes sense now."

How? How does it make sense for Mongo to have a flamethrower but not me?

I chose to let it slide. "Tell me what you're thinking."

She tapped something against her teeth. I assumed it was a pencil. "I'm thinking whoever they are, they found the sub first, and they're protecting their claim. Did you see any vehicles?"

I turned to my team. "Did either of you see any vehicles?"

Kodiak said, "I caught a glimpse of what could've been a few snow machines behind the gunners—maybe five or six hundred yards."

I passed the info and turned back to Kodiak. "Do you think they were trying to scare us away or trying to kill us?"

He furrowed his brow. "That's an interesting question. If they were trying to scare us off, that would explain why they appeared so disorganized. Maybe it was a gambit. Maybe they want us to think they're sloppy shooters when, in fact, they're hard-core."

Mongo said, "They weren't shy about hitting the sub, so either they never plan to use it again, or they know it's broken in half. Either way, they probably know more about the sub than we do."

We slid across the ice on our cushion of air until the *Polar Explorer III* came into sight on the western horizon.

"She's making way," Mongo said.

As we drew nearer, the frozen bow wave parted in front of her. "You're right. Look at that. She's making four or five knots."

"Get her stopped," Mongo said. "We can't get close enough for the crane if there's broken ice everywhere."

I called the bridge and gave our azimuth and range. "Heave to so we can approach."

The officer said, "Roger. Approach from astern, and the engineers will ready the crane."

Mongo brought us past the ship and slid from the ice onto the surface of the frigid water.

"Won't the water cause the pontoons to inflate?" I asked.

He shook his head. "No, they only inflate if they become submerged. We're good on water with less than one-meter swells."

We moved to within a few feet of the stern of our ship, and a pair of cables appeared above our heads. We rigged for the hoist and gave the signal. A minute later, we were on deck with the turbine of the hovercraft at flight idle and awaiting shutdown.

We shucked our survival gear and poured ourselves into the CIC, where the rest of the team waited with Skipper on the monitor.

"Welcome home," Clark said. "I hear you had a little adventure out there."

I rubbed a hand across my shoulder just to make sure there wasn't any blood. "It got interesting for a few minutes, but we're good."

"Good to hear. We've been talking strategy."

I raised an eyebrow. "With Skipper?"

She huffed. "What's wrong with talking strategy with me?"

"Nothing," I said. "But you don't have the authority to approve anything sketchy, and what we do next is definitely going to be sketchy."

"It sounds like you've already got a plan," she said.

"I have the initial sparks of a plan, and you know what sparks become."

The room erupted. "Fires!"

Kodiak shook his head. "I've been here three days, and I've already been attacked by two polar bears, shot at by a bunch of communists, got to watch a giant with a flamethrower, and now we're planning a real fire. I believe I've found myself a home."

"How many did you put down?"

Kodiak scanned the room to find the voice who'd asked the question, and his eyes fell on our sniper.

A long moment of appraisal followed before Singer asked again. "How many?"

"Six," Kodiak said.

"How many rounds did you fire?"

"Four magazines."

Singer turned to Mongo. "Did you have any kills?"

"Two, and before you ask, I pressed the trigger eleven times."

Singer looked up at me, and I said, "One, and maybe a dozen rounds. No more than half a mag."

Singer turned his attention back to Kodiak, and the new guy said, "I get it. My dead-guys-to-bullets-spent ratio is out of line with my teammates'."

Singer let his eyes linger on Kodiak longer than anyone would've described as comfortable. "And that's why the rest of us are glad you're here."

Kodiak screwed up his face. "What? You want me here because I shoot too much?"

Singer smiled for the first time. "No, my friend. We want you here because even though you shot too many rounds, you didn't try to justify it. You just gave the numbers, and then you shut up."

Clark knocked on the table with a knuckle. "Let's quit kissing the new guy's butt and get back to work. If you remember, we're under a presidential endorsement to solve this thing, no matter what it is or what it takes. We put down half the bad guys we saw today, and we lost no one. That's a pretty good day, no matter how you grade it out. Now, I want to hear Chase's idea."

I cleared my throat. "First, we have to make some assumptions. We need to assume there's something about that submarine that someone doesn't want us to find. Agreed?" Nods and groans of agreement followed, so I continued. "Second, whatever it is, it's worth dying to keep hidden. That alone makes me want to know what's so special about that broken-up sub. How about you?"

Clark said, "Keep going."

"I say it's time we get the ship's weapons officer down here and find out for sure what kind of punishment this tub is capable of dishing out."

Kodiak closed one eye and glared at me with the other. "Are you saying you don't know the capabilities of your own boat?"

Clark cut in. "Let's put it this way. We're still getting to know each other."

Kodiak nodded and leaned back, once again, silent.

Disco pressed a button on the console. "Bridge, CIC."

"Go for bridge," came a disembodied voice.

"Send the weapons officer to the CIC."

"Roger."

As if materializing out of the mist, an unassuming face that I remembered well stepped through the hatch.

I said, "Lieutenant Commander LaGrange, it's good to see you again. Why don't you come in and give us a rundown of just how hard this old girl can punch?"

The man nodded behind a blank expression. "Retired lieutenant commander. Just call me Weps now."

He spun a stainless-steel seat from beneath the console and brought up a list of weapons systems on the screen. "Here's our complement. Let's start with the Mark Forty-Five, five-inch gun. It carries a seventy-pound round thirteen miles with a fully automated fire control system. I can drop a seventy-pound shell in your shirt pocket from thirteen miles."

He seemed to expect applause, but my team sat in silence.

"Okay, continuing on. We have a cut-down version of the Aegis Combat System, which is made up of three essential elements: Aegis Weapon System, which is the fast-reaction Aegis Anti-Aircraft Warfare System; the Phalanx Close-In Weapons System, and the Mark Forty-One Vertical Launching System with the strike package."

I wanted to clap after that presentation, but instead, I asked, "What about anti-submarine weaponry?"

Weps met my gaze. "Are you expecting a submarine engagement?"

"Maybe," I said. "But I hope not. Hopefully, we'll only need to sink an already mostly sunken sub."

Weps put on an evil grin only issued to naval weapons officers. "You're going to like this one. We have four Russian APR-3E airborne light anti-submarine warfare acoustic homing torpedoes."

I leaned way back in my chair. "How did we score four Russian torpedoes?"

Weps glanced up at the environmental panel. "It's a balmy six degrees Fahrenheit with a gentle breeze from the northwest at twenty-six knots. That's perfect weather for an afternoon stroll. Wouldn't you say?"

I shook my head. "Okay, I get it. I probably don't want to know anyway, but I do want to know what else you have tucked away that might make us look like a red commie fighting force."

"We have a nice array of surface-to-air and surface-to-surface missiles with authentic Russian and Chinese markings with the appropriate chemical signatures. We can shoot down anything that flies, and if we can find it, we can sink anything submerged up to a thousand meters and make it look like the People's Liberation Army pulled the triggers."

It was my turn to grin. "How close can we get to the grounded sub? I need to get a look at it."

Weps said, "As long as the ice is less than sixteen inches thick, we can pull alongside and toss over a line."

"Not that close," I said.

Mongo jumped in. "We just need to get close enough to launch the ROUV."

I said, "Not so fast. I want to put *my* eyes on the sub."

Mongo ducked his chin. "Are you talking about going into the water?"

"That's exactly what I'm talking about, and I plan to take you and Clark with me."

We steamed for the next twenty-four hours and closed our distance by eighty miles. By the following morning, I believed Captain Sprayberry would lay me alongside the ground sub at pistol-shot range. And we would know without a doubt whose submarine was stuck to the frozen bottom of the Northwest Passage.

Chapter 17
A World Askew

It wasn't exactly pistol-shot range, but through my Swarovski binoculars from my position on the navigation bridge, the submarine was in sight.

"Is this close enough?" Captain Sprayberry asked through a mouth full of pulled pork.

"Where did you get a barbecue sandwich inside the Arctic Circle?"

"I made it. Big Bob down in engineering rigged up a smoker for me in the engine room."

I turned to the navigation officer. "Did he offer you any?"

She rolled her eyes. "He never does, sir."

The captain shrugged. "It's a small smoker, and these young kids don't appreciate the fine art of perfect barbecue."

I asked, "What if they get froggy one day and snatch it from your hand?"

He puffed out his chest. "There's not a man on this tub who can take a sandwich from my—"

Before he could finish his ridiculous claim, I lunged forward, feigned a punch to his temple, and lifted the sandwich from his hand like taking candy from a baby.

It was my turn to speak with barbecue sauce dripping from my chin. "This is just fine. We'll swim in from here. And you're right . . . this is pretty close to perfection."

I passed the remains of the sandwich to the navigation officer and made my exit. I doubt she had the courage to nab a bite before returning it to her captain, but I hope she at least licked her fingers.

In the moonpool, Singer, Clark, and I suited up in state-of-the-art, heated arctic undergarments beneath the best dry suits money could buy. Our Dräger tactical rebreathers came next, and finally, our full-face masks with integrated communications. Nothing about the coming hours of our lives would be pleasant, but there was no better way to learn exactly what those gunmen on the ice were defending than to see it firsthand.

Both Clark and Singer were graduates of the Army's Combat Diver Course. In fact, Clark had been an instructor during a convalescent period a decade before, so I would be in good hands beneath the ice. I'm not claustrophobic, but swimming for a mile beneath a layer of impenetrable ice was enough to give anybody second thoughts.

The moonpool operator lifted a handset from a comms panel. "Request permission to open the doors and splash the divers."

A few seconds later, he said, "Aye, sir."

The operator turned to me. "The captain ordered me to tell you not to come back without a pork butt, but I don't know what that means."

I had a good chuckle and eased my diver propulsion device into the icy water. Clark was first in. I followed him, and Singer stepped into water world a second behind me. The heating elements in my undergarment gave me the feeling of diving in the tropics, but even the high-tech gear had its limits.

Clark said, "Radio check."

"Loud and clear, how me?" I asked.

"I have you the same."

Singer's comms checked out perfectly as well, and Clark gave the order. "On me, boys. Let's go snuggle up to a busted Russian sub. Remember, we've got two hours before the batteries for our heaters take a dive, so we're back on board the *Lori Danielle* in one hundred minutes. Got it?"

I pressed the timer on my dive computer and watched the seconds begin piling up.

Our DPVs pulled us along at slightly less than five knots, so we'd make the sub in less than fifteen minutes. That gave us seventy minutes on target to identify, film, measure, and explore the wreck.

Many non-divers believe SCUBA diving is a thrill-seeker's endeavor. However, nothing could be further from the truth. The underwater world is one of serenity and breathtaking beauty. I've dived in waters all over the globe and witnessed landscapes and creatures far too beautiful for words. In its own way, the world into which I'd stepped on that day was more beautiful than any tropical coral reef I've ever seen. I expected sheer darkness, requiring artificial light to navigate our way to the sub, but my expectations were little more than ignorance. I never could've anticipated or even imagined the color of blue that made up the world around me. It was like no other color I'd ever seen, and it absorbed me as if welcoming me into its calling abyss and begging me never to leave. As we approached the sub, the bottom sloped sharply upward to meet us, and the astonishing beauty of the environment became gray, empty, and ominous.

The massive black wall that was the hull of the submarine rose before us like a barrier between realms. Some force I'll never understand drove me to slide my gloved hand across the gentle curve of the hull. She had once plied the depths in near silence with her deadly payload sheltered deep within her bowels, the intercontinental ballistic missiles straining against their restraints to be freed to do Satan's bidding against the freedom of the land above.

Clark's voice crackled in my ears. "You okay, College Boy? You've been awfully quiet."

"I'm fine. Just taking it all in. This is my first time under the ice."

I wasn't expecting a scolding, but that's what I got. "Keep your head in the game. If anything goes wrong down here, we're a long way from sunshine and fresh air, and I don't want to drag you into sick bay again."

"Again?" Singer asked. "I need to hear that story."

"We'll tell it over cigars and bourbon," I said. "For now, let's start at the bow and work our way astern."

We turned our DPVs to the north and skimmed along the side of the sub until we came to its rounded, blunt prow and drifted to a stop. Clark shone his light on the writing on the hull, and my stomach tied itself into a knot.

I laid a hand against the characters painted on the hull. "I don't know what this is, but it's definitely not Russian."

Singer said, "I think it's Chinese."

Everything about the mission exploded in my head, and I flashed back to the president's mandate: . . . *authorized to use deadly force.*

"Get some pictures," Clark said, and Singer took both video and stills.

The prow of the once-mighty weapon of war appeared undamaged, apart from slight deformation. There was no visible rupture. About a hundred feet from the bow, the upper deck of the hull rose sharply and leveled out well above the foredeck elevation.

I studied the hull design. "I guess that's where they keep the nukes, huh?"

Singer said, "Yep."

Clark spun and stared into my mask. "You're sure there was no radioactivity?"

"I'm sure, but we only took a reading above the ice, so I have no idea what the conditions are like down here."

Singer said, "Mongo would know for sure, but I doubt that a ten-inch sheet of ice would stop radioactivity from penetrating."

"That's good enough for me," Clark said. "Let's have a look inside."

We motored our way to the midsection of the hull, where the vessel had broken into two halves. We hovered by the razor-like shards of metal where the ship had separated and stared into the depths beneath us.

Clark said, "How deep do you think it is?"

I said, "The chart shows a hundred fifty feet, but the charts for this part of the world aren't great."

He said, "I guess we'll find out. Hang your DPVs here, and we'll fin our way through the interior."

We clipped our machines to anything we could find and followed Clark into the sub. The interior was far less welcoming than the water outside. Our lights were crucial, and Singer clipped a line to a loop of cable and unrolled the string as we penetrated deeper into the hull. Finding our way back out was on my list of things to do, so I was thankful Singer remembered to bring the reel of line.

We swam beside the launch tubes, likely containing submarine-launched ballistic missiles, and I fought back the fear of the havoc such weapons could cause in the wrong hands. As we neared the forward bulkhead separating the missile tubes from the forward section of the sub, a massive form appeared at arm's length ahead of me, and I threw myself aside. As the form came ever closer, I felt my lungs convulsing in fear and confusion of what I'd discovered . . . or what had discovered me.

The nose of the creature resembled that of a great white, but the color was wrong, and I'd never heard of a white shark as massive as what I was now nose to nose with.

Clark dived beneath the leviathan, and Singer joined me against the inner hull as the beast drifted slowly by. It never seemed to notice any of the three of us, but I couldn't resist reaching out and letting the creature's sandpaper flesh slide against my gloved hand. At my touch, the monster turned slowly as if to acknowledge the interaction and then continued through the missile section.

"What was that?" Clark almost yelled.

Singer said, "I don't know, but I got enough video to identify it when we get back to the ship."

I huffed. "*If* we get back to the ship with that thing guarding our only exit."

I wanted to keep an eye on the beast, but I needed to know what was in the forward section of the sub. With any luck, I'd never see that thing again.

We finned through an opening barely large enough for the shark to pass through, and discovered what had, no doubt, been the target of the animal's attention. Carcasses of sailors drifted like spirits in the near-freezing water, some of them with evidence of the shark's attention left in their flesh.

Singer let himself drift to the deck below and knelt. Although I couldn't hear him, there was little doubt about what he was doing and who he was talking to.

After his prayer, he shot video and stills of the interior and the bodies. We continued forward and found the captain's berth just ahead of the conning tower. Clark pulled a uniform shirt from inside a locker and shoved it into his bag. Further inspection revealed a small metal safe attached to the interior of a cabinet.

Clark gave a tug against the safe, but it didn't budge. "We should've brought Mongo."

"Let me give it a try," I said.

He backed away and motioned toward the box. "Be my guest."

I pulled a metal pole from the frame of the small bed that had been the captain's and slid it between the gunwale and the safe. Pressing my feet against the bulkhead, I pried with all my strength, and the safe moved a fraction of an inch. "Help me."

Clark and Singer wedged themselves into the tight confines of the cabin and laced their fingers around the metal pole. After three concerted pulls, the box popped from its mount and fell on the deck.

I said, "Now, somebody has to carry that thing,"

Clark reiterated, "We should've brought Mongo."

Singer rigged a small lifting bag to the safe and inflated it ever so gently until the box rose above the deck and hovered motionless be-fore us. "Who needs Mongo when we've got buoyancy?"

Our exploration of the forward section revealed little, so we swam back toward the stern, following Singer's line. At the opening of the hull, the enormous shark hovered as if waiting her turn for the bathroom stall. She lazily swam past us and back into the cavern that had been the Chinese submarine.

Clark ran an arm around his DPV and gazed into the depths. "Who's going with me?"

"I'll go," I said, and Singer handed me the camera.

Clark nodded and pulled his DPV from its temporary anchor. "Here we go. We'll stop at one-twenty. I'm not interested in riding Dr. Shadrack's recompression chamber."

"Following you," I said as we drifted away from the sub and Singer.

The inky black world of the depth consumed the angelic blue we'd known on our swim from the ship, and our lights battled to defeat the darkness.

At one hundred feet, Clark stopped his descent. "How you doing?"

"I'm okay. We're at seventy-two minutes."

He said, "Roger. Down to one-twenty and not an inch deeper."

We sank and scanned the area during our descent. At precisely a hundred twenty feet, Clark came to a hover and shone his light in every direction. "There she is."

I followed the beam of his light and added mine to double the illumination. Resting on her side lay the stern section of the formerly ferocious submarine. Seeing her lying there in the muck made me think of how Goliath must've looked after David felled him on the floor of the Valley of Elah. As threatening as the sub had been, she was reduced to little more than rubble on the cold, dark ocean floor, albeit rubble with up to twelve intercontinental ballistic missiles with nuclear payloads.

Chapter 18
Blow It Up?

Back aboard the *Polar Explorer III*, Mongo leaned toward the display in the combat information center. "Show me the video of the stern section again, then I'll tell you about the shark."

Singer played it back until Mongo stopped him. "Freeze there. Can you blow it up?"

I shuddered. "Let's not use phrases like *blow it up* when we're watching video of nuclear weapons."

"Good point," Mongo said. "Can you zoom in?"

Although he'd never be as good as Skipper, our sniper did a nice job managing the video playback.

Mongo slid from his seat and moved to within inches of the display. "What's that on the underside of the sub?"

Every eye in the room stared at the screen, and I said, "I don't know, but it doesn't look like anything I've ever seen on the hull of a sub. Get Weps down here."

Clark squinted at the screen. "Why didn't we see that when we were down there?"

I shrugged. "I don't know, but whatever they are, I'm glad the video caught them."

A few minutes later, the weapons officer peered through his glasses perched high on his nose and studied the sub video. "Did you get any video on the way back up from depth?" I shook my head, and Weps leaned back. "You know that's not a Russian boat, right?"

"Yeah, we figured that out from the writing on the bow and the markings inside."

He steepled his fingers. "Were any of the missile tube doors open?"

I looked to Singer and Clark, and they both shook their heads.

"So, we don't know for sure if there are missiles in the tubes."

I asked, "Why would a boomer set to sea without SLBMs in the tubes?"

Weps sighed. "An American boomer wouldn't, but I can think of a bunch of reasons the Chinese and Russians might do it—not the least of which being the ability to carry undetected cargo. Who's going to open up a missile tube to make sure it contains a missile?"

Mongo spoke up. "Can GPR see through the tube doors?"

Weps seemed to consider his question before saying, "Maybe, but how do we get a ground-penetrating radar system to function underwater?"

Mongo smiled. "Give me a torch and some stainless steel, and I'll show you."

Weps turned to me as if questioning the sanity of our giant.

I said, "If he says he can build it, either help him or get out of the way."

"That reminds me," Clark said. "How are the engineers coming on the safe?"

Weps pulled a radio from his belt. "Engineering, Weps."

"Go for engineering."

"Do you have the box open yet?"

"Affirmative. We're cooking the books now."

Weps almost laughed. "Run the contents up to CIC when it comes out of the oven."

"Roger, sir."

He replaced the radio on his belt. "It sounds like they're drying everything out now."

I asked, "Do we have anybody on board who can read Chinese?"

He narrowed his gaze. "Mandarin or Cantonese?"

"I'd guess Mandarin, but I don't know for sure. Whatever's written on those documents is what I need translated."

Weps waved his hand. "Don't worry about that. We've got software that'll make short work of it."

I checked my watch. "Our analyst back at Bonaventure can do it, but I don't want to wake her up at this hour. She gets grouchy."

Clark gave me a wink. "I'm telling her you said that."

"She won't believe you."

Weps chuckled. "You guys are quite a crew. I'll have the contents of the safe translated before the sun comes up. Do you need me anymore tonight?"

I said, "Before you go, let's talk about some options. If there are nukes on that sub, they have to come off, and we're not qualified to move them."

Weps said, "We're qualified to haul them, but getting them off the missiles and onto the ship is outside our collection of skills."

Mongo rolled forward in his chair. "There's a mechanical procedure to remove the warheads from the delivery vehicles, right?"

Weps shot a thumb toward Mongo. "Check him out, calling missiles delivery vehicles. Yeah, there's a procedure, but not underwater."

The big man wasn't fazed. "With the right tools, anything that can be done on the surface can be done underwater."

"How about starting a fire?" Weps asked.

"With an underwater torch, I can melt a ball bearing down there. Show me the manual, and I'll decide if we can lift the warheads off the submerged 'delivery vehicles.'"

"I like this guy," Weps said. "The procedure will vary depending on which delivery vehicle is in the tubes. First, we need to know what's underneath those doors, and then I can get the procedures for you."

Mongo nodded. "I'll get started on the GPR rig, but before I go, how much can the cranes on the stern lift?"

Weps shrugged and then put on a smile. "I don't know, but I'm certain they can lift more than a delivery vehicle."

Mongo threw up his hands. "Look at us solving problems already. But I have one more question for you before you hit the hay. Can the doors be opened manually?"

Weps chewed on his mustache for a moment. "Before the boat broke in half, they could be opened manually, but there's likely a safety mechanism that locks them closed in the event of a catastrophic failure of the hull. That's all supposition based on what I know of American boats. Predicting what the Chinese do is not one of my skill sets."

The weapons officer left the CIC, and Mongo wasted no time. "I say we take a torch down there and cut open a door. I could waste a lot of time building a penetrating radar, but if there are nukes in there, we're cutting the tops off anyway, right?"

"You're right, as usual," Clark said. "Forget about the radar, and let's cut our way in."

The big man let out a little chuckle. "Okay, now, let's talk about your shark. That thing is believed to be the largest of all living sharks. It's called the Greenland shark, and believe it or not, they can live to be five hundred years old. You probably encountered one of the oldest living creatures on Earth down there."

"Are they dangerous?" I asked.

Mongo shrugged. "Nobody knows. They're a mystery. Other than knowing where they live and approximately how long, we don't know much more. Did that one exhibit any aggressive behavior?"

Clark laughed. "If you could've seen the look on Chase's face when he came beak to beak with that thing, you wouldn't have been able to convince him the fish wasn't dangerous."

I rolled my eyes. "Go ahead, laugh it up. We're going back down there, and you may get a little one-on-one time with Mr. Sharky."

Mongo said, "Based on what you found down there, the shark wasn't hungry, so he's probably no threat, but since we just don't know, try not to let him get behind you."

Clark slapped a hand on the table. "That's enough for tonight. Let's get some sleep and reconvene after breakfast."

* * *

I expected a night of lying awake and trying to reconcile how an orphan kid from Georgia found himself at the rooftop of the world, getting shot at by mysterious figures on the ice, while melting ice off a Chinese submarine that should've been Russian. But that's not what happened. Instead, I lay in my bunk wondering if I would ever rejoin polite society after uncovering whatever was happening beneath the ice a mile away.

Breakfast was eggs, bacon, toast, and coffee. A lot of coffee. Discussing missions over meals wasn't something the team and I often did, but the weight of our current mission made it worthy of words between mouthfuls.

I pulled a slice of bacon from Clark's plate. "This thing has become enormous. Have you briefed the Board?"

He pressed his fork to the back of my hand. "Touch my bacon again, and you get four holes in your claw."

I chuckled. "Go ahead. That hand is full of man-made parts. You might draw blood, but it's going to take a lot more than that fork to do any real damage."

I destroyed my right wrist and crushed most of the bones in my right hand during the final play of the 1996 College World Series in Omaha, Nebraska. If that accident hadn't happened, I'd be wearing an Atlanta Braves uniform instead of an arctic survival suit, but I would've never met the men sitting around that breakfast table who'd become closer than any sports team ever could be. They'd become even closer than family. We'd bled, fought, and won all over the world, and we bore the scars to prove it. No, Clark's fork couldn't hurt me, but the volume of the mission on which we sat had the potential not only to hurt every one of us, but also to turn the world into a trembling pit of horrors for the millions of innocent souls who had no idea such treachery lay only feet beneath the frozen waters of the Northwest Passage.

Clark lifted his fork from my hand. "Yeah, I brought them up to speed after our powwow last night."

"Are they committing any more assets?"

"Not yet," he said. "But they're briefing the Joint Chiefs this morning. This thing may become a military mission before it's over."

I sighed and hid my face behind an upturned coffee mug. "That'd be a mistake."

Silence consumed the room, and when I looked up from my mug, every eye was focused on me.

"If the military gets their hands on this thing, so will the media, and missing nuclear weapons is not what the world needs to see on the evening news."

No one moved, and no one spoke.

"Am I wrong on this? I'm the civilian here, so somebody speak up if I'm way off base."

I expected some wisdom from Mongo or common sense from Clark, but instead, I got the soft baritone voice of the team's spiritual center and moral compass. "You're not wrong, Chase, but you're looking in the wrong direction. The warheads locked aboard what's left of that submarine aren't the immediate issue. You touched on the human element, and you're right. The world doesn't know there's a wrecked Chinese nuclear submarine in the Arctic. They don't need to know we're here poking around. In fact, they don't need to know we exist."

I swallowed his words with another sip of coffee, and he continued.

"The people who shot at us were protecting a secret. Now they know the secret is out. Desperation is a catalyst for irrational behavior. We've all seen it. We have to find those people, find where they're surviving, and either rescue them or quell their desperation. If we don't eliminate the human factor in this thing, none of us will live long enough to tell the truth about what happened up here, and the world will be left with the story told by the Communist Chinese—if the story is ever told at all."

I'd swallowed my last bite of breakfast for that morning. "We've got no satellite coverage, no reinforcements, and no idea how big the force is we're facing. If we run out on the ice locked and loaded, we're playing cowboys and idiots with no way to know which team we're on."

Disco said, "We do have a tool we've not pulled out of the shed yet. We've got one of the finest FLIR systems in the world mounted on the nose of our Little Bird."

Forward-looking-infrared could find the slightest variation in the temperatures of surfaces ahead of the chopper, and if humans were alive on the ice, they were definitely warmer than the frozen seawater below.

"How about the drones?" I asked. "Do we have any thermal imaging hardware on those?"

Mongo said, "We do, but it's not as good as the chopper."

I stood from the table. "Maybe not, but if something is going to get shot down, I'd much rather lose a thousand unmanned drones than one crewed helicopter."

"Don't forget," Disco said. "The helicopter can shoot back."

Chapter 19
Black the Sky

Skipper's face appeared on the monitor in the CIC just as I settled into my chair. "It sounds like you boys have been busy little beavers up there."

"That's one way to put it," I said. "I've come up with a new set of priorities."

"This ought to be good. Let's hear it."

I slid my notepad in front of me and wrote as I dictated our new priority list. "First, we're going to find, identify, and neutralize the opposing force, whoever they are. Second—"

"Hold on," Skipper said. "You can't just say you're going to kill an entire fighting force and move on."

"I didn't say we were going to kill them. I said we're going to find them, figure out who they are, and neutralize them . . . in that order. Who knows? We may have the same goal as whoever's out there."

Clark jumped in. "College Boy is right. This could be a case of the left hand not knowing the right hand is kicking its butt."

Skipper shook her head. "I'm so glad Tony didn't get whatever language disorder you have. I definitely married the smarter brother."

"He may be smarter than me, but I'll always be better looking."

"Let's get back on track," I said. "We're going to fill the sky with as many drones as we can launch and find out *where* these people are. After that, we'll move on to figuring out *who* they are. The neutralization method will be determined when we answer the *who* question."

"That's reasonable," Skipper said. "What do you need from me?"

"I need you to collect and catalog the drone video. You're the smart one. We're likely to miss something with our knuckle-dragging eyes."

"You got it. What's next?"

I made a few more notes on my pad. "After we neutralize the threat, we'll identify the exterior structure on the sunken sub. When that's done, I have a feeling we'll turn this over to someone else. It's getting bigger than our little team can manage already."

"I don't like the sound of that," she said, "but I tend to agree, especially with what Tony and Hunter are learning. That's a conversation we need to have ASAP."

I said, "Let us get through the drone launch and data dump, then we'll do that briefing within the next forty-eight hours. They're not finding anything that ties this mission to the banks, are they?"

Her one-word answer made me question my new priorities. "Maybe."

That's not what my brain needed, but I brushed it off. "Have them ready to brief us tomorrow. Does anyone else have anything?" Heads shook, and I gave the order. "Launch the drones."

It took an hour to get everything linked, programmed, and the drones in the air. Our full inventory of autonomous aerial vehicles, as Mongo insisted on calling them, consisted of one dozen flying machines with cameras, thermal sensors, and inertial navigation systems that didn't require GPS data.

The AAVs were the size of a pizza box and made a buzzing sound like a thousand annoying gnats as the fleet spread out over the seemingly endless plain of ice at fifty feet above the frigid landscape. Data feeds were pouring into the CIC faster than any human eye could process them, but the computers linked through the ship to the Bonaventure op center made the data collection and analysis child's play.

An hour into the process, Mongo said, "Bingo fuel for flight number one."

"Bring 'em home," I said.

He gave the command for the first six AAVs to return to the ship, and their video feeds powered down to save the battery power for the flight home against the prevailing wind. The first wave made it back to the deck without incident, and I found myself enthralled watching them land without colliding with each other.

Skipper's voice yanked me from my mesmerized state. "Tallyho!"

I spun back to the main screen and stared into a scene I could've never imagined. "What is that?"

Skipper said, "It's a camp of igloos."

I leaned in with disbelief pouring from my face. "Igloos? I didn't know those were real."

Clark said, "Oh, they're quite real, and those particular igloos are bad news. Those aren't Inuit fur trappers. They're Russian Spetsnaz."

"Russian Special Forces?" I asked. "Why?"

"Maybe not Russian, but they're definitely Russian-trained operators. Nobody builds igloos like that unless they learned it from the Spetsnaz."

"Wait a minute," Kodiak said. "We were in a gunfight with these guys, and there's no way Chase, Mongo, and I survived a fight with a Spetsnaz squad. We're good, but two dozen hard-core commandos against the three of us? That only ends one way, and it ain't good news for the good guys."

Mongo said, "I agree. The guys who hit us were barely better than the California National Guard with their low-capacity mags. There's no way those guys were Spetsnaz."

Every eye turned to me, and I said, "You guys are the experts. I'm the civilian, but we were in a gunfight with a Girl Scout troop, at best."

Clark leaned back in his chair and pondered our conflict. "Then, the guys in the igloos aren't the same guys from the gunfight. That means we've got two unfriendly neighbors up here in this tropical paradise. Does anyone see any other possibility?"

Skipper chimed in. "If there are two groups of aggressors, and the igloos are full of Russian Special Forces, where are the others, and how are they staying alive?"

"Some of them aren't staying alive," Kodiak said. "I noticed there aren't any dead bodies lying around by the sub this morning. At least the drones didn't spot any."

"Polar bears?" Singer asked.

Kodiak shrugged. "Maybe, but we put down nine shooters. It's not likely the bears cleaned up nine bodies in twenty-four hours."

I stared at my boots. "Are we suggesting that somebody cleaned up after us?"

Kodiak said, "It looks like it. My guess would be that the surviving gunmen collected their dead and wounded."

"But where did they take them?" Skipper asked. Before anyone could answer, she said, "What is that?"

The monitor turned from Skipper's face to drone footage of a lump in the snow.

I asked, "Where is that?"

"Give me just a second," Skipper said. "Okay, got it. It's two miles north of the sub, but I still want to know what it is."

Everyone leaned toward the monitor. As usual, our big brain was first to answer the tough question. "That's white camo netting, and based on the outline, I'd say it's hiding a helicopter . . . A big helicopter."

Clark spoke barely above a whisper. "The terrain looks like it rises in the background."

I leaned even closer. "I noticed that. Do we have battery life to fly a pass over that rising terrain?"

Mongo said, "We do, but we don't have enough battery life to fly that pass *and* make it back to the ship. We'd have to sacrifice a drone."

Kodiak said, "Uh, it looks like somebody's trying to help us with that sacrifice."

Every eye shot to the screen just in time to see small-arms fire streaking by the drone cameras.

Mongo frantically stroked some keys, and the screens went dark. "What's happening?" I demanded.

Mongo said, "The drones are in defensive retreat. They power down every system except radar and rotors to hightail it out of there. When they escape the threat, they'll come back online, if they survive."

It felt as though everyone in the CIC was holding his breath and staring into a blank monitor. After what felt like hours, but was likely only minutes, the monitor once again filled with an ocean of white.

Mongo said, "We lost one, but the others are safe and headed home."

I asked, "Are there any markings that would identify the drones as American?"

"It doesn't matter," Mongo said. "They're hardwired with a self-destruct circuit and three ounces of C-Four. It turned itself into powdered bits of plastic the same instant it took a hit."

"I guess it doesn't matter. The gig's up, and they know we're coming for them."

Clark said, "Hang on a minute, College Boy. That's not what they know. They may suspect that, but what they know is that they've been spotted by a flight of drones. Did we get any footage of the actual shooter?"

Skipper said, "Give me a minute. I'm compiling."

A few seconds later, she sent us an image of a pair of commandos firing into the air.

Kodiak said, "Those are PKMs."

"What's a PKM?" Skipper asked.

He said, "Pecheneg machine gun. It's a Russian seven point six two by fifty-four that'll run over six hundred rounds per minute. It's usually fired from a bipod or vehicle mount, but those guys are hard-core."

Mongo squinted at the screen. "Those are definitely not the guys we mixed it up with."

"That's about to change," I said. "Get Weps down here."

The weapons officer slipped through the hatch, took his seat, and studied our faces. "Nothing about this looks good."

"We're good," I said. "We're putting on the warpaint, and we need your input, so to speak."

"Whatever you need."

I pointed toward the monitors. "Take us back to the igloos."

Skipper ran the video back to the scene with the eight ice structures, and I said, "We suspect this to be a Spetsnaz camp, and we're going to rattle their ice cubes. Tell us you can put a round down a stovepipe."

Weps rubbed a hand across the console. "I can do it without scratching the sides of the pipe. Do you want to level it?"

"Not yet," I said. "I just want to let them know we can."

He gave me a nod. "I like where your head's at, boss. Just say the word."

Clark reached over and slid my notepad from beneath my fingertips. He studied my scribbling and sighed. "Really?"

"Have you got a better idea?"

He flipped the pad back toward me. "Yeah, I do. I say we sit right here, where it's nice and warm, and blow that camp off the planet."

I said, "I don't want to kill 'em. I want to scare them a little and talk to 'em."

Clark huffed. "You think you're going to scare a camp full of Spetsnaz?"

"They may be Spetsnaz, but none of them wants to die out there on that ice."

He shrugged. "Okay, you're in charge. We'll do it your way."

I slid my pad toward Disco. "Get your girlfriend suited up, and tell her to wear her shooting gloves."

He read through my notes, and a smile overtook his previously somber expression. "This is going to be fun."

I'd stood toe to toe with more Russians than I cared to remember, but the coming encounter promised to be an experience like none other and an unadulterated exercise in sheer fortitude. If I survived it, the afternoon would burn itself into my soul and never surrender its place as the gutsiest stunt I'd ever pull.

Chapter 20
Take Me to Your Leader

Two hours later, I stood in the hangar bay with my team huddled up and geared to the teeth. "Gentlemen, we're not chasing gang-bangers holding pistols sideways. We're stepping right into the face of one of the most highly trained commando units on Earth. I know I don't have to tell any of you how dangerous the Spetsnaz are, but what I do want you to know is this. Everybody—every single one of us—is coming home tonight, and we're coming home vertical and still breathing. Every man is responsible for every other man, and there are no exceptions. Brothers, bring each other home. Whatever this is, it will not be the death of us."

Once again, back aboard the hovercraft and dressed like the Michelin Man, the bitter, bone-chilling cold cut at every living thing, but my mind already saw my body walking into the fire that would either consume me or deliver the Russians into the palm of my gloved hand.

We soared across the ice at the upper limit of the hovercraft's impressive ability, and I watched our limited GPS equipment with one eye while scanning the internal navigation system with the other. If the drones had correctly recorded their position when they befell automatic-weapons fire, we'd be within mortar range in less than ten minutes. My plan was to maneuver well south of the igloo encampment and position my team in the rising terrain to the east of the Russians. Low, overcast skies and light snow were a gift from the sky that particular morning in the Arctic. Visibility was limited to less than a mile, and the incessant wind blew hard and loud enough to drown out at least some of the noise we'd make with the hovercraft. Getting into position would be the easy part. Surviving my solo on the Bolshoi stage would be the performance of a lifetime.

Watching the navigation screens closely, I leaned against Mongo at the helm. "Put me one klick north, and I'll lighten your load."

He let out a long sigh. "I still don't like it, Chase."

I gave his enormous shoulder a reassuring pat. "Trust me, big man. I'm a doctor. I've got this."

He shook his head. "If you're lucky enough to survive, you're going to wish you had a real doctor before this is over."

He brought the hovercraft to a stop precisely on the spot I plotted on the chart, and Clark stepped in front of me and grabbed a fistful of my parka. "Listen to me, College Boy. This is a stupid plan, but I don't have a better one. You've never been as alone as you're about to be."

I pulled my rifle sling off my shoulder and extended the weapon toward him.

He stepped back. "What are you doing?"

I swallowed the fear I should've been strong enough to hide. "I'm going unarmed. It's the only way I'll stay alive."

He pressed a hand against the rifle still waiting in my outstretched hand. "You're not going out there without a rifle and half a dozen mags. It's that simple."

I rested the butt of the M4 on the deck and let the muzzle lean against the console. "It's the only way, and besides, you've got my back if things get weird."

"If? What do you mean, if? Things are already weird, and you walking out there without a rifle is not only the stupidest idea you've ever had, but it's also the stupidest idea *anybody's* ever had."

I gave him a playful shove. "Relax, old man. I've got this. I'll see you when it's over. Let me know when you're in position."

Before he could protest further, I shoved an extra canteen beneath my parka and stepped from the hovercraft. Mongo and the rest of my team disappeared into the snow before I could take my first step, and Clark Johnson had never been more correct in his life. I was alone on a frozen ocean with only three canteens of water and a couple thousand calories worth of protein bars scattered in various pockets. Standing between me and the warm southern breeze off the North River at Bonaventure was billions of acres of arctic landscape in every direction and a platoon of Russian Special Forces commandos armed to the tooth.

In shorts and running shoes, even with my prosthetic foot, I could put a mile of distance astern in less than six minutes, but that same mile felt like a marathon in my layered survival suit, electric socks, and arctic boots. I'll never know why the thought entered my head or precisely why it made me laugh, but it occurred to me that I'd pulled on a *pair* of electric socks back aboard our ship. If I died in the coming hours, I'd leave my mortal body and one toasty warm fake foot behind.

It may have been my pace count, or perhaps I'd plotted my position incorrectly, but that mile turned into seven thousand arduous feet before the igloos appeared through the snow-blurred scene ahead. I took a knee and emptied one canteen of water down my throat between bites of a protein bar to provide the calories my body needed to keep itself warm and capable of efficient movement.

My earpiece crackled, and I turned my head against the wind. "Alpha One, Alpha Team, over."

I pressed the transmitter beneath my chin. "Alpha One has visual on the camp. Say status."

Clark said, "Alpha Team is in position, and conditions are improving. The *Polar Explorer III* reports clearing to the west."

"Roger. I'm pressing on. Alpha One, out."

The earpiece went silent as I considered the weather prediction. Improved visibility wasn't my friend. I needed to get inside the Russian camp before they spotted me, and diminishing snowfall would not make that possible.

A lone soldier dressed nearly identical to me paced as a sentry at the southern edge of the camp. I assumed there would be at least three more just like him patrolling every side of the bivouac site, but I couldn't see his comrades. Interception was inevitable. It was only a matter of time or my willingness to draw the guard's attention. I opted to let the scenario play out without raising an alarm.

He let me get closer than I expected, but when I broke a hundred meters, he shouldered his Kalashnikov and yelled, "*Stoy!*"

Following his order to halt, I did exactly that, but what I hoped the guard didn't see was my hand pressing the transmitter. "Game time. I'll keep the mic hot as long as possible."

Clark said, "Roger, Alpha One. Stay alive."

I slipped my gloved hands into the air above my head and knelt on the frozen ground. The guard was joined by two others who flanked him with rifles bearing on my skull.

"Identify yourself," came the command in harsh Russian.

Rather than yelling, I waited for the trio to continue their approach. They came to a practiced, three-man offensive formation ten meters in front of me.

"Who are you?" one of the men demanded.

I answered in my best Russian. "My name is Fulton, and I'm an American."

"*Slozhit'! Ruki podal'she ot tela!*"

I followed his order and lay face down on the ice with my arms spread wide.

The men moved like lightning, and they were on me before I could stiffen. I expected flex-cuffs for my ankles and hands, but I should've known the hard-core warriors wouldn't resort to tiny strips of plastic while wearing heavy gloves.

Instead of the plastic strips, they bound my feet and hands with thin rope, and one of the men placed a knee in the middle of my back. "What do you want, American?"

Trying to relax and appear as unthreatening as possible, I turned my head toward my captor. "I want to see the man in charge."

The three laughed, and the man on my back increased his knee pressure. "I am in charge."

It was my turn to laugh, and I continued in Russian. "Let's not play games, comrades. The man in charge doesn't walk perimeter guard. Take me to your leader."

The knee left my back, and four hands rolled me onto my back. When I came to rest, I looked up into the muzzle of an AK-47.

"*Vy vooruzheny, Amerikanets?*"

I shook my head. "No, I'm not armed."

He gave a sharp order, and his subordinates searched every inch of my body. They threw my canteens and protein bars onto the ice and ripped my commo gear from my head. The heel of a Russian boot crushed my earpiece and mic.

"You shouldn't have done that," I growled. "Now, I have no way to stop them."

"What are you talking about?" the man demanded.

I raised my head from the ice and listened to the wind. "Can you hear that?"

"Hear what?"

"You boys might want to hit the deck."

At least that's what I think I said. My casual Russian was a little rusty.

What wasn't rusty was the General Electric Minigun mounted on the MH-6 Little Bird. The chopper raced across the ice at a hundred fifty knots, and Ronda No-H cut a swath around my three captors and me that looked as if it had been carefully measured and carved. Chunks of ice exploded into the air, and her prowess on the gun continued to shine as she laced 7.62mm rounds through the igloo camp without touching a single structure.

The sentries turned their muzzles skyward and opened up on our Little Bird, but Ronda's quick hands spun the minigun on them and sent the men diving to the ground.

The precision flying told me beyond any doubt that Gun Bunny was at the controls as the chopper circled the camp again before flying a thousand meters to the west and pouring pounds of lead onto the ice.

I raised my head again. "Keep an eye on that spot, gentlemen."

Although I couldn't see it without my night vision, I had no doubt there was an infrared laser pinpointing the exact spot Ronda had marked. The eye of the guided missile saw the invisible beam only seconds after the weapon left the tube aboard the *Polar Explorer III*.

Everything in my frozen world rattled as if God Himself had pounded the ice with His hammering fist when the high-explosive warhead impacted the marked position. The sky filled with shards of razor-like ice and geysers of near-freezing salt water.

Exactly as I hoped they'd do, the soldiers hoisted me onto their shoulders and sprinted for their camp, likely believing the igloos would be safe if I were inside.

They deposited me back onto the ice near the center of the makeshift home away from home.

A man with his survival suit pulled from his torso and tied at the waist emerged from the nearest igloo and yelled in punishing Russian.

The sentry answered, but the only word I caught was *Amerikanets*, and the hook was set.

The man who wore the face of experience and command stood over me and yelled, "What do you want, American?"

I smiled up at him. "I want you to watch your helicopter get blown to hell and Stalingrad if you don't order your men to untie me in the next three seconds."

"Who are you?" he growled again.

"We've already done this," I said. "The clock is ticking, Ivan. Cut me free or kiss your helicopter goodbye. I'm not here to hurt you. I simply want to know what's happening."

One of the sentries sent a thundering kick to my ribs, and I bucked against the pain of the blow and the wind leaving my chest.

As I lay there, desperate to refill my lungs with air, the commander took a knee beside me and whispered in English, "You made terrible mistake, American. You are alive only because I have not given order to kill you."

I gasped and finally caught my breath, then I looked up into the commander's dark eyes. "*Vertolet.*"

The Russian word for *helicopter* obviously reminded him of my threat to destroy his only means of leaving the icy world around us, and he motioned for his men to lower their weapons. "What do you want from me?"

With my breathing restored, I said, "First, I want you to order your goons to cut me free. If that goes well, we can move on to how I can help you."

He let himself laugh. "What could one unarmed American possibly do for me?"

"Cut me loose, and I'll explain it. Otherwise, get your second-in-command out here."

The threat seemed to baffle the man. "Why do you want my second-in-command?"

"Because my sniper is one twitch away from turning your head into pink mist."

"Do you know who we are, American?"

"Yeah, comrade, I know who you are. You're Russian Spetsnaz sent up here to recover your stolen submarine."

"Kill him!" the commander ordered, and the first man performed what would be his final act on Earth. He pulled his Kalashnikov to his shoulder, but before his gloved index finger could press the trigger, a supersonic, .338 Lapua round entered his torso an inch below the right shoulder blade and exited the center of his chest, taking with it every ounce of life the man had possessed.

Chapter 21
Take No Prisoners

With the confidence in my Russian language skills regained, I said, "No, Commander, it is you who's made the *uzhasnaya oshibka*—the terrible mistake. You doubted I could keep my word, and now you've lost not only one man, but you can kiss your helicopter goodbye."

"You are a fool," he bellowed.

"Perhaps, but I'm the fool who's holding the cards. Shoot me if you want, but you've set in motion something that only I can stop. I command a helicopter gunship, a naval missile platform, and a team of American commandos who can walk through your men as if they were nothing. Cut me free, or the next bullet takes off your head, and I'll deal with your second-in-command."

With a nod of his head, the order was given, and the sentry sliced the thin line from my ankles and wrists. He wasn't exactly gentle with his work, but despite the shallow slices to my wrists, I was free of my restraints, and the commander knew he wasn't dealing with a man who made empty threats.

I rubbed my wrists and rolled onto a knee. "That's not your submarine out there, Lieutenant."

He scowled. "I am Captain Yuri Abramov, and I assume you are suggesting the submarine is now your prisoner."

"Sorry, Captain. I should've known the Kremlin wouldn't deploy a mere lieutenant on a mission of this magnitude. And no, I am not claiming your boat as prisoner. I'm telling you that's not your boat. I don't know where yours is, but that one"—I motioned toward the derelict submarine—"that one is Chinese."

"How could you know this?"

"I've been aboard her."

"*Bred sivoy kobyly!*"

"It's the truth, Captain. I led a team of divers. The bow section is intact with the remains of the Chinese sailors still aboard. The stern section is resting thirty meters deeper on a shelf. I have video of the dive."

He seemed to consider my claim, but the look in his eyes said he didn't believe me. Before the intensity of the moment could grow any stronger, I said, "There are structures welded to the keel of the Chinese submarine. They extend from the hull about two meters and appear to be about three meters wide. There are six of them that we can see, but I suspect there are more. The *Pantera* doesn't have those structures, and her instrumentation is definitely not written in Chinese like that boat."

Naming the missing Russian submarine changed the doubt in his eyes to cautious consideration. "How do you know I am searching for the *Pantera*?"

"Why else would you be here? Every other boat in the Russian fleet is accounted for. Our Pentagon can drop a pin within fifty miles of every ship and sub that Putin owns, with one exception— the *Pantera*."

A distant look rose in the captain's face, and he covered an ear with one hand. I silently cursed myself for not noticing the thin wire leading to his ear from beneath the collar of his shirt.

When the message was received, the captain gave the last order I ever expected. "*Ne brat' plennykh.*"

Panic rose in my chest, and the frozen hades around me exploded into distant 7.62mm gunfire and a Spetsnaz captain drawing his pistol only inches in front of me.

I lunged for the Russian's wrist and trapped it in my gloved hands, but his strength and training made him a formidable opponent. My survival suit limited my mobility, and the damaged ribs in my chest only added to the quickly mounting cards stacked against the good guys.

Captain Yuri Abramov sent a powerful elbow strike to the base of my skull, sending stars circling my head, but somehow, I retained limited control of his gun hand. The sentry who'd delivered me to his commander raised his rifle, and I twisted with all my strength to force Abramov's body between me and the sentry.

Timing, luck, or the hand of God made it happen, and the sentry's pair of rounds pierced his commander's back. The rotational force of my maneuver sent me continuing to spiral back toward the gunman. I had delayed the inevitable for only an instant, but I was still alive and in the fight. As Clark told me a thousand times, I had the rest of my life to figure out how to get out of the mess I was in.

My gloved fingers were too bulky to slide into the trigger guard of the Makarov pistol still clenched in the dead commander's hand. In desperation, I gripped his lifeless hand and crushed his fingers in my grip. By some miracle, it worked, and the pistol thundered twice. The first 9mm round hit the sentry in the center of his chest, and the second demolished his chin. Blood filled the air where the man's head had been only an instant before, and I snatched the rifle from his corpse.

Spetsnaz commandos poured from the igloos at the sound of the gunfire, and I dropped the first one I could target with a pair of rounds to his chest.

I was inside a deadly beehive of highly trained warriors, but the only buzzing I could hear was the main rotor of the MH-6 Little Bird screaming in from the south. Gun Bunny had the nose of the chopper barely above the ice, and Ronda No-H poured lead from the minigun like fire from the heavens.

Igloos exploded, and bodies fell in every direction as I ran for the only cover I could see—a partially finished igloo with blocks of ice three feet high on its perimeter base.

The AK-47 in my arms bucked with each press of the trigger as I picked off every soldier aiming at our chopper. Bunny drove that Little Bird through the camp, time after time, in brutal defiance of the lead being sent skyward. Between No-H's minigun and my stolen AK, we relentlessly punished the soldiers until the few who remained alive ran for their covered helicopter in what I believed was fear for their lives . . . but I was wrong.

When they reached the chopper, no one climbed into the cockpit. Instead, the men yanked a pair of heavy machine guns from their mounts on the sides of the machine. The commandos weren't learning as they went. They were bringing practiced tactics to the battlefield. My team was the ones who were calling audibles and scrambling for options.

A stream of heavy-caliber lead streaked skyward, and Bunny maneuvered like a terrified hummingbird, throwing the chopper from side to side and making it impossible for No-H to put bullets on target.

I yelled into the hidden microphone covertly stitched into my survival suit. "Kill the chopper!"

I didn't know the flight time of the missile from the *Polar Explorer III*, but it felt like an eternity. Our Little Bird maneuvered away to the northeast an instant before the missile hit its mark, reducing the grounded Russian chopper into flaming shards of metal and sending the Spetsnaz soldiers on the machine guns to meet their maker.

After two more gun-runs with No-H pulverizing what remained of the igloos and camp, Bunny brought the chopper to a hover fifty feet over my head with the minigun bearing on the former Russian Special Forces camp.

Although I couldn't hear it over the rotors of our chopper, I watched the hovercraft race across the ice from the east and come to a stop a hundred feet behind me. Singer and Kodiak raised their rifles to add their firepower to the Little Bird's as they covered my retreat.

I bounded up the side of the hovercraft and over her rail just as No-H let loose a long volley of fire on the camp, eliminating any living thing that had survived the initial onslaught.

I caught my breath as I lay on my back on the deck of the hovercraft, and we roared across the colorless landscape. My ribs ached, but the real agony was the inescapable truth pounding inside my head.

* * *

Back aboard the ship, Dr. Shadrack insisted on taping my ribs before our debrief, but I refused. "You can tape me up, doc, but we're debriefing while you do it."

Clark said, "No casualties for the good guys . . . just a few bruised ribs."

Dr. Shadrack cleared his throat. "They're a little worse than bruised."

Clark huffed. "Rub some dirt on it and soldier on."

I winced against the pressure of the doctor's tape job. "When was the last time you saw any dirt, Einstein?"

"Shut up and pretend to be tough, College Boy. The only other casualty was some shrapnel Ronda No-H took during the fight. She's got a few shiny new stitches and some cool war stories to tell, but she's not whining like Chase."

Gun Bunny reported. "Only minimal damage to the Little Bird, and the ship's engineers are already hard at work patching bullet holes and replacing everything that was anywhere near the path of a bullet."

"Did we kill them all?" I asked, trying to quiet the thundering roar of failure in my skull.

"Yeah, the team that came to hit us in the rising terrain was good, but they were fighting uphill, and we prevailed. There were eight of them, and we estimate fifteen to twenty in the camp. That sounds like a platoon to me."

I pulled my shirt down over the tape surrounding my torso. "I blew it, guys, and I'm sorry. I never dreamed they'd hit us like that. I thought I could talk my way in and maybe even broker a deal to figure this thing out together, but I've never been more wrong."

Singer said, "It wasn't your fault, Chase. It was a decent plan. I got a little trigger-happy and dropped the guard who drew on you. If I hadn't put him down, it might have worked."

"If you hadn't put him down," I said, "you guys would be debriefing without me. He was an instant away from wasting me. You saved my life . . . again."

Clark held up a hand. "It doesn't matter. What matters is that we're all alive. Good plan, bad plan, mediocre plan . . . it doesn't matter. It failed, but we survived to fight another day."

Grumbles of agreement sounded, and Weps stepped through the sick bay hatch. He said, "You guys will debrief anywhere, won't you?"

I said, "We had to come down here and lick our wounds. Good shootin' out there. Without you, we would've been in a mess. You saved the Little Bird and her crew, at a minimum. You probably saved at least some of us knuckle-draggers, too."

"I just put steel on target."

"Yeah, well, your steel is a little heavier than most. Nice job."

He gave me a nod. "All in a day's work, but we're likely to suffer a little fallout when this gets back to Moscow."

I said, "I'm sure you're right, but maybe we can wrap this up before that fallout reenters the atmosphere."

Chapter 22

Bait and Switch

I spent precious little time truly alone. If I was home and between missions, Penny and I spent nearly every minute together when she wasn't on the West Coast. If she was working, I trained with some or all of the team to stay in top physical condition and keep our battlefield skills razor-sharp. The rare times in my life that I was truly alone were spent in small moments of reflection and sometimes prayer. I preferred such moments to happen in the Bonaventure gazebo overlooking the North River, but the environment in the high latitudes wasn't conducive to time in an Adirondack chair under the stars.

The *Lori Danielle*—temporarily named the *Polar Explorer III* —offered little in the way of unused space. She was an efficient ship with capabilities far beyond the typical research vessel, and such an existence means making the absolute most of every inch of space. The one exception was the hangar bay. That particular space was void of any clutter, with enough space to house the helicopter, a few tool chests, and my favorite fixture—a pair of sky chairs. The chairs were hanging, fabric seats suspended by short pieces of line affixed to a spring and situated near the forward starboard corner of the space. The sky chairs offered not only solitude, but also remarkable comfort. I never remember sitting in one of those chairs without sleep tugging at my eyelids. That day, sleep called, but it was kept at bay by the torturous thoughts colliding inside my head.

I'd been the direct cause of death for a platoon of Russian soldiers whose only sin had been trying to kill an invader in their camp. They didn't have to die, and the weight of their eternal souls fell solidly on my shoulders. It had been my plan, my idea, my belief that it would work, and I was wrong. Now, two dozen elite soldiers lay on the frozen ground, their bodies stiffening as their blood froze and the harsh arctic world consumed them. I could've used back channels to the Kremlin to garner the information I needed, but instead, I hatched a terrible plan that left me weary beneath the burden of what I'd done.

As if dispatched by the Almighty Himself, Singer—our Southern Baptist sniper and moral compass—slid himself into the second sky chair without a word. I didn't look at him, and neither of us said a word for a long moment. I listened to the soft squeak of the heavy spring above my head and tried to imagine what the man by my side was about to teach me.

Finally, as if talking to someone else, Singer spoke in his gentle baritone. "It's eight."

I chewed on his words, unable to piece together what he was trying to say.

Without a word from me, he continued. "That's the number of men I killed today who weren't directly trying to kill me. Three of them would've killed you, and the other five were devoted to the mission of killing our ground team. None of the men I killed was pointing a weapon directly at me. In fact, I suspect there was only one, maybe two, who knew I was there."

"What's the point?" I asked, sounding more sarcastic than I meant.

He propped his boots in the small hammock suspended in front of the sky chairs, specifically for that use. "The point is hard to swallow sometimes, but it's always true. When we take another human life, it's never done in malice. It's only done to protect ourselves or those we love."

"But we wouldn't have needed protecting if I hadn't insisted on wandering into that camp thinking I could talk them into joining forces with an American covert ops team."

He touched the tip of his index finger to his nose. "That, my friend, is why you were sitting out here all alone and beating yourself up."

I turned to face the sniper. "You're wrong this time. I'm up here kicking myself because I should've known better. I should've listened to Clark and Kodiak. I should've . . ."

He laid a hand on my forearm. "Maybe all of that is true. Perhaps you should've done those things, but you didn't, and there's nothing you can do to un-ring that bell. I need you to answer one question for me, though."

I was in no mood for a pep talk, but I indulged him. "What's the question?"

"It's actually more than one question, but we'll start with this one. What would those Spetsnaz troops have done if they'd caught us messing around on that submarine?"

I didn't hesitate. "They would've lit us up."

"And what order would you have given when they started pulling triggers?"

"I wouldn't have given an order. It wouldn't have been necessary. Everyone would've reacted and laid down as much fire on them as possible."

He picked an imaginary irritant from between his teeth. "How many of us would've been hit?"

"There's no way to know."

He lowered his chin. "Would the number have been zero?"

I slowly shook my head, and he asked, "Would we have let them escape?"

His point hit me like a truck, and apparently, he saw it on my face.

"That's right," he said. "Those guys were sent up here for two equally important missions. Number one was to find their missing sub, and number two was to kill anybody standing in their way. We were already on their hit list, even if they didn't know it. Confrontation was inevitable, but instead of it turning into the shootout at the frozen O.K. Corral, we managed the battlefield, separated the superior force, and eliminated the threat."

I'll never know how Singer is always right when I start to crumble, but he'd done it again.

He said, "Your plan may not have achieved the original goal, but what happened out there today saved our lives, and in turn, we'll do whatever is required to save the lives of those millions of people we'll never know who rely on us for exactly that."

As his words washed over me, the speaker above my head rang out. "Chase to CIC, ASAP."

Singer and I stood, and I said, "Thank you."

"Don't thank me. Just keep on keeping me alive. Now, let's get down to the CIC."

We made our way from the hangar bay, down two ladders, and into the combat information center, where the rest of the team waited with Skipper's face plastered across the monitor.

As soon as we were through the hatch, Skipper said, "Sit down. I know what the structures on the bottom of the sub are."

By the time Singer and I planted ourselves in our seats, Skipper was gone from the screen, replaced by a picture of a Chinese submarine in dry dock for repairs.

"Does that look familiar?" she asked.

I studied the cradles supporting the massive submarine as it sat stoically in the dry dock. "But why would they keep the cradles attached to the sub outside the dry dock?"

Our analyst reappeared on the screen. "That's the best part, and that's why the Chinese icebreaker showed up in record time."

"Spit it out," I said.

She widened her gaze. "Easy, Dr. Impatient. I'm getting there. But first, we have to talk about the *Pantera*."

I said, "This isn't the *Pantera*. It's a Chinese boat."

She rolled her eyes. "Yeah, I know, but we're supposed to *think* it's the *Pantera*. I've been sifting through the dive video, frame by frame, and I discovered some very interesting missing objects."

I groaned. "Come on, Skipper. Quit stalling. Tell us what you found."

"It's what I didn't find that's important. The Chinese always set to sea with eighteen torpedoes aboard their boomers. There were only twelve in the video you took of the forward section of the sub."

"Okay, so they left off some torpedoes. Big deal."

"It *is* a big deal because they never set sail without a full complement of weaponry, and they didn't for this mission, either. The identification brackets that come off each torpedo when it's loaded into a launch tube are still in the racks. They fired six torpedoes at something since they left port in China."

Mongo was the first in the CIC to piece it together, and he palmed his forehead. "Oh, no."

Skipper sighed and relaxed. "I knew you'd be the first to figure it out, Mongo. The whole world—including us, the U.S.— thought the sub in the Northwest Passage was the Russian *Pantera*, but that's because that's exactly what the Chinese wanted the world to believe. I think the Chinese boat shadowed the *Pantera* and sank her someplace far too deep to ever see her again. Then the Chinese kept sending coded daily position reports that we intercepted and took as authentic. Moscow apparently made the same assumption and believed their *Pantera* was alive and well."-

Clark let out a gasp. "The old switcheroo."

"Precisely," Skipper said. "The structures on the exterior of the sub were to serve the same purpose they served in dry dock. They were designed to support the Chinese ballistic missile sub on the bottom of the Northwest Passage after it dropped off the bulk of its crew on the ice and descended back to launch depth."

Mongo said, "That's brilliant. They offloaded the officers and operations crew, who were to be rescued by the icebreaker, while the launch crew rode the sub back to the bottom to rest on the cradles while they unleashed their complement of nuclear ballistic missiles on the United States."

It suddenly felt like an elephant had stepped on my chest. "And the whole world would believe it was the Russian sub, *Pantera*, that launched the missiles."

Skipper sat and silently nodded.

Weps said, "It would've been World War Three, and China would've sat back and watched the whole thing."

The room was silent except for the whir of cooling fans inside the computers and equipment.

My mind raced. "We were minutes away from nuclear war with Russia, and we're the only Americans who know."

"That's right," Skipper said. "But that's only half of the puzzle. Just wait 'til you hear Tony and Hunter tell you about the bank robberies."

"Wait a minute," I said. "Something isn't adding up. The Chinese sank the *Pantera*. Then, they pretended to be the *Pantera*. Then they dropped off most of their crew on the ice and descended back to launch depth and parked the sub on the bottom."

Skipper jumped in. "No! That's where it went wrong. The crew that was left aboard the sub after most of the sailors and officers got off weren't competent to submerge the boat back to the bottom. That's how it ran aground and broke up before they could launch the missiles."

"Okay, I've got that," I said. "But what were they going to do after the missile launch if everything went as planned?"

"That's the terrifying part—as if nuclear war isn't scary enough. Based on some circuitry that was visible in your video, Hunter and I believe they were going to blow the sub to kingdom come and sacrifice the launch crew."

"Like kamikaze?"

She said, "Well, kamikaze is Japanese and means 'divine wind,' but yes, it's the same idea. A few devoted sailors were dedicated enough to sacrifice their lives to start World War Three between Russia, the Middle East, and the U.S."

"If you're right," I said, "I agree, it is terrifying. But what if you're wrong?"

"Listen to me, Chase. The Chinese embassy in DC is closed for a year-long massive remodel, so the ambassador and his staff have been temporarily recalled to Beijing."

My heart sank. "Okay, that's compelling."

"There's more. The Chinese consulate in Chicago was ravaged by fire three weeks ago, and it's been abandoned until a new building can be constructed. The San Francisco office has been cut to a skeleton crew, and Beijing is claiming budget cuts as the justification. They're recalling their diplomats, Chase. This thing is real."

I stared at the overhead. "Does the Board know?"

"Not yet. That's Clark's call."

I blew out the chest full of air I'd been holding. "Give us an hour, then get Hunter and Tony in the op center for the bank briefing. CIC, out."

Chapter 23
What Could Possibly Go Wrong?

It took twenty minutes for Clark to brief the Board and deal with their questions. When he'd shared everything he knew, and possibly a little more, the spokesperson for the Board asked, "So what do you suppose we should do next, Mr. Johnson?"

Clark leaned back as if his conscience were clear. "That's above my pay grade, sir. I'll do whatever you ask, but I'm not going to make the decisions for you."

"Give us a moment," the man said, and the monitor went dark.

Clark gave me the look.

I said, "There's only one thing left for us to do."

He nodded. "I agree, but let's see what the brain trust in DC hatches."

Kodiak leaned toward Clark and whispered, "Is this typical of what you guys do?"

Clark sighed. "No, not at all. We usually deal with important stuff and leave this petty nuclear war business to the amateurs."

The monitor came back to life. "Gentlemen, we want you to hit the icebreaker."

Clark nodded. "That's what we expected you to say. ROE?"

The man said, "The rules of engagement are simple. Don't get killed, salvage any intel you can find, and roll up anybody you think the interrogators at Guantanamo Bay might be able to squeeze."

Clark started to speak, but the man cut him off. "Oh, and one more thing. Sink the ship. If the Chinese want plausible deniability, we'll give it to them with a big red, white, and blue bow on top."

"What about the nukes?" Clark asked.

"We'll let you know, but for now, the objective is the icebreaker."

Clark said, "Roger that, sir."

The monitor went black again.

My handler turned to me and raised an eyebrow. "What do you think of that?"

"I think we're about to walk into a hornet's nest masquerading as a derelict ship."

Every head in the room nodded, and Clark said, "I've got a feeling we'll be praying for hornets when we discover it's really a den of vipers."

He pressed an intercom button. "Bridge, CIC."

"Go for bridge," came Captain Sprayberry's voice through the speaker.

"The mission has changed. Put us within two miles of the crippled icebreaker."

"I thought that might happen. We already have the best route planned with the least amount of ice, but it's still going to be slow-going."

Clark said, "Do the best you can, Captain. CIC out."

I checked my watch. "It looks like we've got just enough time to hit the head before the bank briefing."

With our bladders empty and our heads full, Skipper appeared on the monitor with Tony and Hunter by her side. "Okay, guys. Get out your best crayons and take good notes. This is going to get tricky."

"Who's the new guy?" was Hunter's first question.

Clark fielded it beautifully. "That's Kodiak. He's an Arctic operations specialist and a brother from my Green Beret days."

"Nice to meet you, Kodiak. Are you my replacement?"

Kodiak turned to me as if caught completely off guard, but I tossed him a lifeline. "No, Hunter, you can't be replaced. But we do need an extra trigger-puller since Tony's out of the game. We'll just say Kodiak is on a probationary period."

Tony took the floor. "I know Skipper told you this was going to be complicated, but I'm keeping it simple. Our bad boy, would-be bank robbers from Saint Marys turned out to be precisely who the DNA testing said they were. We interviewed Christen from the post office. You remember her, right?"

"Yes, keep going."

He said, "Anyway, I think she turned out to be more of a handful than they wanted. Apparently, the original plan was to force her to give them access to the postal service computer system, but—"

"Wait," I said. "Why did they want access to the computer system?"

"Keep your shirt on, man. I'm getting there. When they nabbed her, she put up a pretty good fight but refused to let them inside the secure area in the post office. From what we've been able to piece together, the whole suicide vest thing at the bank was just retribution for her not giving them access to the computer system. They wanted to make her pay, but they couldn't kill a postal employee on the loading dock at the post office in a small town like Saint Marys and not cause enough stir to ruin their bank job."

I said, "That's a little sadistic, but I'll buy it."

Tony took a sip of water. "Every bank that was hit as part of that day's fiasco resulted in zero cash being stolen."

He had my attention. "That's interesting."

"Yes, it is," Tony said. "But the really interesting part is the fact that all they wanted was short-term access to the computers. They needed to implant a virus into the system that would start a domino effect of wire transfers into a thousand accounts in the Middle East."

I leaned toward the monitor. "Why wouldn't they do that remotely without pretending to rob banks?"

"That's the thing," he said. "They needed physical access to the computers so they could plug a physical key into each computer to stagger the system's clock. It's crazy complicated, but think of it like clocking on GPS. In order to make the international banking system believe the wire transfers were legitimate, the clocking had to be precisely measured. Otherwise, red flags would pop up all over the place, and the wire transfers would become hard-locked."

"What's hard-locked mean?" I asked.

"It means the transfer and the account from which it was coming would be shut down. This is a fail-safe built into the banking system. They simply needed to place a key on a dozen computers inside a dozen seemingly unrelated banks across the country. These keys would then communicate with each other and fool the wire transfer system into believing everything was legit. If you want to know the details that will melt your brain, Skipper can explain it, but those are the basics."

I asked, "Did it work?"

Hunter took the reins. "It did, but not very well and not for long. They weren't able to get all twelve keys in place, so it was kind of like driving on one of those donut tires after you've had a flat. It works, but just long enough to get you to the next exit. They ended up transferring about eleven million dollars, but that's just a drop in the bucket compared to their original plan."

I said, "I guess it's good they were only able to score eleven million."

"I'm not finished," Hunter said. "The transfers were all blind transfers into nine accounts."

I said, "I thought Tony said it was a thousand accounts in the Middle East."

Hunter continued. "We're getting there. The transfers from the States went to nine accounts, all of which are owned by the Kremlin, and like I said, they were blind transfers."

"What does that mean?" Clark asked.

"It means it's impossible to know which accounts the transfers came from. The FBI believes it came from millions of accounts in small amounts, but it only worked for about ninety minutes before the legitimate software figured out something didn't smell right. When the FBI techs dug into the code, they discovered a self-destruct code at five-point-five billion dollars."

I let out a low whistle. "So, they were going to steal five and a half billion dollars, dump it into eleven Russian accounts, and then disseminate it into a thousand accounts in the Middle East. Is that right?"

"You got it," Hunter said.

Mongo spoke up. "That makes perfect sense. Those are further attempts to make Russia look like the bad guys."

"They sort of are the bad guys," Skipper said.

Mongo continued. "Yeah, but not in this case. In this scheme, the Russians are the scapegoat, and China is the real bandit, but there are two lingering questions. Why Saint Marys, and why a bank on a military base?"

Skipper said, "I'll take this one. Saint Marys because there are seven people who live inside the city limits, and each has over three million dollars in net worth. In case you're wondering, seven of the eight are on this video call, and number eight is married to number one. That'd be you, Chase."

Kodiak's eyes raced across the faces in the CIC, but his obvious question remained unasked.

I said, "Okay, that answers question number one, but what about the bank on the military base?"

"That one makes sense, too, once you work it out. It was the only bank on Fort Rucker in Alabama, and it was a credit union. Over seventy percent of the soldiers on the base receive their direct deposit from the Department of Defense into that bank. That deposit hits the bank through the on-base branch every month at the same time, and the total deposit into fifteen thousand accounts is over one hundred fifty million bucks of taxpayers' money."

I shrank in my chair. "Who's the mastermind?"

Skipper rang an imaginary bell. "Ding! We have a winner! That's exactly the question the FBI is asking, and they aren't any closer than we are to finding out."

"Whoever it is," I said, "I bet he lives in the People's Republic."

"I'd put my money on that, but there's one more thing. I couldn't make a connection between a dozen banks and the U.S. Post Office computer system until I saw a postal money order on your desk downstairs."

"Why would there be a postal money order on my desk?"

"That doesn't matter," she said. "What matters is the fact that the post office sells over two hundred thousand money orders every day, and the average dollar amount is two hundred thirty-five dollars, for a daily grand total of forty-seven million dollars per day. That's pass-through money, but it still exists temporarily on the books. Although, that's small potatoes. The revenue the post office takes in is over seventy billion dollars a year. That's almost two hundred million dollars every day. And as you know, the federal government doesn't do anything original or efficient, but what you probably didn't know is that they piggyback their financial transactions on the same networks the banks use."

The magnitude of the situation exploded in my head as I tried to expand my mind enough to understand just how enormous this scheme was and how close it came to working.

I ran my hands through my hair. "Please tell me that's all the data you have. I don't think my brain can manage any more."

"Oh, no. That's just scratching the surface. But I am the data queen. You don't need to know the details—just the bottom lines."

"Thank you! Now, if there's nothing else, I have to go start a fight with an unknown number of combatants aboard a ship I've never been aboard in an environment that will freeze the life from a human body in minutes. Oh, yeah. I'm doing that with an old retired Air Force pilot, a washed-up former Green Beret, a choir director, a giant, and a new guy who looks like a wild-eyed woolly-headed mountain man. I almost forgot. If we survive that fight, we're under orders to sink that twenty-one-thousand-ton ship in water that's only fifty feet deep with two feet of ice on top. What could possibly go wrong?"

Chapter 24
The Real Deal

Weps drummed his fingers on the console and chewed his bottom lip.

"What's on your mind?" I asked.

He stopped drumming. "Maybe I wasn't supposed to be here for that briefing, but . . ."

"If you weren't supposed to be here, somebody would've kicked you out. What's eating you?"

He looked away. "I don't know. I guess it's that thing you said about taking a pilot and a choir director on a maritime assault. I don't know where the line is that separates the crew from you guys, so I don't want to overstep my bounds."

"I never figured you for the timid type. Spit it out, man."

He said, "We're not tier-one operators, but we've got some guys on board who've seen a little action and who know how to handle themselves under fire. Not me, mind you. I'm a naval surface warfare officer, not a SEAL, but if you need some extra muscle and a few more guns in the fight, I've got six or eight guys who'd fit the bill."

I thought about his offer and checked Clark with a glance. His look said *No, thanks,* so I turned back to Weps. "I'll keep that in mind, and we may need them, but I can't justify taking half a team into a fight having never seen them train. It's too much of a gamble for the first penetration, but if the interior of that icebreaker looks anything like I expect, our first peek inside won't be our last, and we may need all the muscle we can get."

"Do you want me to spool them up?" he asked.

"Sure. There's no harm in drawing their weapons and doing some stretches. Set them up as a quick-reaction force in case we get pinned down."

"Consider it done. Oh, and when it comes time to sink that tub, just say the word, and I'll cut her into bitesize pieces that all the king's horses and all the king's men couldn't put back together again."

I slipped my notepad from my pack and flipped to a fresh page. "When we get within range, I want you to park a few drones over that boat and tell me what they see. If there's life on that crippled old girl, I want to know about it."

"I'll fly a drone right down the main corridor, if that's what you want."

"That's not a terrible idea," I said, "but let's keep that one inside our little bag of tricks for now. Just look for signs of life. You know, heat signatures, motion, lights, anything like that."

He checked our position on the navigation monitor and ran some numbers in his head. "We'll be in drone range in sixteen hours if we can maintain this speed. I'll find you when we're getting close. Anything else?"

"Just one more thing. I was kidding about taking a ragtag bunch of guys into a fight. Those misfit toys put down a platoon of Russian Spetsnaz without any casualties and with only a little help from you. I'd wade through Hell in gasoline underwear with these guys."

He gave a nod and rose from his seat. "I guess that's my cue to bug out. I'll have my radio if you need me."

When the hatch closed behind Weps, Kodiak said, "I realize I'm the new kid, but I know a little about maritime ops. Your analyst saw my résumé, but I thought you'd want to know that I did a rotation with the SEALs out of Little Creek when I was drawing a SAD check from Langley."

Clark perked up. "You were with Special Activities Division?"

Kodiak drew a figure eight on the table with his fingertip. "Yeah, for a while, but I wasn't cut out for the Agency. I'm not a dog who behaves well on a leash."

"I've noticed," I said. "And you're in good company around here. We don't spend much time worrying about permission *or* forgiveness."

"That's one of the things I like best about you guys, but I won't lie. The net-worth disclosure during the bank robbery briefing caught my attention, too."

"Don't worry about the money. We do this because somebody has to, and it's the right thing to do. The money just comes with the territory."

"I've obviously been digging ditches in the wrong territory for most of my life."

It was time to change the subject, so I glanced at the clock. "Let's shove some chow down our gullets and get a little sleep. We're going to need the calories and the rest. We've got a ship to take."

* * *

Sixteen hours later, a knock came at my cabin.

"Come on in."

Weps stuck his head through the hatch. "Drones are airborne, and they'll be on target in fifteen minutes."

"Thanks," I said. "I'll be down in a few minutes."

I didn't expect much from the drones, but I was hopeful there might be a detectable heat signature.

Half an hour later, I pushed my way into the CIC. "Anything yet?"

Weps looked over his shoulder. "I've got something, but it's faint. If there's somebody living on that ship, they have to produce heat to stay alive, and the only way to do that is with one of the generators or the main engine. The problem is, the exhaust stacks are cold. There's no smoke, no discernable temperature difference . . . nothing."

I slid onto a chair beside the weapons officer. "Have you ever owned a boat, Weps?"

"Several. Why?"

"Where was the exhaust stack on every outboard engine you've ever owned?"

He leaned back in his chair. "Why didn't I think of that? If they have a way to redirect the exhaust below the waterline, there's no way to detect the heat signature."

"Sure, there is," I said. "We've got an ROUV, and exhaust gas always makes bubbles."

We continued our dreadfully slow movement toward the Chinese icebreaker, and I grew less patient with every passing hour. I finally called the team together.

"All right, Kodiak. Give us your take on boarding that beast."

He flipped his pad sideways and sketched a rough outline of the icebreaker. "See how she's perched high at the bow and low at the stern?"

Eyes flitted between the monitors showing the drones' views and Kodiak's sketch.

I said, "She'll be easy to board with the stern sitting so low."

Kodiak pointed at my chest. "That's exactly what I'm banking on the Chinese thinking. Any aggression would surely come across the stern. You'd have to be some kind of masochist to want to climb over the bow stuck up in the air like that."

In my book, Kodiak just earned his salary, and I was a little embarrassed. Our arctic survival specialist was proving to be a lot more than a snow bunny. He was morphing into a SEAL right before my eyes.

He continued. "I say we penetrate over the bow. That gives us two distinct advantages. In addition to being the last spot anyone would expect to see a boarder, once we're on deck, we'll have the high ground. Given the choice, I always want to fight downhill. Don't you?"

Heads nodded, and he flipped the page. A few seconds later, he showed us a sketch of the likely layout of the ship. "We can't know for sure, but this is the typical deck plan for the weather deck of any icebreaker. It's wide open to the superstructure, but we can cover that distance in seconds, and there's no reason to believe there will be a lookout up front." He leaned back and met my gaze. "I'm not dictating procedure. That's your job. But if I were in command, we'd clear in two-man teams."

"I'm okay with that," I said. "But I want everybody to change decks together. Whatever deck we're on, I want all of us on that deck. We have no idea how many or how much resistance we'll encounter. I don't want a two-man team standing toe to toe with thirty armed Chinese in the galley."

Kodiak said, "I heard the rules of engagement, but I'd like to hear them again, straight from your mouth, in plain language."

He was talking to me, but Clark fielded the request. "The ROE are simple. If you believe you or any member of your team is in mortal danger, you're authorized to eliminate the threat by any and all means available. We capture officers or anybody who looks like he may know something we want to know. Is that clear enough?"

A chorus of affirmatives rose, and Clark said, "All right, Chase. We're ready to go. I briefed the quick-reaction force, and they're solid guys. They'll stage two thirds of the way between our ship and the icebreaker, and they'll be armed to the teeth. One of the gunners is a former Force Recon Marine, and two are former Rangers."

Weps called out, "Movement!" and every eye in the room turned to the live drone feed.

I studied the screens inch by inch, but our drones were retreating. "Where?"

"Starboard side amidships. Two men exited a hatch and held up their hands against the sun. I think they were looking for our drones."

"So much for the element of total surprise," Clark said. "At the very least, they know somebody's watching. That means we have to tighten up. We're not boarding a cruise ship, boys. This is downtown Hanoi."

Mongo rolled his eyes. "Hanoi is in Vietnam, and that's a Chinese boat."

Clark laughed. "Ha! Shows how little you know. I was talking about the top-secret underground city of Hanoi outside of Beijing."

The big man kept shaking his head. "Nice try, but that's not a thing."

I checked the nav screen. "We've got ninety minutes, men. Let's gear up."

Everyone pushed themselves from their seats, but Kodiak asked, "How close are we parking this thing to the icebreaker? If they're already nervous and looking at the sky, they'll go to general quarters at the sight of us."

I gave him half of a grin. "We've got a cloaking device."

He shoved a bushel of hair under his hat. "You've been watching too much *Star Trek*."

I pulled a handheld radio from the charging stand. "Come with me."

Our newest team member followed me through the hatch, up the ladder, and onto the weather deck.

I led him to the bow and pulled the radio to my lips. "Bridge, Alpha One."

"Go for bridge," came Captain Sprayberry's instant reply.

"Show our new shooter your whiteout."

"Roger, Alpha One. Whiteout in three . . . two . . . one."

The haze-gray hull morphed before our eyes and mirrored the endless world of white surrounding us.

Kodiak stumbled and grabbed a rail. "Are you kidding me? How?"

I keyed the mic. "Thanks, Captain. Feel free to resume normal ops."

Captain Sprayberry said, "I think we'll keep our invisibility cloak in place for the foreseeable future."

Kodiak's face still wore a look of awe and disbelief, so I said, "It's called electrochromic coating. Depending on the electrical current applied to the surface, the ship can become any color we need, anytime we need."

He stared at the ultimately camouflaged hull and superstructure. "You guys are the real deal."

Chapter 25
My Gut

Captain Sprayberry positioned the *Polar Explorer III* bow to bow with the *Xue Long*, giving the crew of the icebreaker the smallest possible target. Our relatively narrow beam, coupled with our ability to blend in seamlessly with our environment, made the mile separating the two ships more than enough veil for us to hide in plain sight.

The team and I stepped over the rail and onto the ice at the same moment the engineering team launched the ROUV from the moonpool. The rover would arrive at the icebreaker and begin gathering intelligence long before my team reached the objective. I was relying on that intel to give me at least some indication of what we might face when our boots hit the frozen deck of the Chinese vessel.

A one-mile run for my team of operators was a six-minute endeavor at most . . . when in shorts, T-shirts, and running shoes. That same undertaking while wearing forty pounds of survival gear and carrying fifty pounds of combat equipment on ice at ten degrees below zero would be a miracle in anything short of fifteen minutes.

A miracle didn't occur. It took just over seventeen minutes to make the crossing between our boat and theirs—whoever *they* were. With perimeter security set, I took a knee on the ice at the bow of the mighty ship, pulled off my helmet, and pressed an ear to the hull. No matter what the rover had to report, the low rumble of a diesel engine deep inside the vessel rang like a bell inside my head. There were humans on board that ship, and they were being supplied with heat, desalinated water, and maybe communications.

I pulled my head away from the hull. "Gentlemen, we've got a rumble. It looks like we've got some potential playmates in there."

I couldn't see them, but I had little doubt that every member of my team was wearing a smile.

I keyed my mic. "CIC, Alpha One. Sitrep."

Weps answered. "Send it."

"Crossing complete. Prepared to board. Mechanical sounds detected through hull. Over."

"Roger, Alpha One. Rover located a pair of small exhaust stacks near the stern, but it's not enough to be the main engine or one of the ship's onboard generators. If they're making power, it's not much power."

I said, "Roger. Show us boarding now and start the clock."

"The clock is ticking. Godspeed, Alpha Element."

Without a word, I locked eyes with each man, one by one, and the warriors inside each of them spoke loud and clear with one unified voice. They were ready, and nothing short of death would stay their hands.

Singer stepped from beneath the towering bow of the *Xue Long*, raised the launcher, and fired a grappling hook over the rail five stories above us. With the messenger line retrieved and the boarding ladder hoisted into place, I gave my gear one final glance and took to the ladder.

The point man is often synonymous with being first to die, but there was no way I would let anyone other than myself be the first head over the railing of the big ship. Without looking down, I could feel the weight and sway of the next man, and there was no question whose head was only inches beneath my boots. Mongo, the enormous man who'd taken my personal safety as his purpose for living, wouldn't let anyone else follow me aboard.

When I was one rung from the top of the ladder, I felt Mongo's shoulder pressed against the backs of my legs, pinning me in place so I could raise my rifle with both hands and scan the deck for resistance. Taking full advantage of his strength and steadfast position, I rested on his shoulder and raised my head and rifle an inch above the toe rail. Starting a gunfight from my position would qualify as one of the dumbest moves I could make, but getting my skull pierced by an AK-47 round would be slightly dumber.

Through my whisper comms, I said, "Foredeck is clear," and I let my sling, once again, carry the weight of my rifle as I used both hands to cross the bow rail.

Once on deck, I took cover behind the ship's massive windlass to provide security for the rest of the team to board. No targets presented themselves, and for that I was grateful, but everything was progressing far too smoothly, and that left a sour feeling in my gut.

"Let's move," I whispered.

As if we were connected at the joints, the whole team pressed toward the superstructure like a machine. Rifle barrels protruded in every direction, giving us the look of an enormous porcupine crossing the open deck. Probing eyes scanned every inch of the environment, alert and anxious to locate a target, but by all indications, no one outside of our world had any idea we were aboard the Chinese ship.

For a moment, my mind flashed back to the last time I'd been aboard a Chinese vessel. Along with a South American ninja named Diablo de Agua, Clark and I boarded the AAS *Pearl*, owned by Advanced Asian Shipping in the Miraflores Locks at the Pacific end of the Panama Canal. I spent the most horrifying seconds of my life inside a shipping container with a pin-pulled hand grenade rolling around on deck. How we survived that mission will forever remain a mystery, but there was no time for my mind to wander into the past and onto any other ship than the one frozen to the earth beneath me.

We pressed ourselves against the front of the superstructure, and I turned to Kodiak. "Can you climb?" He nodded, and I said, "You and Singer get those commo antennas down."

Without a second's hesitation, the sniper and our own version of Nanook of the North scampered up the exterior of the structure, snapping antennas as they climbed. The rest of us stood in stalwart defense of our vulnerable teammates until they returned to the deck.

Singer said, "That'll shut down their radio comms, if they had any, but if they're using sat-phones, we've got another hill to climb."

"Did you see any signs of life on the bridge?" I asked.

"The windows are frozen over, so we couldn't see in, but that also means no one can see out."

"Let's clear the weather deck," I said. "Clark and I will take starboard. The rest of you clear to port and report all contact. Move out."

I remained on point, and Clark took position two, half a stride to my right and a full stride behind me. We'd moved mile upon mile in precisely that formation for a decade, so we moved almost as one. Our slow progression around the superstructure exposed us to the howling wind that left our comms all but worthless. I wouldn't hear the other teams if they reported contact with the

opposing force, so I'd have to rely on the gunfire to serve as a report.

The instant I stepped from beneath the overhang at the stern
of the superstructure, a white shape consumed my vision and sent
me backward into Clark. As if the instinct were hardwired into
our heads, we recovered and stepped away from the bulkhead with
our rifles aimed skyward.

Just as I'd ordered the rest of the team to do, I spoke into my
mic. "Possible contact, starboard stern corner of the superstructure. Cover from astern."

It sounded like Mongo's voice in my ear, but the unceasing
wind drowned out his reply. We'd worked together long enough to
know he would do exactly as I ordered. There was no need for me
to even glance astern.

As Clark and I continued progressing away from the towering
section of the ship in hopes of seeing what had pushed the mass of
ice and snow on me, I caught a glimpse of our remaining four
fighters moving astern, three of them with weapons raised into the
air while Kodiak scanned the open deck for threats.

Clark lowered his rifle. "Singer, did you dislodge anything aloft
while you were breaking antennas?"

"Possibly."

We continued astern until we'd reached the rail with no sign of
life. In fact, ours were the only footprints on the snow-covered
deck.

I motioned toward the superstructure, and we moved in a col-
umn to begin our interior search. When we reached the portside
hatch, I gave the dog a tug, but it was frozen in place. Without a
prompt, Mongo stepped beside me and took the wheel in his massive hands, but even his strength couldn't budge it.

Clark said, "The drone caught two men exiting the starboard-
side hatch."

"Let's move," I said.

We made short work of transitioning to the opposite side of the ship. I gripped the dog, and it spun easily and silently. Someone had definitely been maintaining that hatch.

I slipped inside and broke left. Clark followed and moved to the right as our eyes adjusted to the relative darkness compared to the reflective white world of the exterior.

Singer glanced to me and then up the ladder, and I answered his wordless question with an equally silent hand signal. He and Kodiak started up the ladder until they were out of sight. I could hear their measured, regular breathing through their open-channel whisper comms, and neither man showed any sign of stress in their consistent breathing.

I listened intently as they progressed through the ship's tower until Singer finally said, "Clear to the crow's nest."

Sound travels in vibrations through every medium in existence, and steel railings and ladders were some of the best conductors of sound waves in the world. I expected Singer and Kodiak to telegraph their descent down the ladder, but they were as quiet as church mice.

Once reunited, we moved downward into the belly of the beast and split into three teams of two. Clark stayed pinned to my side, Mongo kept Disco under his watchful eye, and Singer moved away with Kodiak. We slowly descended the metal stairs in a wasted attempt to remain as quiet as possible, but six men in arctic boots, survival suits, and full battle-rattle on a metal staircase were the antithesis of silence. I held up a fist, halting our squad in place, then gave the hand signal to move two at a time while the rest of the team remained in place. The action tripled the time it would take us to reach our objective but reduced our overall noise signature exponentially.

Reaching the first deck, Clark and I moved to separate sides of the corridor and pulled security for the rest of the team's descent. Everything about the ship felt and looked abandoned. Without our night-vision devices, the interior of the vessel would've been a black chasm into a frozen abyss.

I was no stranger to operations in the dark, but nothing about this penetration felt right. My gut told me we were walking into an ambush of epic proportions, but I had nothing material on which to base my feeling. It was just that—a gut feeling.

I motioned for Mongo and Disco to clear toward the bow while the rest of us pressed to the stern.

Ten steps into our clearing run, Clark whispered, "I don't like it. It doesn't feel right."

I said, "I agree. Let's put the quick-reaction force in place." He nodded once, and I whispered to the CIC, "Put the QRF on the ice. Something isn't right in here."

Weps replied, "Roger. Launching QRF. Report contact."

I said, "Negative contact so far, but something doesn't smell right."

"Roger."

The corridor ahead continued toward the stern and intersected corridors left and right with hatches along each bulkhead. Clark and I moved left, Singer and Kodiak took the branch to the right, and I called Mongo and Disco to clear the center corridor when the bow section was clean. For the first time since boarding the Chinese ship, each two-man team was out of visual contact with everyone else, and the division of forces significantly reduced our lethality, but anyone who stepped in front of any of the teams with malice in his eyes would taste death's sting before his next breath.

Two-man room-clearing is a tactic we'd practiced countless times and is an area in which we were supremely confident, but cabin-clearing on a ship was an entirely different animal. The typical bold, loud, dynamic entry we practiced was the extreme opposite of the technique we'd use while clearing the small cabins. *Stealth* and *silence* were the words of the day. Sooner or later, we'd be discovered, but later was a much better option.

At the first cabin, Clark pulled the latch, and I pressed the hatch inward with the toe of my boot. The bow-high angle of the ship made the hatch want to close by the pull of gravity, but Clark steadied it as I pressed the muzzle of my M4 into the space. The infrared illuminator mounted atop my barrel turned the darkened environment of the cabin into a bright, sunny day.

Boots aligned neatly beneath the bunk, a few photographs on a small desk, and coveralls on hangers completed the contents of the space. We continued down the corridor, clearing every space we encountered until we rendezvoused with the rest of the team at the stern.

I reported to Weps in the CIC. "Deck one is clear. Moving to deck two."

"Roger. QRF is under the bow."

I took a moment to consider the potential of an ambush. "Is the QRF on open-channel comms with us?"

Weps said, "Negative, but they can be."

"Make it so, and have them check up."

"Roger. Stand by."

A few seconds later, a new voice rang in my ear. "Alpha One, Bravo One. QRF is up."

"Bravo One, Alpha One. Board the vessel and stage at the superstructure on the port side."

"Roger. Bravo Element is moving. Verify weather deck is clear."

I said, "It was clear when we made entry, but it's been twenty minutes. Proceed with caution."

He said, "Roger. We'll re-clear the weather deck and stage by the superstructure."

I gave the hand signal, and the six of us continued down the steel noisemaker to deck two. Just as we'd done before, we moved only two at a time until everyone was on deck. Clearing the second deck became as monotonous as the upper deck. Not a living soul other than my brothers-in-arms was anywhere to be found, but that was about to change.

The instant my left boot hit the third deck, the dark, cold, metallic world around me exploded with blinding white light, sending me swatting at my night-vision devices and battling temporary blindness.

Chapter 26
Russkiy?

Fumbling in the now bright-white world while my eyes worked double time to narrow my pupils enough to piece together any semblance of vision, I shoved a palm toward what I hoped was the center of Clark's chest and ordered, "Retreat!"

We staggered up the stairs and collided with Mongo halfway back to the second deck just as thundering hooves sounded in the third-deck corridor. Those hooves just happened to be boots, but whose feet were in them and how ready they were for the fight of their lives remained to be seen.

While we regrouped at the top of the stairwell, the boots kept coming, and I tried to estimate the size of the force, but the echo chamber that was the ship made that an impossible task. Singer and Kodiak took up prone positions with their muzzles trained on the bottom of the stairs. Clark and I knelt just behind them and focused as far down the lower corridor as possible. Mongo and Disco formed rear guard in case we missed anyone on the sweeps. Being flanked in a choke point was the worst possible position we could find ourselves in, but if they were coming from both sides, we'd make them pay with their lives.

My earpiece came to life, and Weps said, "Sitrep."

I spoke as quietly as possible but still loud enough for him to hear and understand. "We tripped an alarm on deck three and retreated to deck two in a defensive position. Oncoming aggressors from below. Insert QRF to deck two immediately."

The QRF leader answered before Weps. "Bravo Element penetrating to deck two."

Clark pulled his mic close to his lips. "Listen up, Bravo. Don't shoot us if we retreat farther. Keep your eyes and ears open, and get out of our way if we come running."

"Roger."

"Why didn't we drop a smoke grenade down there?" I believed I'd only thought the question, but either I said it out loud or Clark had become a mind reader.

He said, "I did, but I didn't get the pin all the way out before you knocked it out of my hand."

I tapped Singer's leg. "Do you see a smoke grenade on the deck down there?"

"Affirm."

"Shoot it," I whispered.

Before another second passed, Singer's suppressor belched, and a 5.56mm round pierced the grenade, filling the lower deck with billowing white smoke. At least half of the cloud escaped up the ladder and into the corridor of the second deck.

"The smoke is ours," I whispered.

Bravo One said, "Roger."

A seemingly disembodied voice from below yelled, "*Huǒ!*"

I assumed the language to be Chinese, but it could've been Martian as far as I was concerned.

Kodiak whispered, "They think it's a fire."

"Are you sure?" I asked.

He said, "That word is *fire*. It could mean a *burning fire* or *fire your weapon*, but it definitely means *fire*."

Our language arts class came to a screeching halt when the meaning of the word was no longer in question. Automatic rifle fire exploded from the third deck, and bullets ricocheted in every direction. I expected Kodiak to press his trigger and empty a magazine through the smoke, but he held his fire as patiently as the rest of us and let the shooters downstairs waste their precious ammunition.

I leaned to within inches of Kodiak's head and whispered, "Tell 'em we're here to rescue them."

A lesser man would've kept his eye on his front sight, but not our new brother. He rolled from his prone position to stare directly into my face. "In Chinese?"

I'd been under enemy fire on five continents. I'd heard the most ridiculous questions imaginable—or so I thought—but in that moment, aboard a stranded Chinese icebreaker in the coldest place I'd ever been, with angry Asians spilling lead in every direction, the culmination of every fight in my past and the collection of every stupid question I'd ever asked or been asked collided into an instant of hilarity, and I laughed. Out loud. Like a deranged psychopath.

Kodiak raised his night-vision nods from his eyes, gave me a wink, and yelled, "*Wǒmen shì lái zhěngjiù nǐmen de bèndàn de, suǒyǐ bié zài cháo wǒmen kāi qiāngle.*"

I'll never know for sure what he said, but whatever it was, it worked. The flurry of gunfire became intermittent echoes, and finally, silence.

From behind the veil of smoke and darkness, a sharp voice echoed. "*Nǐ shì shéi?*"

Before I could intervene, Kodiak was in full-blown conversation with the voice as if they were long-lost school chums. I prayed he wasn't talking us into a kung fu match not even Mongo could win.

After two minutes of conversation, Kodiak looked over his shoulder. "They're laying down their weapons. Have Bravo Element open the hatch."

I gave the order, and the swift wind blowing over the ship's weather deck drew the smoke from between us and the fighters beneath us, revealing six men with their hands extended in front of them and a pile of AK-47 rifles resting peacefully on the deck amidst a flood of spent shell casings.

The same instant the clearing smoke allowed us to see each other well, the sickening realization that they'd been duped swept over the former gunmen, and they lunged for their discarded weapons. Speed of response and violence of action had long been ingrained into my psyche, and my team demonstrated the perfect application of that credo.

Singer and Kodiak were first to deliver crushing blows, sending the fighters to the deck in semi-consciousness. Clark and I were next, and by the time Mongo thundered down the stairs, the remaining two aggressors were on their knees with fingers interlaced behind their heads.

I spoke into my mic. "Bravo One, Alpha One. Come down the aft stairwell to retrieve six detainees."

"Roger, Alpha One. We're moving."

One of the kneeling men looked up and said, "*Zhè shì yīcì fēicháng qíguài de jiùyuán.*"

I turned to Kodiak. "Let me guess. He said he wants me to read him his rights?"

"Not exactly, but he says he's never seen a rescue like this one."

I chuckled. "Tell him we're new to the rescue business, so cut us some slack."

Bravo Element arrived with weapons at the low-ready position, and Clark waved them down. "Relax, guys. We've got 'em trussed up. Get 'em off the ship and onto ours, but have an element come get them. We still need you guys for QRF."

Perhaps it was the energy I'd spent, but I thought I detected a small rise in temperature on the third deck, and my team seemed to feel the same. As we patrolled the corridor, gloves and masks came off, and we unzipped our survival suits. We cleared the deck and descended the stairwell amidships to find the fourth deck devoid of any cabins. It was a vast open space with hatches in the deck and two dozen makeshift cots scattered about.

"It looks like we're on top of the engine room," Clark said.

I studied the space and counted hatches. "We need Bravo back down here. There are too many holes, and I don't want to play whack-a-mole with just the six of us."

Five minutes later, Bravo One had a man stationed at each of the six hatches on an oversized hatch near the starboard bulkhead.

The vibration I'd heard through the hull was loud enough to hear and feel in the cavernous space. "That's loud enough to give us a little cover for entry, don't you think?"

Clark listened for a moment. "You know how my ears are. I can feel it in my feet a lot louder than I can hear it in my head, but I'll take any cover we can get."

I motioned to the largest of the hatches. "All right, Mongo. Ring the doorbell for us, if you please."

The mountain of a man spun the wheel and yanked the heavy hatch from its jamb. Singer and Kodiak took point, and the rest of us followed them down the stairs and into the engine room, where massive machinery lined every wall and provided perfect cover and concealment. My team and I had just stepped into a labyrinth of the unknown. We had no idea how many people were in the space and no way to know what lay beyond and behind each piece of machinery, but most of all, each of us knew the only way to learn the answers to any of those questions was to clear the room with precision, speed, and caution, just like we'd done on the upper decks.

The space emitted a dim glow that gave our nods just enough light to turn the room into a well-lit shooting gallery. Even though we could see, the last thing I wanted was for the space to turn into a gunfighting arena. Everyone was alive so far, and I was determined to keep all the good guys on my side of the great divide between the living and the long gone.

I flashed two fingers in rapid succession, and the six of us split off into our previous teams of two and began our meticulous search of the engine room that had enormous potential to become a gigantic floating coffin.

Clark stepped in front of me with his rifle shouldered, and I fell in behind him just like we'd done countless times. Being eight inches taller than him and in second position made a lot of sense in the complex environment of the engine room.

We moved in measured steps, cutting the pie in wedges around every corner, exposing as little of ourselves as possible while taking in the environment and assessing threats. At the first intersection, we committed to movement to the right, and Clark leaned around the edge of the machinery with his muzzle barely protruding around the corner. He held up one finger but didn't press the trigger.

I followed my handler around the corner to within inches of a man resting against the wall with a blanket wrapped around him. Clark prodded his shoulder with the muzzle of his rifle, and the man slowly opened his eyes. Instead of a loud, violent reaction, a look of relief seemed to take over his face.

Clark pressed a finger to his lips, and the man spoke in a soft, one-word exhalation. "American?"

In unison, Clark and I shook our heads, and the man closed his eyes. "*Russkiy?*"

Our headshaking continued, and my partner extended an ungloved hand and laid it against the man's forehead. A few seconds later, Clark gave me a small nod. I didn't need to feel his skin to see the fever inside of him.

I took a knee beside the man, and Clark backed up against me to provide security while I tried to communicate with the dying Asian. "English?"

He nodded in small, slow motions. "A little."

I pulled a canteen and pressed it into his hand. "How many people are on this ship?"

He struggled with the lid until I finally twisted it for him, and he pressed it to his lips. Water dripped from the corner of his mouth, and he tried to hand the canteen back to me.

I pushed it back toward him. "It's yours now. How many?"

He strained to say, "Twelve. Five or six are sick like me."

"Where?"

Without speaking, his eyes moved to the right.

I leaned back against Clark's leg and said, "Toward the stern."

The man furrowed his brow and asked again, "American?"

"Who were the men with guns?" I asked.

"*Russkiy.*"

His answer didn't make sense. The men who were on their way to the *Polar Explorer III* were clearly Chinese, not Russian. Perhaps the man's fever left him delusional.

"No, the Chinese men with guns. Who are they?"

"Dead," he breathed.

I was wasting valuable time trying to speak with a dying man, so I pulled an injector of morphine from my med kit and held it up in front of him. "Medicine. Needle."

He moved in ultra-slow motion as he pulled the blanket from his shoulder and exposed enough skin for the injection. I pressed the pen against his pale flesh and listened for the clicks. When I pulled the needle from his skin, he looked up at me as if I were an angel of mercy. "Thank . . . you. *Ostanovit' Russkikh.*"

I tried to digest his charge to me, but it didn't make sense. I watched until he closed his eyes and his body fell limp against the bulkhead. My fingertips detected a weak pulse in his carotid artery, but Clark was right. The man was on fire with fever.

I stood, and Clark asked, "What did he say?"

"He told me to stop the Russians."

"That makes sense. He must know they have the sub and what they plan to do with the nukes."

"Maybe, but it felt different. I can't explain it." I spoke into my comms. "We've got one who's almost dead with fever. He indicated there are twelve others, and half of them are sick like him. He said they're aft of amidships."

Singer said, "We have eight in sight fifty feet astern of the stairwell. Wait . . . make that ten. We're blown."

Chapter 27
Live and Let Die

Singer's whisper comms couldn't pick up ambient sounds, but the tone of his voice said they were in serious trouble, and seconds later, no microphone was necessary.

"Drop weapons or we shoot!"

The Chinese-accented English was impossible to ignore, and my heart sank at the sound of Singer and Kodiak dropping their rifles.

Singer whispered, "They're taking our comms. Hop freqs. Two shooters at eleven and two, maybe more. Come get us, Chase."

The rustling sounds of the communication gear being ripped from their heads told me we'd heard the voices of our brothers for the last time until we liberated them from the hands of the Chinese gunmen.

The rest of us switched frequencies on our comms, and I said, "Bravo One, Alpha One. Are you up?"

"Go for Bravo One."

"Move half of your men to the base of the stairs in the engine room and stand by."

"Roger, Alpha One. We're moving."

I didn't wait for Bravo Team to be in place before calling Mongo. "You and Disco get eyes on Kodiak and Singer and kill anyone who gets in your way."

"Roger," came Mongo's reply.

Clark and I headed aft without concerning ourselves with clearing the room as we moved. The only people who mattered were fifty feet away, and nothing would stop us from liberating them from the hands of the enemy.

It was rare to hear Disco's voice during a non-flying operation, but what he had to say left me encouraged. "Eyes on two gunmen in addition to the two who've got Singer and Kodiak pinned down."

"Can you take them without firing?" I asked.

"I can take one of them, but Mongo's too big to get to the second."

"Hold your position. We're moving to you."

Clark and I crept athwartships and stepped silently behind Disco and Mongo. Without a word, Disco pointed out the two covering gunmen pinning down our brothers, and then he motioned toward their backup.

Clark leaned in and laid a hand on Disco's shoulder. "You take the guy on the left, and I'll take righty. Move."

Mongo and I covered their movement as the two of them advanced on the gunmen. Any sound louder than the generator twenty feet away would set off the powder keg of armed, tense gunmen in the belly of the ship. Taking the two shooters alive was our best bet to keep bullets out of everyone's body, and I didn't want or need any more dead bodies to deal with or explain.

Watching Disco move precisely as Clark and Hunter taught him reminded me how much everybody on the team learned from each other. We were far more than a collection of disconnected parts. When anyone bled, we all felt it, and when any of us was successful, we all celebrated. Call us a team, a family, a machine . . . it didn't matter. We were one unit, moving in choreographed precision with one goal in mind—mission completion with every heart still beating.

When I was certain Clark and Disco were in position to take the backup gunmen, Mongo and I moved to firing positions with the best visibility and greatest angle of fire.

Once situated, I whispered the command, "Hit 'em!"

Disco pounced on his prey, jerked the Kalashnikov rifle from his hands, and twisted the fabric sling around the defeated man's neck.

Clark drove a knee into his foe's back and sent a crushing elbow strike to the base of his skull, rendering the man unconscious and completely out of the fight.

Mongo and I leapt to our feet, revealing our superior position of fire.

I yelled, "Lay down or die!"

Widened, disbelieving eyes shone upward where Mongo and I held the high ground, and a few of the crew followed my instructions.

Immediately sensing the necessity, Kodiak repeated my order in Chinese. "*Tǎng xià huò sǐqù!*"

The two men covering Kodiak and Singer flashed between the four of us and their two targets.

Kodiak yelled, "Drop the weapons! *Fàngxià wǔqì!*"

I'll never know who fired the first shot. It could've been me. Of all the tense situations I've experienced in my life, that moment was near the pinnacle.

AK rounds ricocheted through the engine room with American 5.56mm flying in the opposite direction, but the rifle rounds weren't the mystery. It was the snap of the pistol fire that perplexed me.

My earpiece roared. "Bravo Team advancing!"

I welcomed the additional firepower, but the confusion of the scene playing out in front of me was like a psychotic dream. Bodies spilled to the deck, and the American rifles fell silent. When the pistol fire hushed, the carnage beneath me was almost unfathomable. Nothing about the scene made sense.

I ran an inventory of what I knew. I'd killed gunman number one, and Mongo undoubtedly dropped number two as they opened fire on us. Disco and Clark held their positions over their prisoners. Singer and Kodiak escaped and recovered their rifles, but I don't think either of them fired a round. The final thing I knew that made absolutely no sense was the fact that at least seven dead bodies lay on the deck, but none of them had American bullets in them.

Regaining command of my senses, I called, "Bravo Team, hold position! Alpha Team, report."

"Clark's up."

"Singer's up and unhurt with Kodiak."

"I'm good," Mongo barked.

And finally, our last man said, "Disco's good."

I climbed down from the piece of machinery that had been my firing point. "Check for living."

We regrouped and cautiously stepped through the throng of bodies, each with a single gunshot to the head and discarded Chinese QSZ-92G pistols resting silently beside them.

I tried to understand the scene. "They killed themselves?"

Clark poked the toe of his boot against the shoulder of one of the bodies. "It looks that way."

"Why would they do that?"

Singer took a knee and talked to God, and I wished He'd talk back and tell us what had just happened and why.

When the battle-damage assessment ended, only two of the Chinese sailors remained alive. The man Clark silenced with a powerful elbow to the skull was still unconscious, but Disco's man was wide awake and terrified.

He spoke in rapid-fire Chinese as if trying to explain what was happening, but only Kodiak could understand him.

"What's he saying?" I asked.

Kodiak held up a finger and spoke as calmly as the language could be spoken in an obvious effort to get the man's heart rate back into double digits.

"Slow down and tell me your name," he said in patient Chinese.

To my surprise, the man spoke in broken English. "Will no be prisoner."

I said, "We're not here to take you prisoner," but the man made no sign of understanding.

Kodiak took over and translated between exchanges. "He keeps insisting he will not be a prisoner."

"Make him understand that he's *not* a prisoner. Tell him we'll take him to a Chinese embassy."

"I'll try," Kodiak said, but the interaction looked and sounded as if it were little more than frustration for both sides.

Finally, Kodiak threw up his hands. "I'm out of ideas."

"Let's try another approach." I turned to Clark. "Give me a safe pistol."

While Clark unloaded and cleared his Glock behind my back, I drew my fully loaded pistol and pressed the muzzle against the man's forehead. Ninety-nine point nine-nine percent of people on Earth flinch and pull away from a pistol pressed to their noggin, but not our non-prisoner. He leaned forward, practically begging me to press the trigger.

I lowered my weapon and leaned toward the man, staring into his dark eyes with my pistol held behind my right hip. "Do you want to die? Is that what this is? Death before dishonor, or some crap like that?"

Clark lifted my pistol from my palm and replaced it with his identical but empty weapon. I raised the Glock back to the man's face and flipped it in my palm, offering it to him, butt first.

He stared into my face and then down at the pistol.

"Go ahead," I said. "Take it."

I had no reason to believe he understood my words, but he understood the gesture. Narrowing his gaze, he wrapped his fingers around the pistol and lifted it from my hand. I learned more about that man in the next two seconds than I could've learned in a lifetime as his psychologist.

Without hesitation, he lifted the pistol, raised it to within inches of my nose, and squeezed the trigger. The thunder of the falling firing pin made my heart skip a beat and made the sailor close his eyes in disgusted disbelief. Instinctually, I snatched the pistol from his hand and shoved it back toward Clark.

Disco almost gasped. "I expected him to point the gun at himself."

I said, "Instead, he pointed all of our guns at himself."

We were running out of people to interrogate, so I called the ship. "CIC, Alpha One."

"Go for CIC," Weps replied.

"Say status of the six detainees."

"Stand by."

Several minutes passed before Weps came back on the air. "Uh, we've got a little problem over here. Five of them are dead, and one is unconscious with a severe head wound."

"Keep him alive," I ordered.

My second order was to Bravo Team. "Clear the rest of the ship and report all contact."

"Aye, sir."

I led the team back to the position where I found the dying man wrapped in a blanket. When we reached him, his heart was still beating, but barely.

"Wrap him up and get him to the ship, then put him in Dr. Shadrack's hands and make sure he stays alive. He's got a nasty fever and is pumped full of morphine."

Mongo lifted the small man into his arms. "Who is he?"

I tucked the man's arm under his blanket. "Right now, he's the only person who knows what's going on up here and who doesn't want to die."

Mongo and Disco headed for the weather deck with our singular cooperative combatant, and the rest of us joined Bravo Team in clearing the remaining sections of the ship.

I got lucky picking the lock on the ship's safe, and we retrieved everything inside, including a stash of Russian, Chinese, Canadian, and American cash. I didn't count it, but judging by the weight alone, it was well into the millions of each currency.

The two-hour-long search of the vessel revealed four more bodies. Each was dressed in full military regalia with a single gunshot wound to the head, just like the men in the engine room. We collected identification cards, took pictures, and met Bravo Team on the weather deck.

"Let's go home, guys. It's time to put this one to bed."

We descended the same ladder we'd used to board the ship nearly four hours before and found ourselves back on the ice. We climbed aboard the hovercraft and crossed the mile separating the *Polar Explorer III* and the icebreaker, *Xue Long*.

Back aboard our temporary home, I found myself beside Singer, just outside Dr. Shadrack's sick bay. "How'd you let a couple of malnourished PLA sailors get the drop on you?"

He examined his fingernails. "I was watching the new guy instead of watching for threats."

I leaned back in my chair. "That's my fault. I shouldn't have dragged him onto the dance floor until we'd trained with him."

Singer shook his head. "No, that's not it. He's solid, and I hope he stays. We could use him with Tony sidelined and Hunter on the mend. It's just that I got wrapped up in babysitting him, and I lost my focus. It won't happen again."

"Sure it will," I said. "It may not be you next time, but we all let our guard down sometimes. That's why we do this as a team. So, what's your take on the mass suicide over there?"

He stared at the ceiling and bounced the heel of his boot on the deck. "I could be way off the mark here, Chase, but I don't think any of this is what it appears to be. I think we're neck-deep in a billion lies and sinking fast."

Chapter 28
To Wrestle a Shark

Dr. Shadrack stuck his head through the door to sick bay. "Okay, guys. Come on in."

Singer and I stepped inside to see two patients I expected and one who I most certainly did not expect. As interested as I was in the Chinese patients, the third curtain held my immediate attention. "Is she okay?"

The doctor said, "She'll be fine. Go on in if you'd like."

I stepped past the curtain, and Ronda No-H looked up as if embarrassed. "Oh, Chase. Hey. I'm sorry about this—"

I cut her off. "Don't be sorry. You saved a bunch of lives out there. Are you okay?"

"I don't know about that. I just did my job."

"No, that's not exactly what you did. You stepped up and did a job we're not paying you to do. You're the purser, and it's pretty rare to have a purser who's a killer door-gunner like you. You kicked some butt out there."

She shrugged. "It's nice to be part of the team."

"And we're glad you're on our team. I wouldn't want you shooting back at us. What's going on with you?"

She touched her neck. "I took a little shrapnel, but Dr. Shadrack is taking care of it."

I stepped closer and spoke barely loud enough for her to hear. "We're wrapping this thing up. If you need a medivac to Alaska, we'll make it happen."

She smiled against the pain. "You're sweet, but I'm in good hands here. Oh, and don't worry about the books. I won't neglect my real job while I'm healing up."

"Stop it. You've never neglected anything. I'm not concerned about the books. I'm sure you'll get everyone paid on time. If you need anything, just let me know. Every resource we have is at your disposal."

She ducked her chin. "That's nice, but really, I'm okay."

"Has Disco been down to see you?"

She blushed. "I had to run him off. He smelled like a filthy mule, but I'm sure he'll clean up and come back."

"We're all a little dirty after our excursion. He's a good one, though. Hang onto him. He's a lot easier to live with when you're around. He can get a little grouchy sometimes."

She chuckled. "I'll take that as a compliment, and I have no intention of letting him go."

I gave her a wink and stepped back through the curtain. Dr. Shadrack was listening to the man's breathing behind curtain number one.

"How's he doing?" I asked.

The doctor looked up. "His fever is coming down, but his lungs are full of fluid. I've got him on everything I can pump into him, but I can't make any promises."

"Pneumonia?"

"Yeah, to say the least. The morphine you gave him made him more comfortable, but it wasn't a good choice. It slowed his breathing and reduced his oxygen saturation. I've got him on oxygen now, but he's still a long way from stable."

"Can I talk with him?"

The doctor looked back at his patient. "I don't think he speaks English."

"He speaks a little English and some Russian," I said. "If all else fails, our new guy has some pretty good Mandarin."

"You can try," he said, "but don't push him too hard. If we're going to keep him alive, he needs to rest. Keep in mind that his fever is severe enough to cause some delusions, so don't expect anything you get out of him to be the gospel truth."

"Thanks, doc. I'll keep it light. Now, how about the other guy?"

"He's a horse of a different color. It was necessary for me to sedate him. Physically, he's okay, but psychologically, he's a mess."

I let out a chuckle. "Yeah, I noticed that. I'll get to him, but in the meantime, keep him restrained and medicated. How about the head wound from the first group they brought aboard?"

Dr. Shadrack took a long breath. "I've never seen anything like that, Chase. It looks like they killed each other with their bare hands until only one man was left alive. Then, he pounded his head against the deck until he was unconscious and bleeding out. Who *are* these guys?"

"Where is he now?"

The doctor motioned toward the back of the sick bay. "He's in the morgue. He suffered a severe concussion and bled out before we could get him stabilized." He paused and pulled off his glasses. "Look, Chase. I know I'm not an operations guy. I'm just the medical officer. But what in the world is going on up here?"

It was my turn to take a long, deep breath. "I wish I knew, doc. The only thing I know for sure is this . . . Nothing makes sense, and I think that guy with the fever is our only link to the truth."

Dr. Shadrack pulled back the curtain and studied the man. "I'll do my best to keep him alive, but his is the worst case of pneumonia I've ever seen."

"Can we fly him to a hospital in Alaska or Canada?"

"He'd never survive the flight, and there's nothing they could do for him in a hospital that I can't do here. Something tells me you don't really want either of those guys exposed to the rest of the world."

I laid a hand on his shoulder. "You may be more of an ops guy than you think, doc. Before I go . . . is Ronda okay?"

He peered around me. "She will be. A couple of pieces of shrapnel got pretty close to her vocal cords and the associated nerves. I'm keeping her under observation for a couple of days, but she's going to be just fine."

"Thanks, doc. We'll be back in a couple of hours to talk with your pneumonia patient."

The team assembled in the CIC for the after-action review, and if we went into the room confused, we were confounded by the time we dismissed.

There wasn't room for the entire Bravo Team, but the team lead squeezed in, and I said, "We couldn't have done it without you. Did everybody come home without new holes in them?"

He said, "Proud to help, Chase. No bullet wounds, but a few of us got scraped up a little. Dr. Shadrack says we'll live, and we all trust him."

"Glad to hear it. I don't anticipate another raid on this mission, but honestly, I don't know what to expect. I'd like for you to keep your men spooled up, just in case."

"We'll be on standby. Just call if you need us."

Clark took the floor. "Nice job keeping everybody alive. In my opinion, we learned only one thing on that ship, and that's the fact that those crewmen were dedicated to a cause they refused to divulge. They protected it with their lives."

I cut in. "Most of them did. We've still got two of them alive in sick bay, but we don't know who they are yet. I think the troublemaker isn't important, but there's something about the older guy with pneumonia. He said something to me that I can't get out of my head. '*Ostanovit' Russkikh.*'"

Mongo furrowed his brow. "Stop the Russians?"

"Yeah, exactly," I said. "If we're operating on the theory that the Chinese are behind all of this—and that's where the evidence was pointing—it doesn't make sense for him to tell us to stop the Russians."

Kodiak said, "It might make sense. These guys are obviously willing to protect some secret with their lives. The guy you found could be doing the same thing. Maybe he wants us to look hard at the Russians for all of this so we're distracted from the fact that it's all on the Chinese."

"Maybe," I admitted, "but there's something about the guy that makes me want to listen to him."

"He spoke Russian?" Skipper asked from the monitor overhead.

"Yes, Russian and English, but not much of either."

She tapped the stem of her glasses against her teeth. "How many Chinese sailors speak both Russian and English?"

"How should I know?" I said. "You're the smart one."

"Digging up that statistic might take a while, but about eighty-two million Chinese citizens speak English, and about seven hundred thousand speak Russian. That means about six percent for English and point zero five percent speak Russian. Based on those numbers, the chances of a common Chinese sailor speaking both languages are astronomical. Whoever your guy is, he's not a common sailor."

We finished our briefing, and Singer prayed when it was over. There was always something comforting and reassuring about him praying for us. We survived on a combination of skill, ingenuity, dumb luck, and miracles, and if we could keep only one of those things, Singer and I would pick the same one.

As we stood to leave the CIC, the quartermaster opened the door and stuck her head inside. She recoiled. "Oh, I'm sorry. You're not who I was expecting. I'll come back later."

"Wait," I said. "Who were you expecting?"

She paused. "The captain ordered a drill, and clearing the CIC is part of my checklist."

I turned to Clark and grabbed his shirt. "Did you get a look at any of the faces in the submarine?"

He pulled away. "Do you mean the icebreaker? Sure, I got a good look at all of them."

"No, not the icebreaker. The sub. The dead bodies in the sub. Are you sure they were Chinese?"

He closed his eyes, apparently replaying the scene in his head. "I think they were Asian, but I can't be sure."

I turned to Singer. "How about you?"

"We've got the video, but I don't know. What are you thinking?"

"You and Clark pore over that video and get as close to as many faces as you can. I need to know who they were."

"You got it, boss. We'll call you when we find something definitive. But what if we can't tell?"

"Then we're going back to wrestle a dead submariner away from that five-hundred-year-old shark."

As the rest of us filed out of the CIC, I grabbed Kodiak. "Come with me. We've got a date with a dying sailor, and I'm going to need your language skills."

"Whatever you need. But do you mind if I grab a shower first? I'm a mess."

"That's a good idea for both of us. I'll meet you at sick bay in twenty minutes, and try to do something with your hair, will you?"

He pulled off his cap and shook out his mane. "It's alive . . . It's alive!"

I gave him a shove and turned to Weps. "I guess it's time."

He nodded. "She's only in two hundred feet of water. I need to cut down her superstructure before sinking her."

"Do whatever you have to do, but don't create a hazard to navigation for surface vessels."

"Consider it done."

The explosions from a mile away rocked the *Polar Explorer III*—and my heart. I'd just given the order to put a dozen men on the bottom of a frozen ocean forever, with their ship as a coffin. Burning bridges is rarely the work of happy men.

Chapter 29
Not My Boat

Kodiak was waiting for me when I made it to sick bay. "Ain't it amazing what a shower can do for you?"

I laughed. "I see you didn't find a razor."

"What's a razor?"

"Come on. Let's go to work. The first order of business is to find out who this guy is. Do you have enough Mandarin to get that deep?"

He said, "I'll try. My Chinese is the street variety. I wouldn't pass a grammar test, but I can get him to talk."

"Go gentle at first. There's something inside that guy making him want to talk."

"Whatever you say. You're the boss. Let's do it."

I poked my head around the curtain and into the partition where Ronda No-H was resting.

She glanced up. "Hey, Chase. Back again, I see."

"I just wanted to check on you. Do you need anything?"

"I'm good. Thanks."

I pulled a stool beside the curtain to the man's space, and Kodiak stepped inside.

He began in English. "How are you feeling? I'm Kodi."

"Where is other man?"

"What other man?" Kodiak asked.

"Man in command."

"His name is Chase. What's yours?"

"He is wise man. Where is he?"

"Chase asked me to have a little talk with you to make sure you're feeling okay and to find out if you need anything. Is there anything I can get for you?"

"I do not understand. English is not so good."

"My Mandarin isn't great, either, but we can give it a try."

They switched to the man's native tongue and continued.

"Tell me your name," Kodiak began.

"Call me Hépíng."

"So, you're a man of peace. Is that right?"

"Peace is good. Everything else is bad." Hépíng paused and finally asked, "May I have water with lemon and honey?"

"I can get that for you, but that's a strange request."

He said, "This is something I wanted since I was a small boy."

Kodiak asked, "You've never had lemonade?"

Listening through the curtain, I couldn't understand a word they were saying, but the tone was good.

Kodiak stuck his head through the curtain. "Can you get us a couple of glasses of lemonade?"

"Lemonade? Why?"

He shrugged. "That's what he wants."

Five minutes later, I returned with two cups of lemonade from the galley, and I stepped through the curtains.

It wasn't exactly a smile that came to the man's face, but it was the most pleasant expression I'd seen from him since we met on the icebreaker.

He took the cup from my hand and pulled his oxygen mask to the side. "*Spasibo*."

"You're welcome, Mr. Hépíng."

He almost smiled, but it was hidden behind the drink. He smelled the contents and then held the cup in both hands in front of him as if offering it back to me. I took it and drank a mouthful of the lemonade. He reached for the cup before I'd swallowed, and I placed it in his hands. His first drink was small, and he smacked his lips several times. He seemed to drift off into his thoughts, but I didn't want his mind anywhere except right there with the three of us.

I said, "A beautiful Russian once made that drink for me, and I slept for two days."

In broken Russian, he said, "Never trust gift of big horse. Enemy inside."

Kodiak took a drink from his cup and sighed. "No Trojan horses here, my friend. Just good old-fashioned lemonade."

I let Hépíng finish his drink in peace before taking the empty cup from his hand. "Would you like some more?"

He frowned, and Kodiak translated.

"No, thank you."

We pieced the conversation together over the next twenty minutes until Hépíng asked, "You are American commander?"

I braced myself. "Yes. I am Chase, and I am in command."

Hépíng bowed his head and softly said, "*Zhang Yìchén Zhèngzhì shìwù gànshi.*"

Kodiak's face flushed pale, and he planted his cup on the small table beside the bed. He was on his feet in an instant and had me by the collar. "Outside, now."

I stood, and we stepped through the curtain together, but Kodiak didn't stop. He kept moving through the door to sick bay and into the corridor. He scanned the space and locked eyes with me. "He's the freaking political affairs officer."

"What?"

"You heard me," he said. "He's the highest-ranking official who's ever been on any icebreaker. Especially that one." He shoved a finger in the direction of where the ship had been only moments before.

The contents of my skull exploded as I ran through the possibilities of what Zhang Yìchén's presence could mean and what must be done next.

I stared into Kodiak's head. "Get back in there and keep him talking and breathing."

I followed him through the door, but I split from him as soon as we were inside the bay, then I turned for Dr. Shadrack's office while Kodiak made a beeline behind Zhang Yìchén's curtain.

The doctor's door was closed, but it was no barrier for me with my new information. I pushed it open, and Dr. Shadrack looked up in surprise as he pressed his telephone receiver to his ear.

I motioned toward the phone. "Hang up. Everything just changed."

Without a word, the doctor slid the handset back onto the desktop base. "What's going on?"

"Your pneumonia patient has a name and a title."

"A title?"

I nodded. "Yeah, a title. His name is Zhang Yìchén, and he's the political affairs officer."

The doctor's chin fell. "Are you kidding me?"

"Listen to me, doctor. If we let that man die, World War Three will be the last of our worries. He's the key to this whole frozen debacle. If we can flip him and hand him off to Defense Intelligence, or maybe even the Agency, he's a bottomless well of intelligence."

Before we could finish our conversation, a cacophony of sound poured through the open door. I spun on a heel and sprinted from the office like a hurdler springing from the starting blocks. What I saw couldn't be happening. Kodiak and the lone surviving sailor were fighting in the center of the sick bay.

The sailor held a piece of a metal IV pole in one hand and a broken shard of glass in the other. He lunged at the wild-haired Kodiak, barely missing with a slicing swing of the glass, and as instant punishment for the attempt, Kodiak landed a crushing side kick to the man's left knee, bending it unnaturally and sending the man to the deck. The blow would've stopped most men, but the sailor was hell-bent on getting to Zhang Yìchén.

He dug his heels into the tile, shoving himself toward the political affairs officer, but Kodiak planted a boot heel squarely in the center of the man's face, sending blood and spittle spraying in every direction. The shot should've left the sailor unconscious, but his sheer determination kept him moving.

He swung the chrome pole section, catching the back of Kodiak's wrist, and sent the former Green Beret hopping backward and clutching his forearm. I'd seen Clark fight more times than I could remember, and some part of me believed all Green Berets fought with the same style. I was wrong. Where Clark was violent and unrelenting, Kodiak was meticulous and patient, learning from his opponent with every strike and every miss.

I took a step toward Kodiak's assailant with the intention of driving him through the deck, but before I could strike, my newest teammate stepped back toward the sailor, giving him another easy target with the same wrist, and the man took the bait. Kodiak moved with the speed of a striking viper, stepping into the coming blow and trapping the sailor's weapon and hand beneath his right arm. The blinding motion continued as Kodiak spun on the ball of a foot and launched a massive punishing elbow to his victim's chin. Both the will and ability to continue the fight flowed from the sailor with a stream of blood trailing from his face.

Kodiak stepped on the sailor's other wrist and kicked the glass from his grip. When he finally stopped moving, Kodiak came to rest with one knee in the center of the sailor's chest and his pistol pressed beneath what was left of the man's nose.

"Don't kill him!" I yelled before I could stop myself.

"It may be too late for that," Kodiak breathed as he holstered his Glock.

In an instant, Dr. Shadrack was at the sailor's side with his stethoscope, probing for signs of life. He pulled open the man's mouth and peered inside. With the sweep of a finger, three teeth fell from his bloody mouth, and the doctor rolled the unconscious combatant onto his side. "We don't want him drowning on his own blood. What happened out here?"

Kodiak took a breath and motioned to Zhang Yìchén's bed. "He was trying to kill him. I barely got to him in time. Another second or two, and our whole case would've bled out. We've got to lock that guy up or put a bullet through his skull."

A medic appeared, and he and Kodiak loaded the sailor back onto a rolling bed.

Kodiak produced a pair of flex-cuffs and attached the man to the bed rail. With his binding in place, Kodiak said, "Shoot this guy up with something that'll keep him under control. He's likely to chew off his own arm to get out of the flex-cuffs."

Dr. Shadrack grabbed a phone from the wall, and in minutes a pair of armed guards—whom I recognized from Bravo Team—arrived and took positions beside the sailor's bed.

The doctor said, "Get him clean and prepped, and I'll stitch him up."

The medic went to work on the bloody task, and Dr. Shadrack stepped inside Zhang Yìchén's curtain. The IV pole the sailor had wielded turned out to be the one holding the officer's bags of fluid. The doctor hurriedly replaced the broken IV pole and resituated the hanging bags. A quick check of his vitals showed that the patient was none the worse for wear.

Kodiak leaned in and asked in Chinese, "Are you okay, sir?"

He nodded. "That man was only doing his duty. Killing me to keep me from talking to you is his ultimate responsibility to the president and the Republic."

Of course I couldn't understand anything he was saying, but Kodiak promptly translated.

"Would you like more lemonade?" I asked.

He smiled. "No, thank you."

I softened my tone. "Do you want to talk to us?"

Through Kodiak's translation, our conversation continued until we came to the ultimate revelation.

"I understand your position," I said. "It's your job to keep the Chinese government from suffering embarrassment, but my job is a little different."

He said, "I also understand. You are a man of action. A warrior. This means we are two bulls with only one cow."

The chuckle wasn't intentional, but it pulled me from the conversation. I asked Kodiak, "Is that really what he said?"

He shrugged. "Something like that."

Refocused, I turned back to Yìchén. "I'm not a bull. I'm a dangerous man who chooses peace."

The interpretation seemed to please the man, so I pressed the issue by locking eyes with him and speaking in Russian—our best common language. "Look into my eyes and tell me who is responsible for your submarine."

He considered my words carefully and furrowed his brow. "My submarine?"

It had to be the language barrier that had him confused, so I said to Kodiak, "Repeat what I just said in Chinese."

"I can't," he said.

"Sure you can. You're the only one of us who speaks Chinese."

He shook his head. "Yeah, but I don't speak Russian."

I'd become so engulfed in the conversation I'd forgotten our limitations. "Tell him to look me in the eye and tell me who is responsible for his submarine."

I assume Kodiak did as I asked, but Zhang Yìchén's response didn't change.

Kodiak turned back to me. "He says that ain't his boat."

Chapter 30
Show-and-Tell

"Keep him talking," I said.

Kodiak asked, "About what?"

"I don't care. Just don't let him clam up. Give him whatever he wants, and keep his lips moving. I'll be back."

I stepped from behind the curtain and peeked in on our rambunctious guest. He was sleeping like a baby while Dr. Shadrack worked inside his mouth.

"Is he going to make it, doc?"

Without looking up, the doctor said, "You can bet the farm on it. I'm not letting him die. How's it going next door?"

"Frustrating. But we may be on the verge of some progress."

"How's Zhāng Yìchén holding out?"

"He's tired, but he's either cooperating or playing us. We'll know soon."

The doctor said, "If you run into a wall, I just happen to have a vial of Scopolamine."

"My pharmacology is a little rusty. You'll have to remind me what that is."

He stopped stitching and raised his head. "It's truth serum."

"There's no such thing. Anything learned under any of those drugs is inadmissible."

"Inadmissible? That's funny. Are you planning to take a Chinese diplomat to traffic court? Who cares about admissibility? If you want him to talk and tell the truth, I'll blend up a cocktail that'll turn your new friend into Chatty Kathy."

"I'll keep that in mind, doc, but we're doing okay for now."

It took fifteen minutes to find Weps, but when I did, he said, "Your analyst is really something. She pulled some graphics out of the dive video that aren't good enough for facial recognition, but we can definitely rule out a few ethnicities."

"Show me."

He brought up the video shorts on the main monitor in the CIC and froze on a direct frontal facial shot of one of the corpses in the sub. "Check out that face. He looks a lot more like you and me than our detainees down in medical. Don't you agree?"

"How did we miss that while we were down there?"

He shrugged. "Maybe it was the friendly, five-hundred-year-old shark you were dodging."

"You may be on to something there, but that's not why I need you right now. I need a way to show this video to our detainee downstairs in sick bay."

His hesitance made me miss Skipper. She would've instantly had a resolution, but Weps didn't disappoint in the end.

Two minutes later, he handed me an electronic tablet. "That'll do it."

Back in sick bay, I found Kodiak and Zhang Yìchén in relaxed conversation. I slipped through the curtains and handed the tablet to Yìchén. "Tell him I took that video eighteen hours ago, forty miles east of here."

It took Kodiak a few seconds to formulate the interpretation, but the look on Yìchén's face spelled utter disbelief, and his tone reiterated the sentiment.

"He says he doesn't believe you. He thinks this is a ruse to place blame on China when they're innocent."

"Ask him why I would want to do that."

Kodiak hesitated. "That's going to come across as accusatory."

"That's exactly how I mean it," I said. "I'm not concerned about hurting his feelings. I'm trying to prevent the next world war. Now ask him."

Kodiak shrugged and spat out a string of sounds that meant nothing to me but clearly slapped our guest right in the face.

The man pulled his oxygen mask from his face and peered through my soul. "This cannot be truth."

I played a few mental games to remain calm. "It is truth, Zhang Yìchén. I was down there. I saw it with my own eyes. *Ya videl eto.*"

I stepped into position so I could see the screen at the same instant Yìchén flinched and let out an audible gasp, then I pressed a finger to the small screen. "I saw that shark. I touched that shark."

He looked up at me with a child's wonder in his eyes and gently touched the back of my hand. I looked down as the tips of his small fingers traced the scars on my wrist and hand.

He asked, "Shark did this?"

"No, that wound is fifteen years old. I saw that shark less than two days ago."

He shot a look at Kodiak, and my interpreter quickly turned my words into Chinese.

Kodiak turned back to me. "He wants to know if your scars are from war."

I replayed the afternoon in Omaha, Nebraska, when my dreams of becoming a major league ball player were crushed and burned in an instant on the only battlefield I'd known back then. I said, "Yes, it was war, but I was victorious."

It wasn't completely false. War is a matter of perspective. At least that's what I told myself and what I believed.

I left the tablet in his hands, and I sat on the edge of his bed. "Tell me what you want, Yìchén."

He looked up at me as if he understood but didn't have an answer, so I rolled the dice. "If I can prove to you that your submarine is broken into two pieces under the ice, will you tell me the truth?"

Kodiak translated, and Yìchén said, "You cannot prove this. It is not true."

"How do you feel?" I asked.

"Better. Thank you."

"I'm going to take you to the place where your submarine is aground and broken up. When I show you, I will ask for the truth once again. If I get the truth from you, my country will be very grateful to you, and I will give you a home anywhere you want."

Through Kodiak, he said, "You cannot make such a promise." "Yes, I can. I have no reason to lie to you. I still believe you and I want the same thing in the end." I left that statement hanging in the air and walked out of his curtained prison cell.

I found Captain Sprayberry on the bridge. "How long will it take for us to get back to the submarine site?"

"I'm not sure we can get there. The ice is thickening, and even if we get there, I have my doubts about getting back out."

I glanced around at the three other crew on the bridge. "We need to talk, Captain."

He motioned toward the rear of the bridge with his chin. "Come with me."

I followed him into his private cabin, and he settled onto the edge of his bunk while I propped myself against his small desk.

"Let's have it," he said.

"I have the Chinese political affairs officer from the icebreaker downstairs. He's got the worst case of pneumonia Dr. Shadrack has ever seen. I've also got a pissed-off Chinese sailor who insists on killing everybody who gets close to him, including the political affairs officer. Everybody else from that ship is already dead. These are the only two I have left. The sailor is meaningless to me unless the officer dies."

Captain Sprayberry said, "All of this is fascinating, Chase, but my number one priority has to be the safety of this ship and crew."

"I understand, Captain."

He shook his head. "Let's drop the *captain* and *mission commander* crap. We're just two guys, okay? Tell me what you need, and I'll tell you what this ship and I can do."

"Fair enough. I need to show that submarine to that man downstairs. He needs to . . . no, that's not right. *I* need him to see it with his own eyes. He may be the only person on Earth who knows what's really going on up here, and I'm not going to get anything out of him with threats. I need the ultimate show-and-tell. I'll show him his sub, and he'll tell me the truth."

The captain leaned back against the wall and laid his head back until he was staring directly overhead. Finally, he said, "If I get you there, there's a better-than-good chance this ship won't move again until the spring thaw, and I'm not willing to strand a good ship and crew in the ice for six months just so you can make a point with some Chinese political affairs whatever."

I pulled the chair from beneath the desk and sat facing the captain. "If we show that derelict submarine to that man downstairs, and if he comes clean, you and your good ship will have prevented the war to end life as we know it on this planet. But if you don't get me there, you can rest assured a stuck ship and crew won't matter when mushroom clouds are rising over every major city on the globe."

"That's a touch dramatic, don't you think?"

I locked eyes with my friend and master of the *Polar Explorer III*. "Barry, that's not drama. It's the world we inherited, and it's ours to lose if that's the choice we make."

He turned and lay back on his bunk.

As the most important decision he'd ever make weighed on him, I asked, "How long will it take for the trail we leave behind us to freeze over as thick as the surrounding ice?"

With his eyes closed, he said, "If we're going to do it, that's our only hope. We have to turn this thing around in ice that's three feet thick and push our way back out, in exactly the course we took in. I honestly don't know if it can be done."

"Who does know?" I asked.

Without hesitation, he said, "Big Bob in engineering."

Barry sat up and pressed a button on his desk phone.

Seconds later, Big Bob's gruff voice boomed through the speaker. "Engineerin'."

"Big Bob, it's the skipper. I need to put us back on the sub site for . . ."

He glanced at me, and I whispered, "Ten minutes."

"Ten minutes, and then back out of there. Can your super boat pull that off?"

"How thick is the ice?" he growled.

The captain said, "Enviro estimates thirty-six inches."

"No, she can't do that. Even if we got in there, we'd never get her out."

Captain Sprayberry sat on the edge of his bunk and stared at the phone for a long moment until Big Bob said, "You still there, skipper?"

"Yeah, I'm here, Bob. Get the hull as hot as you can make it and make ready to break ice."

Big Bob said, "But, Captain. I said—"

Captain Sprayberry pressed the button, and Big Bob's protest was silenced.

I said, "You made the right decision, Barry."

"The hell I did," he said. "I just buried my career and the finest ship that's ever set to sea, and I did it on your hunch. You better pray you're right, Chase."

I stood from the chair. "Instead, Captain, I think I'll pray that you're wrong."

Chapter 31
Fire-Breathing Giant

As we inched our way eastward through the ever-increasing barrier of ice, I stood against the rear bulkhead of the navigation bridge and watched Captain Sprayberry's expression morph from hope and faith in his ship to regret and self-loathing for having allowed a tactical operations officer to talk him into a fool's errand.

The helmsman scanned the panel in front of him and reported the ice thickness. "Thirty-one inches, Captain."

"Thirty-one," repeated the captain in his best imitation of an unconcerned, seasoned man of the sea. But his face told a different story.

I stepped toward the master and commander of the Research Vessel *Lori Danielle* turned *Polar Explorer III*, but he held up a hand.

"Not now, Chase. I'm in no mood for a pep talk."

Although prudence wasn't always my strong suit, I made the best possible decision in that moment and stepped from the bridge, leaving the pros to deal with punching through the frozen barrier separating me from the scene that might prevent global nuclear war.

Back in sick bay, I found Kodiak sitting beside Yìchén, who appeared to be sleeping like a newborn.

"How's it going?"

Kodiak started to rise, but I waved him down. "Don't get up. Just catch me up on what I missed."

He glanced at the sleeping man and motioned through the curtain, so I stepped aside and followed him from the space.

Kodiak said, "He's a widower. His wife died two years ago when she couldn't get the medical care she needed for a cancerous tumor on her spine."

"What else?"

"His only son was killed in a military training accident just over a year ago. He was a junior infantry officer in the PLA."

Just as Captain Sprayberry attempted to hide his concern on the bridge, I tried and failed to hide my optimism.

Kodiak eased my pain. "I know, man. As crappy as it is, he's easier to flip when he's got nobody to go home to. That's the plan, right? To flip him?"

"Unless a better option arises, that's all I've got left. We've run out of people to kill."

He leaned around the troublesome Chinese sailor's curtain. "Ah, we've got one more if we need one."

"Is he stable enough to lock up yet?"

He nodded. "Yeah, the doc said we could move him whenever we want."

"Good," I said. "I'll make that happen. Why don't you go get some chow and some rest? We've got a long, slow trip ahead of us, and nothing about it feels good."

He checked his watch. "I could use some chow and shut-eye for a couple of hours. Yìchén is out cold. Doc gave him a little something to help him sleep, so he'll be down for at least eight hours."

I stepped through the curtain, where the two Bravo Team gunners were watching over the sleeping troublemaker. "Let's put him to bed downstairs and keep him medicated. I need him to be missing when Yìchén wakes up."

"You got it, sir. We'll take care of it."

Lying to a detainee while trying to get him to betray his country is both accepted and expected, but I preferred to stick as closely as possible to the truth—at least the truth as the detainee perceives it. The coming hours would be no exception.

* * *

I slept in short bursts and ached every time the ship creaked and moaned against her frozen foe. My head was clearer, but my body still needed sleep. There would be time for sleeping through as many sunrises as I wanted if I could pull off my plan, but if I failed, sleep would become eternal for millions of innocent people whose lives lay in my hands.

Back on the bridge, Captain Sprayberry's first officer was nervously pacing the deck, but he paused when I stuck my head through the hatch and asked for access.

"Come aboard, sir."

"Thanks," I said. "Is it getting any better?"

"No, sir. We're in thirty-four inches of ice, and thirty-six is the designed maximum penetration depth."

"What happens if we hit thirty-six?"

"In theory, we'll slow down three quarters of a knot and keep pressing on, but if we hit thirty-seven, we have no choice but to come about and run for warmer water."

"Coming about sounds challenging in those conditions."

"It is," he said. "That's why I'm swinging the bow every half mile. That makes a wider swath in the ice where we can begin a turning maneuver. That way, we'll never have to steam astern more than half a mile to reach a turning point."

"That sounds reasonable to me. I'm sorry to put you and the ship through this, but—"

He interrupted. "Don't be sorry, sir. This is our job and the job the ship was designed to do. I don't have the clearance to know everything that's going on, but everybody—officers and crew alike—trusts you. If you say this is what has to be done, we put our heads down and push. It's that simple."

I gave him an appreciative smile. "The captain may disagree."

"He doesn't," the young man said. "He's the captain. He's supposed to worry. The rest of us simply follow orders."

Before we could take the conversation any further, a lookout from across the bridge called out, "Captain's on the bridge!"

"Carry on," Captain Sprayberry said. He glared at me and then at his first officer. "Report, Mr. Lamb."

"Two and a quarter knots, sir. Ice is holding at thirty-four inches, and engineering reports the hull is at a hundred and ten percent maximum temp and holding. Pumps and seawater heaters are holding. Fuel is at eight-thousand-mile range. No contacts, and we're three and a half miles from the target."

The captain stuck out his hand and shook the first officer's. "Thank you, Mr. Lamb. You're relieved. I have the ship."

The lookout echoed, "Captain has the ship."

One by one, every sailor on the bridge was replaced by a fresh-faced seaman eager to see how far Captain Sprayberry and I would push the vessel.

"Well, Chase, it looks like we're going to make it, but there's a storm approaching from the southwest with sustained wind of forty-five knots and blinding snow. Finding our way out of here when we can see and hold the old girl true would've been hard enough, but in zero visibility and wind like that, we're asking more of the ship than she was ever designed to do."

I scanned the bridge, surveying the new crew. "Maybe so, Captain, but when they designed this warhorse, they had no way of knowing just how tenacious and capable her crew would be. Keep the faith, Barry. I'm going to light a fire and try to talk Dr. Shadrack into a little field trip."

"Good," he said. "I don't want you on my bridge anyway."

My first stop was CIC, where Weps had Skipper on one monitor and weather radar on the other. I pulled up a chair. "Nice to see you, Skipper. How are things in the land of no ice?"

She said, "I'm in no danger of getting stranded a thousand miles from the nearest help, and I speak the same language as everyone around me, so I'd say that makes things here better than there."

"That's a rather pessimistic way to look at our situation," I said. "We're simply making the most of the ship's capability and saving the world. It's just another day at the office."

She put on her all-business face. "Seriously, Chase, you're in a tenuous situation. I've got a commercial icebreaker headed your way, but she's at least fifty hours away. She does have a pair of choppers aboard if we have to fly you out of there. The Navy is on alert and moving north in the Pacific. Oh, and Penny says if you don't make it home in time for her premiere, you have no idea what cold is going to feel like."

"When's the premiere?"

Skipper laughed. "I do love your priorities, Chase. Don't worry. You've got plenty of time, and I won't let you miss it. How's the new guy working out?"

"Kodiak? He's great, and his Chinese is good enough to make this operation possible. If he's interested, I think we may keep him around."

"In that case, I'll run a deep background check and start looking for a house for him."

Changing subjects, I said, "Tell me about the weather."

Weps pointed toward the monitor. "It's coming fast, and we don't have the speed to run in ice this thick. It'll be on us in less than five hours if nothing changes. Fortunately, it's a fast-moving system and should pass within forty-eight hours. Even so, a storm that strong can do a lot of damage in that length of time."

The ship shuddered beneath us as if hit by an earthquake, and our forward motion ceased.

"Show me our position, Weps."

He stroked a few keys, and the weather radar screen was replaced with a navigation display. "We're just over a mile from the target site and making no headway."

The ship's intercom came to life. "Attention on deck. Fulton to the bridge, immediately."

"Duty calls," I said on my way through the hatch. I stepped onto the bridge without permission, but no one seemed to care.

The captain motioned out the window. "There's your sub. This is as close as I can get you."

I peered through the thick glass at the mound of ice and snow in the distance. "Thank you, Captain. I'll make it as quick as possible."

He lowered his gaze. "If we're not underway an hour before the storm hits, we're shipwrecked, Chase. I'm not being dramatic. I'm briefing you on a certainty."

"Then there's no time to waste."

The argument with Dr. Shadrack didn't come. Instead, he said, "If you have to take him out on the ice, just know that he's frail and not likely to survive more than a few hours out there."

"Thanks, doc. If all goes well, I'll have Yìchén back in his nice warm bed within an hour."

I met the team on the stern deck and watched Mongo test-fire his favorite new toy. Fire belched from the muzzle, and the roar could've been a raiding dragon, which somehow seemed an appropriate nod to Yìchén and his one point three billion countrymen.

Our giant doused his flame and loaded his gear aboard the hovercraft, and Singer slung his .338 Lapua rifle across his shoulder and climbed aboard.

"Who are you going to shoot?" I asked. "There's nobody left."

"There's always one more, and I'm not letting that one get a free shot at Mongo. He's hard to miss."

Clark mounted the hovercraft and stepped to the controls. "Don't worry, Chase. I'll have everybody back on deck inside an hour."

"We'll be on your tail as soon as you give the word," I said.

Clark gave a salute and then the hand signal to hoist the hovercraft over the side. He brought the turbines to life and set off across the ice the instant the crane's lifting cables were cut loose, and I turned on a heel to see the MH-6 Little Bird emerging from her warm, dry hangar with Disco inspecting every surface.

I gave Kodiak a nudge. "I guess it's time to check our patient out of the hospital."

"Let's do it," he said. "Chase, is this going to work?"

I threw an arm around him. "If it doesn't, the next northern lights we see will be intercontinental ballistic missiles flying over the North Pole."

Chapter 32
The Feet of a Man

Back in sick bay, Dr. Shadrack had Yìchén dressed in every layer of clothing he could wrap around the small man. If not for his thin, dark eyes peering from beneath the hood, it would've been easy to believe he was nothing more than a pile of cold-weather gear.

A medic rolled a wheelchair around the corner and situated it behind Yìchén, but he shook his head. What came out of his mouth was meaningless until Kodiak said, "He's a man, and a man should walk on the feet of a man."

"I wish I was smart enough to understand that," I said.

Kodiak sighed. "It sounds a lot better in Mandarin."

I faced Yìchén and asked, "Are you sure you want to see this?"

Kodiak interpreted and said, "He says he's sorry for not trusting you, but he believes you understand."

"I do. Let's go."

We walked the slow walk of men who dread what lay ahead, but Yìchén never missed a step. Outside the hangar, Kodiak and I helped the man into the rear of the chopper, and I was pleased to see Ronda No-H standing with one arm draped across the General Electric Minigun.

"You must be feeling better."

She gave me a wink. "Just don't tell the doctor. Deal?"

I chuckled. "Just don't let anybody shoot us down. Deal?"

She lowered the visor on her helmet and clipped the sling from her harness to the airframe.

I climbed onto the left front seat, and Disco took the driver's perch.

Working meticulously through the start-up checklist, our chief pilot brought the sleeping machine to life and watched the temperatures rise. He pulled his microphone close to his lips. "Seal it up, folks. We don't have a heater big enough to keep the polar ice cap warm."

We closed all the doors, and Ronda situated herself in a position that would allow her to slide the door open and man the gun in an instant should the need arise.

After sitting on the pad for fifteen minutes, the call we so desperately wanted to hear finally came.

Clark said, "The package is unwrapped. Launch the spectators."

Disco rolled the throttle to the appropriate power setting and pulled the collective. The rotors chewed at the frigid air, and a second later, we were flying away from the *Polar Explorer III* and toward the grandest production of my life. Suddenly, I knew how Penny felt when the theater lights went dark the moment before her premiere.

As soon as we cleared the superstructure of the ship, the black smoke and orange flame from Mongo's flamethrower stood out in stark contrast to the endless world of white before us.

I shot a glance over my shoulder. "How are you doing back there?"

Yìchén said, "I fear this is terrible day for my country."

I gave Kodiak a glance. "Tell him that I fear this is a terrible day for the world if we don't do what's right."

I don't know what Kodiak told him, but whatever it was, it gave the old man a reason to bow his head. Something told me he wasn't praying to Singer's God. Perhaps he was taking a journey deep inside, in search of ultimate truth, and surrendering himself to the weighty reality of the coming experience that would likely be the defining moment of his time on Earth.

The blunt bow of the black submarine shone in the bright, reflected light from every icy surface, and Disco touched down fifty feet from the site where Clark and Mongo stood awaiting our arrival. Perched high atop the mound of white covering the sub, Singer lay with his rifle and eagle eyes scanning the horizon for threats the rest of us would never see.

I unbuckled my harness, stepped from the Little Bird, and slid Yìchén's door open. "Are you ready, sir?"

Kodiak and I helped him onto the ice and away from the rotor wash of the chopper.

Disco and Ronda lifted off and flew a circling patrol pattern overhead, adding an additional layer of security to our sniper's already-hefty surveillance.

The three of us walked slowly toward the exposed bow of the sub until we were within a few feet of the massive hull. Yìchén first looked up at me and then at Kodiak before pulling off his gloves and shoving them into his pockets. The exposed flesh of his hands would experience frostbite in minutes, but the coming ritual demanded his touch.

The man stepped away from us, shuffling his feet carefully across the sheet of ice that had refrozen almost instantly after Mongo melted it away.

"What's he doing?" I whispered, but Kodiak shrugged and threw up his hands.

I watched the bizarre scene unfold in front of me, and it's a sight I'll never forget. The man leaned toward the sub, placed his hands on the black hull, and cried. I watched his shoulders rise and fall in shuddering staccato until his hands were nearly frozen to the hull of his nation's once-stealthy ship of war.

Kodiak laid a hand on his arm and spoke quietly and slowly as he encouraged the man to turn his back on the sub.

I gave the signal, and Disco touched down on the spot he'd vacated only moments before. Yìchén felt somehow heavier when I lifted him back aboard the Little Bird. Perhaps it was the weight of his decision and agony over all that had been taken from him.

We landed on the helipad without Ronda No-H firing a single round, yet I felt as if we'd waged a war of magnificent proportion in the fleeting moments we'd spent on the ice. Bullets are rarely the answer to the greatest battles of mankind. Learning unthinkable truths about the masters we serve pierces deeper than any dagger, and surrendering to our own conscience is oftentimes more agonizing than raising the white flag in the face of insurmountable odds. Zhang Yìchén, Chinese political affairs officer, bore the pain as a true warrior should. He stood on his own feet—the feet of a man betrayed and robbed of everything he loved. No matter the color of his skin or the language of his thoughts, fears, and dreams, he was a man of ultimate truth, honor, and strength, whose world had opened beneath him and threatened to devour his immortal soul. But a team of brave men and women stood beside me and took Zhang Yìchén by the hand before he could be consumed by a reality he could scarcely understand.

The storm raged on the western horizon and inside the combat information center aboard what was, once again, the *Lori Danielle*.

Zhang Yìchén sat stoically in his chair and faced me as if we were players in a game with cosmic consequences. He cleared his throat. "First, I am sorry for lying to you. My English is good, but this was a tool I did not wish to reveal when I deceived you. Please forgive me."

Although I likely failed, I tried showing no reaction other than offering my hand, which he took. "There is no reason to apologize, sir. I may have been less than honest with you at some point, but I've dealt fairly with you since the moment we first encountered each other."

"You have little reason to believe me, but I have nothing to gain from lies. You offered a home to me if I would turn from my loyalty to the Republic. Was this offer a lie?"

"It was not, sir. It was sincere. If my government will not do that for you, I have the means to keep my promise without governmental intervention."

"I believe you for one reason. Your men obey you not out of fear but out of well-earned respect. This is proof of your honor. In addition to this, you were kind to me when you believed I had nothing to offer you. This is also the way of an honorable man. I am correct that you are a CIA case officer, yes?"

"I am not associated with the CIA in any way. I work for an independent agency, but before this is over, it is likely you will speak with a number of intelligence officers who may work for any number of agencies within the U.S. government."

He took in the bevy of equipment and technology around him inside the CIC. "Independent agency, you say? And this ship is yours?"

"I'm not the captain of this ship, but I am commander of the tactical operation teams who work from aboard her."

He said, "I did not ask if you were captain. I asked if the ship is yours."

Rather than lie, I said, "Let's talk about what's going on with your submarine."

He lowered his head again, just as he'd done in the helicopter, but a few seconds later, he looked into my eyes. "You should record what I am about to tell you."

"I'm listening," I said, but there was no way I could've ever expected the volumes of Chinese intelligence he poured out before me. He spoke uninterrupted for ninety minutes, stopping only to reposition his oxygen cannula beneath his nose or ask for more hot tea.

Finally, when I was on the verge of believing Zhang Yìchén was going to tell me everything except how their ballistic missile submarine ended up in two pieces on the floor of the Northwest Passage, he said, "I am hungry, and your analysts need thirty minutes to verify many of the details I have told you. In that time, if you will allow me such privilege, I will eat, and then I will tell you everything about the submarine."

While Clark ate with Yìchén, I headed back to the bridge. "Permission to enter?"

"Come aboard," Captain Sprayberry said. "I hope you're having more luck than I am."

"Things are going far better than expected with the debrief."

He pointed out the window. "It's going to get very uncomfortable very soon. The storm will be on us in minutes, and it's far worse than we believed earlier. Sustained wind is up to sixty knots with gusts in the high nineties. But that's not my greatest concern."

"That doesn't sound good," I said.

He leaned against the console. "Big Bob reports that we burned out at least half of the hull heaters. The pumps and saltwater heaters are still functioning, but we can't heat the hull above forty degrees Celsius."

"I'm a tropical sailor, Captain. Break that down for me."

He picked at a fingernail. "It means our capability to break through ice greater than twenty-eight inches thick is all but nil. We're in trouble, Chase."

I checked my watch and tried to ignore the storm on the bow. "Do what you can. Skipper has an American icebreaker headed this way, but . . ."

"I know, but if we get hung and I can't keep our bow in the wind, that storm will lay us on our side and tear everything off the weather deck and above."

I wanted a solution, but more than that, I wanted to know the truth about the parted sub that lay behind us, still with nuclear weapons aboard.

Captain Sprayberry's concerns rested solidly on the task of saving his ship and crew, and there was nothing I could do to make that task easier.

Back in the CIC with the recorders humming, Zhang Yìchén reclaimed the floor and spoke in clean, polished English.

"On twenty-one September, the Russian ballistic missile submarine *Pantera* rendezvoused with the Chinese submarine northwest of the Azores in the North Atlantic Ocean under the guise of a joint training mission, but instead of initiating pursuit operations, the *Pantera*'s captain asked to have an opportunity for each crew to tour the other boat. After gaining approval from PLA naval command, the agreement was made, and approximately fifty crewmen from the *Pantera* boarded our vessel, killed the officers and crew, and sent a coded distress message to Moscow. Where the *Pantera* went immediately following the act of piracy is unknown, but we will talk more of her later." He adjusted his cannula, sipped his tea, and asked, "Do you have questions?"

I bounced my pen on my legal pad. "I have about a trillion questions, but I'd prefer you continue your narrative, and I'll save my questions for later."

He continued. "By some strange happening, the Western intelligence services, including yours, began tracking our submarine as the Russian *Pantera*. The Russian crew was unfamiliar with the intricacies of the precise operation of our submarine, but they apparently learned quickly. Chinese intelligence determined the Russians planned to launch a nuclear missile attack on the North American continent from the westernmost reaches of the Northwest Passage, but as the ice formed and currents changed in the passage, the Russian crew lacked the skill to manage the vessel in such conditions."

He paused again and squeezed a lemon wedge into his tea. "Forgive me. My throat is dry from the oxygen."

"Take your time," I said.

After a few sips, he continued. "The rest is supposition on the part of the Chinese government. We . . . excuse me . . . *they* believe the Russians were going to launch the missiles, rendezvous with a Russian supply ship in the Arctic Ocean, and scuttle the submarine in time to be back in Sevastopol before your Yankee Thanksgiving. Every indication would then be that we, the Chinese, launched the attack, and Russia would enjoy the benefits of a war between the two remaining superpowers while they got rich selling natural gas and remaining neutral in the conflict."

He stopped and took a long, full breath as if he were finished, but I was not.

"Tell me about the *Pantera*. Where is she now?"

"She is likely lying off your eastern coast, well within striking distance of New York, Washington, DC, Kings Bay, and New London submarine bases."

As if choreographed in the heavens, the massive storm of Zhang Yìchén's revelations hit me the same instant nature's fury struck the bow of the *Lori Danielle*.

I turned to Weps and ordered, "Nav screen."

He brought up the chart and data showing us making less than one knot against sixty-knot wind and blinding snow.

I hit the comms panel. "Bridge, CIC."

"Go for bridge."

Suddenly, I had no idea what to ask, so I hit the plunger. "Disregard. I'm coming up."

I stood and looked down at the man whose shoulders no longer slumped, and his face looked somehow younger than it'd been only hours before. "If you'll excuse me, my friend, I have things I must attend to, but I'll be back shortly, and I need to know why your crew was so willing to surrender their lives rather than be taken."

"This is a simple answer," he said. "No one believed the West would trust us to tell the truth. Everyone believed we would become prisoners, and would, as such, be murdered immediately upon return to China. Prisoners are not honored and revered in my country. In China, prisoners are believed to have betrayed the Republic and must, therefore, be killed immediately."

The mentality was beyond my capacity to comprehend, but instead of exploring it more deeply, I simply said, "Thank you," and stepped from the CIC.

On the bridge, the melee outside the windows was terrifying. Our ship listed to port, and the wind howled across every surface as if trying to scour the skin from her bones.

Captain Sprayberry squared off with me. "Have you got any fresh ideas, Commander?"

I studied the wind instruments. "How much room do you need to maneuver to hold out?"

The captain shook his head as if throwing water from his hair. "What?"

I said, "If I can make a hole, how big does that hole have to be for you to hold the bow in the wind until the storm passes?"

He blurted out, "Two thousand feet unless the wind picks up, but how, under God's Heaven, are you going to make me a two-thousand-foot hole?"

I steadied myself against the sway of the deck and leaned on the comms panel. "CIC, Bridge."

Weps said, "Go for CIC."

"How many of those missiles do you have left, and can you fly them in this wind?"

"Four, and they can fly against a hundred knots, but only for a short range."

"What is the safe distance from the explosion of all four missiles for our ship?"

I thought I heard him grin across the comms. "Half a mile, bridge."

I turned to Captain Sprayberry. "Can we back up half a mile?"

He smiled for the first time in days and jabbed a finger onto the chart table. "Put 'em right here."

I relayed the coordinates to Weps in the CIC, and the sound of the howling wind was soon joined by the rush of rocket motors propelling four anti-ship missiles from our missile tubes. They flew two thousand feet high, armed themselves, and dived for the ice.

Although we couldn't see the explosion, we felt it, and Captain Sprayberry gave the order, "Helm, all back full, and make for Chase's hole."

It took five minutes to maneuver the ship the half mile through the broken ice field we'd made on our way west, but once inside the big, beautiful hole the weapons officer created with his impressive marksmanship, the captain ordered the bow to be stuck into the howling wind, and the mighty *Lori Danielle* parked herself in the slushy center of her temporary home until the storm raged past.

Epilogue

We rode out the storm with the Azipods and bow thrusters holding the bow of the ship directly into the wind, with the exception of clearing turns made every hour to keep the ice broken up sufficiently for us to maneuver once the torrent ceased. Thirty hours after situating ourselves in the hole, Big Bob had the hull heaters on the mend and operating at seventy-percent capacity. The storm still howled, but it was well east of our position by then. Damage assessment reported minimal harm to the exterior of our beloved vessel, and Zhang Yìchén enjoyed the best night of sleep of his life.

Our push through the heavy ice that remained between us and open water was a mighty battle for our ship and crew compared to the peril we'd been in only hours before, and the arduous crawl felt like a walk in the park. We met up with the USS *Hollywood*—a naval supply ship—in the Beaufort Sea, where we took on fuel and provisions, as well as a pair of Defense Intelligence Service special agents who accepted responsibility for Zhang Yìchén, with the promise of treating him with the respect and kindness he'd earned and deserved.

"Oh, yes," I said. "There's one more thing you should keep in mind. Mr. Zhang will be an American citizen soon, and he likes lemon wedges with his hot tea."

Yìchén then did something I never expected. He looked into my eyes and bowed ever so slightly. His gesture felt like the most sincere appreciation anyone could express, so I returned the gesture as a demonstration of my respect for his courage and willingness to support my mission, but I took the moment further by stepping forward, extending my hand, and shaking his in a wordless exchange of sentiment I believe we both understood well. The wealth of intelligence he would divulge in the years to come would save the lives of countless Americans and weaken China's dam holding back her political secrets we never knew existed. His defection and cooperation constituted the greatest feat of espionage ever accomplished against the Chinese government.

Saint Marys's newest police detective spent three days taking the FBI through the case he built against the nationwide spree of bank robberies orchestrated by the Russians to point blame through the Chinese to the Arabs. Nothing within the federal government flows smoothly, efficiently, or quickly, so Tony was left with nothing more than the self-assurance that he and Hunter had done everything in their power to gather as much intelligence and evidence as possible. Leaving it in the hands of the FBI felt like a hollow victory, but such are the empty rewards of feeding hard-earned information into the monstrous federal government machine.

As for the Russian ballistic missile submarine loitering off the East Coast, that proved to be little more than another day at the office for the U.S. Navy, and it gave the Atlantic fleet a chance to dispatch a pair of Los Angeles-class fast-attack submarines to play a little undersea, silent-service, cat-and-mouse with the *Pantera*. Even with our level of clearance, we'd never know the details of just how much fun our submariners had with the Russians, but rumor has it they chased her all the way to the Baltic Sea.

Our time aboard the ship that had been our refuge, home, and base of operations for what felt like weeks, came to an end, and part of me regretted leaving her behind. She would spend enough time in the shipyard to repair everything we damaged on the excursion, but we'd be reunited again soon in another ocean on another side of America.

Gun Bunny flew us back to Deadhorse Bay, where the *Grey Ghost* waited patiently for us in her borrowed, climate-controlled hangar. Our host, Pecos, met us with a bottle of Gentleman Jack and a box of Dominican cigars, which weren't as good as the Cubans, but they certainly weren't bad.

We landed at Burbank Airport the next afternoon and stepped from the plane into eighty degrees and breathtaking Southern California sunshine. The air enveloped us like a warm blanket and reminded me how different life on Earth is when episodes are separated by only a few thousand miles, or by philosophies and beliefs so vastly different that one could hardly believe humanity could continue to exist beneath such extremes. My team and I may have prevented global nuclear war and untangled a complex and bewildering web of deceit and treachery, but in some corner of the world, perhaps not so far away, someone else would, undoubtedly, plan and execute an even deadlier and more terrifying plan to wreak havoc on perceived enemies, and the very thought of such inhumanity left me choking on the reality of my own necessity.

Without people like my team, how long would it take for the pack of wolves at the gates to push through and pillage life as we know it? How long can so few keep those wolves at bay? And how many lives must be extinguished before greed, hatred, and tyranny can be replaced by mutual respect, love, and shared joy in the human experience? Perhaps I'll never see that day, but as long as there's breath in my chest, I'll stand before those gnarling wolves and beat them back with every ounce of strength I can muster. And maybe . . . just maybe . . . the dead and dismembered wolves I leave in my wake will discourage the next pack against baring their bloodstained teeth, and we can beat our swords back into plowshares and finally learn that our differences are minuscule and insignificant when weighed against our shared humanity and common desire to leave our children a better world than we inherited.

We checked into the Four Seasons in Beverly Hills, and just as promised, Skipper's team of clothiers arrived, measured us, and delivered tuxedos that almost made us look like civilized gentlemen, but the warrior heart and fourteen-year-old-boy mentality inside every member of my team were impossible to hide, even beneath the finest threads in L.A.

Rather than changing and primping in his suite, Kodiak tossed the garment bag across his shoulder. "I'll catch you dudes later."

Perhaps we'd failed at welcoming him aboard, or perhaps he simply wasn't ready to step back into the world in which we lived. Either way, I was thankful he'd been along for our arctic adventure, and I'd never forget how quickly he'd earned our trust and respect as an operator.

When the limos pulled up in front of the posh hotel, we were clean, dry, and warm for the first time in what felt like months. The drivers held the rear doors open and ushered us inside just in time for us to arrive at Penny's premiere.

As the limo in which I sat rolled away from the curb, a knock came at the window, and the driver pressed the brake. The rear door opened, and there stood a man I'd never seen, dressed identically to all of us. His tuxedo fit perfectly, his hair was clean and styled perfectly, and his pale face wore the look of a man who'd lived his life behind a veil of his own making.

Kodiak stuck his head inside the car and said, "You guys weren't going to leave without me, were you?"

Just as the first two premieres had been, Penny's new movie was a raging hit among the gathered Hollywood elite and entertainment reporters. I loved watching Penny's movies and feeling her heart and soul pouring from the screen. She was a brilliant storyteller and one of the movie industry's brightest writing stars.

As enjoyable as the movies were, the afterparties were what I found most entertaining. My team had little, if anything, in common with most of the Tinseltown crowd, but it was always fun to watch how they interacted with each other and boasted about their success on the world's stage. They were oblivious to the harsh reality and bitter truth of the ugliness that crawled just beneath the surface, popping its gruesome head through the mist from time to time, making men and women like my team an invaluable commodity most people would never see and a crucial ferocious force few could stomach.

With Penny's gloved hand laced inside my elbow, she whispered, "Just hear him out and tell him no. Don't laugh at him. Promise?"

That admonition could mean only one thing: I was about to meet an idiot, and I was required to play along.

"I promise."

A gentleman who was perfectly dressed to play the part of the idiot stuck out his hand. "Ah, you must be Chase. I've heard so many grand stories about you. Tell me, are they true, or is Penny the greatest storyteller of our generation?"

I shook his hand, feigned the most sincere smile I could make, and said, "Both."

He roared with laughter as if he were the only person at the party. "Indeed. Well, is it true that you're in the business of international security?"

"That might be a bit of a stretch," I said. "But if I were, I'd be interested in hearing your next sentence."

Penny squeezed my arm as if to say, *Walk away, Chase.*

"Ah, that must be humility I detect. It's such a rare spice in La La Land, but I digress . . . Do tell. Are you available for overseas security on a movie set?"

Again came the arm squeeze, but this one was far more aggressive. I was already invested in the insanity falling out of the clown's mouth.

"I may be available, depending on several factors." I leaned close and whispered, "Not the least of which is in your security budget."

"Ah, how quaint," he said. "A true capitalist."

His temporary silence left me wondering if I was supposed to deny the charge, but regardless of his accusation, I wasn't going to shun the title he found so distasteful.

"Anyway," he continued. "Have you ever heard of Diamond Beach?"

I scrolled through the geographical Rolodex in my head. "I can't say that I have, but I'm an enormous fan of beaches all over the world."

"Brilliant!" he almost shouted. "I'll have my personal assistant call yours, and we'll see if we can tempt you with a little international intrigue, and maybe even a six-figure contract. How does that sound, huh?"

I gasped, and Penny moved from squeezing to pinching.

I said, "Six figures? Oh, my. I'm afraid a fee like that would be well outside of our typical arrangement."

He slapped a meaty hand against my shoulder, "Well, my boy, perhaps it's time you grew up and played ball on the big-boy field."

Author's Note

First, please accept my deepest appreciation for letting my characters and me spend a few hours with you. I'm flattered, honored, and grateful to be on your reading list, and I vow to do my best to continue bringing stories into your lives that provide a temporary escape from reality, a tiny glimpse into the world of covert operations, and a look into the lives of the brave men and women who fight the good fight and sacrifice their time, bodies, financial standing, and far too often, their very lives in defense of the life you and I are fortunate to live. Although Chase, Skipper, Clark, Disco, Hunter, Tony, Mongo, Singer, and Kodiak are fictional characters, please keep the real heroes they represent in your thoughts and prayers when you lie down to sleep beneath the blanket of security they provide.

Now, for the truth. I made it all up. I know less than nothing about ballistic missile submarines, icebreakers, the Northwest Passage, and missile systems, and I don't even know if the Chinese have political affairs officers. As the great novelist, James Lee Burke, says, stories are found things, and writers are but archaeologists charged with digging them up, dusting them off, and sharing them with the world. That's exactly how this story came to exist. It came to me in bits and pieces as I spent hours behind the keyboard, every day, until each piece finally fell into place. I'm thankful and proud to be your personal fiction archaeologist, and I'll do my best to keep digging, dusting, and sharing as long as my fingers can type and my imagination can dream.

I'm certain many scenes from this story are not only implausible, but also impossible. Like most novelists, I invite you to suspend reality for a few hours as I spin a yarn for your enjoyment. I'm madly in love with the art of storytelling and the craft of writing, so please accept my deepest and most sincere appreciation and gratitude for giving me the greatest job on Earth. I take that charge seriously, and I'll never take it for granted.

Thank you for taking this journey into the frozen world of the Arctic with me. I loved having you along for the ride, and I can't wait to invite you back on board for the next adventure, *The Diamond Chase*.

— Cap

About the Author

Cap Daniels

Cap Daniels is a former sailing charter captain, scuba and sailing instructor, pilot, Air Force combat veteran, and civil servant of the U.S. Department of Defense. Raised far from the ocean in rural East Tennessee, his early infatuation with salt water was sparked by the fascinating, and sometimes true, sea stories told by his father, a retired Navy Chief Petty Officer. Those stories of adventure on the high seas sent Cap in search of adventure of his own, which eventually landed him on Florida's Gulf Coast where he spends as much time as possible on, in, and under the waters of the Emerald Coast.

With a headful of larger-than-life characters and their thrilling exploits, Cap pours his love of adventure and passion for the ocean onto the pages of the Chase Fulton Novels and the Avenging Angel - Seven Deadly Sins series.

Visit www.CapDaniels.com to join the mailing list to receive newsletter and release updates.

Connect with Cap Daniels:

Facebook: www.Facebook.com/WriterCapDaniels
Instagram: https://www.instagram.com/authorcapdaniels/
BookBub: https://www.bookbub.com/profile/cap-daniels

Also by Cap Daniels

The Chase Fulton Novels Series
Book One: *The Opening Chase*
Book Two: *The Broken Chase*
Book Three: *The Stronger Chase*
Book Four: *The Unending Chase*
Book Five: *The Distant Chase*
Book Six: *The Entangled Chase*
Book Seven: *The Devil's Chase*
Book Eight: *The Angel's Chase*
Book Nine: *The Forgotten Chase*
Book Ten: *The Emerald Chase*
Book Eleven: *The Polar Chase*
Book Twelve: *The Burning Chase*
Book Thirteen: *The Poison Chase*
Book Fourteen: *The Bitter Chase*
Book Fifteen: *The Blind Chase*
Book Sixteen: *The Smuggler's Chase*
Book Seventeen: *The Hollow Chase*
Book Eighteen: *The Sunken Chase*
Book Nineteen: *The Darker Chase*
Book Twenty: *The Abandoned Chase*
Book Twenty-One: *The Gambler's Chase*
Book Twenty-Two: *The Arctic Chase*
Book Twenty-Three: *The Diamond Chase*
Book Twenty-Four: *The Phantom Chase*
Book Twenty-Five: *The Crimson Chase*
Book Twenty-Six: *The Silent Chase*
Book Twenty-Seven: *The Shepherd's Chase*
Book Twenty-Eight: *The Scorpion's Chase*

The Avenging Angel – Seven Deadly Sins Series
Book One: *The Russian's Pride*
Book Two: *The Russian's Greed*
Book Three: *The Russian's Gluttony*
Book Four: *The Russian's Lust*
Book Five: *The Russian's Sloth*
Book Six: *The Russian's Envy* (2024)
Book Seven: *The Russian's Wrath* (TBA)

Stand-Alone Novels
We Were Brave
Singer – Memoir of a Christian Sniper

Novellas
The Chase Is On
I Am Gypsy

Made in United States
Orlando, FL
05 July 2024

48642704R00162